BREAKING HIM

Scarlett

It was the kind of relationship where I invested more than I had to spare.

I gave it everything.

And so when it failed, I lost myself.

It changed me. He changed me.

I went down with the ship.

My soul, burnt embers in the aftermath.

The fire of him ravaged it all.

He burned me.

Broke me.

Scarlett had always dreamed big. She was headed straight for Hollywood. Destined for silver screen greatness.

But in her wildest dreams she never imagined she'd be broke and single at twenty-eight, doling drinks at thirty-five thousand feet.

She was a glorified waitress in the skies.

It had been yea   ek she'd seen him.

But one day, th   er, ready to set everything al

Dante wanted

Sure, she'd play along…but this time, it was his turn.

She was breaking him.

After all, love is war.

breaking him

by

R.K. LILLEY

BREAKING HIM

ISBN-13: 978-1-62878-040-6
ISBN-10: 1-62878-040-1

Cover photos by Perrywinkle Photography
Cover design by Okay Creations
Edited by The Word Maid
Interior design by Warkitty Formatting

www.rklilley.com

Give feedback on the book at:
authorrklilley@gmail.com

Twitter: @authorrklilley

Instagram: @Authorrklilley

www.facebook.com/RkLilley

First Edition

This book is dedicated to two of my favorite ladies in the world.

Vilma, I feel lucky every day to have you as a friend. You are one of the kindest and most caring people I have ever met. You make me feel less alone in the world, and shamelessly enable my shopping addiction. I crazy stupid love you.

Anna Todd, you are a rock star and a class act. You inspire me and get me writing like no one else. You are my muse and rest assured that I am, and will continue to be, your biggest cheerleader. I love you to pieces.

"I was born for the storm, and a calm does not suit me."
~Andrew Jackson

chapter

one

PRESENT DAY

Scarlett

He was here. He was actually fucking here.

On this plane. *My* plane. In *my* cabin.

How *dare* he?

This was not allowed, and he fucking knew it.

I slapped my rolled up flight paperwork against my palm agitatedly, over and over, like I had a twitch and I couldn't stop.

"Oh my God," Leona muttered, peeking out of the curtain. "What's he doing here?"

Humiliating me was the answer to that, but I didn't say it aloud.

That bastard. I was grinding my teeth. Audibly.

Leona straightened, her kind gaze going sharp as she studied me closely. "I'll take the cabin this time. You can stay in the galley. You don't even need to see him."

Leona worked the number two flight attendant position in our crew, and she knew me well enough to know about *him*.

She was the good girl to my bad, the sweet to my sour, the nice to my vicious, the peacemaker to my ballbuster.

She was all the things I'd never be, and I loved her for it. Adored the ground she walked on.

And she knew about me and Dante. About our history. She knew almost everything, though she was one of the *only* ones besides me that did.

I shook my head sharply, not letting myself even consider it. He knew I was here, of course he did. For whatever twisted reason, he was on this plane, had bought a ticket just to see me.

And I would not give him the satisfaction of knowing how hard it was for me to face him.

Pride had always been my greatest weapon when it came to Dante.

Sometimes my only weapon, so it was honed to killing sharpness.

"I can handle him," I told her. And it was the truth. It would hurt like hell, but it was a pain I was familiar with.

She bit her lip and nodded. She was the sweetest thing. So sweet, I wished I could be more like her. I couldn't. I'd tried once or twice, but the results had been laughable.

Leona had been raised by doting parents that loved her, in a world where being kind was a virtue.

I had not. I had been shaped by petty meanness in a world that had tried from the start to throw me away, and where being hard was the only way to survive.

"Is he alone?" I asked.

"I think so. So far."

The *so far* wasn't without reason. The last time he'd sought me out, he hadn't been alone, the bastard.

In all fairness, I probably shouldn't have taken it so personal. He was rarely alone.

I slipped into the bathroom with my makeup kit and did a quick touchup.

I'd been wearing a nude lip-gloss for work as I usually did, but I dug out my favorite red lipstick for this little reunion.

It was aptly named: *Blood*.

No other color was appropriate when dealing with my ex. I put it on because I was planning to draw some.

It occurred to me then that I was relishing and dreading this confrontation in near equal measures.

You see, it wasn't the first time. It happened every so often. Dante sought me out, confronted me, we each got in our blows and limped away.

I usually spat the last word at his retreating back.

A part of me lived for it.

My shredded heart had been wrapped up in spite for a very long time, wrapped so long and so tight that it was suffocating, and it was almost a relief sometimes to let it vent.

But how much of your life can you devote to spite?

I'd spent a lot of time thinking about this.

The answer, in my case, was sad: Too much.

Great, gory chunks of it. Major, necessary pieces.

And all because of him. Dante the Bastard.

I loosened my tie and undid the top three buttons of my blouse, turning my uniform from professional to more than a touch sexy.

I had outrageous curves. A tiny waist, voluptuous hips, a great ass, mile-high legs, and full breasts.

I had the exact body type that drew him like a kamikaze to suicide, so of course I'd use it against him.

He'd never been able to resist this body, not *once* in his entire life.

I pushed up my breasts, pinching my nipples until they popped perkily through the layers of my blouse and vest.

Go get him, tiger.

I smiled a bloodthirsty smile at my own reflection and headed back out to the galley.

The curtain was still up, but Leona was out in the cabin. Serving the first pre-board round of champagne, I assumed.

I grabbed my manual and made a quick announcement over the intercom, lowering my voice just so, turning it into a near seductive purr.

I did this for one reason. I knew it would get to him.

I wanted to score a hit before I ever even had to look at him.

He'd had the nerve to come into *my* territory.

I'd make him pay.

I always traveled with two pairs of shoes. One on my feet and one in my carryon. Work heels and killer heels. Work heels were for work, i.e. all of the grunt work on the airplane and keeping my balance at 35,000 feet. The killer heels were for the glamorous walk through the airport with my crew of gorgeous girls.

Well, okay, it wasn't glamorous. Nothing about being a flight attendant was. But we made it *look* glamorous, which was close enough, as far as I was concerned.

I yanked my bag out of its spot in a cubby that ran just behind my jump seat and pulled out my killer heels.

Don't get me wrong. My work heels are not hideous.

I wouldn't be caught dead in hideous shoes. They were black, patent leather, three-inch wedges with a cute little bow on the toe.

But this was not the time for cute.

I switched out my shoes in record time, stepping into five-inch red platform stilettos with a peep toe.

My uniform was simple and sleek. A black pencil skirt, white dress shirt, black vest and tie. I'd had every piece custom tailored to fit to perfection, accentuating my figure to its best advantage.

Add to that a sexy pair of red stilettos, and I knew I looked like a million bucks.

I stashed my bag right as Leona returned to the galley.

"I handed out menus, but the champagne could use topping off," she informed me, dashing back into her galley to prep for takeoff.

That was fine. I was ready.

I grabbed the opened bottle of champagne and strutted out into the cabin.

Under my breath I was humming *Seven Nation Army*.

My battle anthem.

Because this was war.

I faltered slightly when I spotted him, but recovered between one step and the next. His face was downcast, eyes pointed away from me, thank God, so at least he hadn't seen it.

His looks had always devastated me.

I was a shallow thing, with a weakness for the superficial. Even now, with all we'd put each other through, his beautiful face moved me.

He was just how I remembered. Every gut-punching, heart-wrenching inch of him.

He'd always struck me as a handsome villain. He

had wicked good looks, with golden hair, ocean eyes, and a perpetual, darkly shadowed jaw. His coloring was interesting, eye-catching, with his brows a few shades darker than his hair. His features were even and sharp, with slanted eyes and a lush mouth. You couldn't look at him without words like sinister or dastardly coming to mind.

Or maybe that was just me.

He was extremely tall, enough so that it was apparent when he was sitting down. If he stood, even in my killer heels he'd tower over me.

He was broad shouldered, muscular, but he was lean enough to pull off looking elegant in the ungodly expensive suits he wore on a regular basis.

Physically, he was just my type. I was a sucker for a sinister looking man.

Another thing that was all his fault.

"Dante," I crooned with a smile when I reached him. "To what do I owe the honor of your disagreeable, unwelcome presence?"

He'd been looking down at his phone when I'd approached, and he sucked in a deep breath at the sound of my voice.

He held it there for a long moment before letting it out and waited another beat still before letting his ocean blue eyes travel up to meet mine.

Ah, sweet torture.

This was the part I dreaded the most.

When our eyes clashed, and everything, every horrible, wonderful, painful, ugly, beautiful, torturous, ruinous, gory bit of us came back to me.

It was bad enough when I didn't have to look at him.

But when I did—exquisite torment, with a touch of

pleasure so concentrated, so brutally pure it had ruined my life.

Broken my heart.

Eviscerated my soul. I'd scraped what was left of that pathetic soul out myself, sawed it into little pieces and left it somewhere far behind.

What you're seeing is what was left.

"Hello, Scarlett," he returned, in that beautiful voice of his that I utterly *detested*. It was the deepest timbre and compelling to an unusual degree.

Compelling to the point of controlling.

When it warmed, I warmed with it. When it cooled, I went cold.

His voice was a dirty trick.

An unfair weapon.

I wanted to wrap my hands around his throat just to disarm it.

Well, if I were honest, I wanted to choke him for numerous reasons. Several came to mind, not the least of which that the thought of it turned me on.

"How flattering that you'd deign to fly commercial just to ruin my day." My tone dripped with venom.

"How flattering that you'd put on your favorite red lipstick just for me," he returned with his own bloodthirsty smile.

Fuck.

Point to The Bastard. He must have gotten a glimpse of me before I'd applied it to notice the difference.

His eyes shot down to my feet and a ghost of a smile lingered on his lips. "And the shoes. I'm more than flattered. Your efforts never go unappreciated, angel."

Another point.

If I was fair, it was two.

Because *angel*. The Bastard.

I barely held my 'eat shit and die' smile.

He didn't call me that because I was angelic.

Obviously. He was being ironic.

He thought I was the devil, and as far as he was concerned, I sure as hell was.

But that wasn't why it burned. It burned because it was a very old nickname, from back in the day when we were just dumb kids in love and he'd actually meant it.

Once upon a time, I'd been his angel. The reminder was yet another reason I'd have loved to wring his neck.

"More champagne?" I asked him, holding up the bottle, wondering if the other passengers would notice if I quietly poured it over his head.

He looked away, and I saw his lip curl up in disdain.

That made me grind my teeth.

It was shitty champagne, cheaper than he was used to, and he couldn't hide his distaste.

God, he was a snob. It was one of the things I hated most about him. At the top of a very long list.

"Oh. The brand too low class for you? You *poor* baby. You should put it up on your blog: spoiledrottentrustfundbrats.com.

Here was the part where he was supposed to make a biting crack about me being from a trailer park, or pointed out how far I'd fallen that I was slinging drinks on an airplane, or asked archly about how my failed acting career was going.

That's how this little play worked.

Only he didn't.

He just raised suddenly tired, sad eyes back to me and said, "We need to talk, Scarlett."

That set me off. Here he was, wasting my time, and he wasn't even giving me the reaction I wanted.

Scratch that.

Needed.

"Oh yeah sure," I said flippantly, fake-distracted eyes traveling away from him to skim leisurely around the rest of the cabin, letting him know that he was barely worth my attention. "Go ahead. Talk." I snapped my fingers. "Be quick about it. There's still time for you to get your privileged ass off my plane before we close the doors." My voice was dismissive and bored.

"Not here," he ground out. I could tell by his tense tone that I'd gotten to him.

Score—another hit for me and my fake nonchalance.

I knew how to push every single button he had.

I'd keep pushing them until my fingers fell off or he left.

I saw one of my other crewmates, Demi, giving me a strange look from the coach cabin.

Dammit, I'd forgotten for a second that I was working. I had at least a hundred things to do in the next five minutes. I didn't have time to indulge in this hatefest just then.

"Excuse me," I told Dante coldly, not even looking at him again, and strode away.

"Why slap them on the wrist with feather when you can belt them over the head with a sledgehammer."
~Katharine Hepburn

chapter two

I approached him again as I was taking dinner orders. I'd skipped him on my first sweep, only getting to his seat when everyone else was taken care of.

With every other passenger, I'd politely inquired what they'd like from the menu.

Dante, as always, got special treatment from me.

"We're out of everything but chicken," I told him flatly. "Take it or leave it, princess."

Dammit, I'd overdone it. That actually made him smile.

"I'll take it," he said, sounding amused.

I hated it when he sounded amused. It made me want to smile, and also perversely, to smash a blunt, heavy object over his head.

"It's good to see you, Scarlett." The fucker actually managed to sound like he meant it. "You look as amazing as you always do. How've you been?"

Shut up, I wanted to say. *Just stop talking.*
Just leave me alone.
Forever.

But I'd never say any of that. It would be too much like letting him win.

And if he won, I lost.

I'd lost enough.

"Peachy," I said through my teeth.

"I saw that commercial you did. The one for the body lotion. You were really good."

He was making fun of me, of course.

"Fuck you," I drawled.

His brows lowered, bright eyes squinting at me. "I wasn't being sarcastic. You were good. Beautiful. Charming. Charismatic. I'd bet a lot of money that the exposure from that is going to get you some offers."

"Offers for what? Go on. Let's hear it. Stripping? Prostitution?"

He sighed. "For an acting job. God, you don't make anything easy. I was trying to say something *nice* to you." He sounded sincere.

"Why?" My tone was outright hostile.

His mouth twisted, his eyes imploring me as he answered with a soft, "Because, insane as it is, I miss you."

He sounded like he genuinely meant it.

It made me feel violent, so unhinged that I couldn't keep it in, couldn't hold back a quiet and vehement, "Go fuck yourself."

I turned on my heel and stormed off.

Add another point for The Bastard.

Make no mistake. He can be a charmer but Dante is every bit as difficult as I am. This is not some scenario where I've tormented a sweet man in love.

I *have* tormented some sweet men. Broken hearts and shattered dreams.

Men are punching bags, and I have a hell of a right hook.

But (unfortunately) none of those broken hearts belonged to Dante. His heart is black and cold and made of sterner stuff than most.

I'd tried once. Given it my all when righteous rage had driven me to do some awful things in the name of revenge, things done for the sole but futile purpose of stomping his lying black heart under my heel, but in the end I'd done more harm to myself than to him.

That wasn't to say I wasn't capable of hurting him. I could and had many times.

But it was never enough.

Breaking him until he was as broken as me was the only thing that would ever be enough.

I tried to ignore him as much as I could for the duration of the flight, but it was impossible to snub him completely.

Still, he was served everything last and with insolence.

I sneered as I handed him his food. It was burnt. I'd left it in the oven for an extra ten minutes. On purpose.

"Thanks," he told me cheerfully. I could *feel* his eyes searching my face, but I refused to look at his. "Would a gin and tonic be too much trouble?"

"Yes," I said curtly and stormed off.

But back in the galley, as I was refreshing another passenger's champagne, I remembered how much I liked to get him stinking drunk.

I made him a triple in the biggest glass I could find, and put a laughable splash of tonic on top.

I didn't add ice, stir it, or give him a straw.

We had limes, but I didn't add one.

I wanted it to be a bitter drink. Let him taste how he made me feel.

Just the thought of getting him good and drunk had me in high spirits, recovered from the debilitating round earlier and determined again to play this game.

I handed him his glass of bitter with a bright smile.

He eyed it warily. "What's this?"

"Your gin and tonic. Drink up."

He tipped it at me in a toast and took a drink. His eyes stayed on me while he did it, so I got to watch them scrunch up as he got a proper taste.

"Not to your liking?" I asked him archly. "Too strong for you? Need something weaker?"

He shook his head. "No, it's fine. I'll drink it. Almost forgot how much you loved to get me drunk for no good reason."

"If you're determined to have that talk about God knows what that you mentioned, then yes, I'd rather deal with you drunk. You're more pleasant."

"Fair enough."

"And clever."

"Really?"

No. It was an insult, you ass.

I hated it when he didn't play along.

"Absolutely. You're actually funny when you're drunk. Hell, inebriated you is almost human."

He winced. That one had gotten to him.

Hit scored. Point for me.

I made another sweep through first class, and a quicker one through coach.

Dinner flights were nonstop busy, and I'd never been more happy about it than I was on that one.

I passed him again on my way up to the front galley.

He was nursing his glass of gin and nothing.

That wouldn't do.

I made him another, delivering it to him with a smile that was all teeth.

I set the second drink next to the first.

He glanced at them, then at me.

"Oh I'm sorry. Did you need me to put a nipple on that?"

He laughed.

"You used to drink like a man," I told him, undeterred.

He finished off the first one, eyes on me all the while.

That was another thing about him. He rarely backed down from a challenge.

I wish I could say it was one of the many things about him that I hated, but frustratingly it wasn't. It had saved me when we were kids. Who knows what added hell I'd have gone through without his cursed stubbornness.

I took the empty glass away, intending to refill it immediately.

When I returned, the second drink was nearly finished.

I set down a third without a word.

I kept an eye on him, delivering a fourth as he was finishing up the third. And then a fifth. And so on.

"You did this on purpose," Dante said to me. Even when he was blitzed, his speech was barely slurred. But I knew the signs. He was trashed in the extreme.

Hit scored. Another point for me.

I stayed busy for the duration of the flight, and Dante stayed drunk.

We were deplaning when I realized he might not even be able to make it off unassisted.

Everyone had deplaned and he was still swaying in his chair.

"What should we do with him?" Demi, the youngest of our crew, asked. She was a sweet little thing, and somehow on her, sweet didn't annoy me.

The cabin crew was up near the door, ready to go, the pilots waiting for us in the jet bridge.

All that was keeping us was The Bastard.

"He's hot," Farrah, who worked the back galley, added. "Like, fuckhot hot."

"He's too drunk," Demi pointed out. "That'd be rape."

"I wasn't being literal," Farrah said wryly.

"Should we call a paramedic?" Leona asked, eyeing him. "That's the protocol for this level of inebriation on the ground."

I rolled my eyes. "No. I'll handle the fucker."

With an annoyed sigh I headed toward him. "Flight's over," I told him, voice stern. "You need to get your drunk ass off this plane."

At that he staggered to his feet.

"We still need to talk," he pronounced slowly.

"If you can't get yourself off this plane unassisted, we're calling a paramedic for you," I told him coldly.

Yes, I had done this to him. Didn't mean I'd help him.

He nodded jerkily and started to move past me.

I stiffened as he squeezed by me in the aisle.

He put his drunk face into my hair and inhaled.

My hands clenched into fists, but he moved away before I could do anything productive, like, say, punch him in the face.

I grabbed his things out of the overhead bin. At least he hadn't brought much. One small carryon that didn't weigh a thing.

"We divided up your bags," Leona called out to me. "You get that, and we've got your stuff covered."

The girls were starting to file off the plane directly behind Dante the Drunk.

I was the last out of the jet way. Dante was already parked in a chair by the time I caught up to the rest of them.

"What should we do with him?" the captain asked me. As the lead flight attendant, he *was* my responsibility.

I rolled Dante's bag over to him, perching it beside him. He was staring at me, but I never even glanced at him directly.

I turned back to my expectant crew. "We leave him. He's a big boy. He can fend for himself."

I got some strange looks, but everyone was ready to be done for the day, so no one argued.

"You won this round!" Dante called to my retreating back. "But I'll find you again!"

I was at the back of our crew, and I didn't break stride as I held up my hand, waving goodbye to him with one expressive finger.

"He's more myself than I am.
Whatever our souls are made of, his and mine are the same."
~Emily Brontë

chapter three

PAST

The first time we ever *really* talked to each other was right outside of the vice principal's office in fourth grade.

We'd both just been busted for fighting.

It wasn't the first time we'd met, or even the first time we'd been forced to spend time together, but I remembered very clearly that it was the first time I realized we were alike. That there was another kid like me, someone who could relate to all of the rage, all of the insecurity and anger I carried around with me every second of the day.

On the outside, we were opposites in almost every way.

I was skinny. He was strapping.

My clothes were too small and threadbare; his fit him perfect, and looked so expensive to my young, untrained eye that I'd have been afraid to touch them with my grubby hands.

Even his hair was perfect. Not short like the other boys, but not long either. Styled with gel and parted on the side. No other boys had hair like him, like a grownup tended to it every single day before school.

Mine was a long, tangled mess that I hadn't brushed in days.

He smelled like soap, fancy soap, something spicy and pleasant.

I just smelled.

He was filthy rich.

I was dirt poor.

But we did have a few, crucial things that matched: Bad attitudes and worse tempers.

I swear I was born with a chip on my shoulder. Full of more hard things than soft ones. And so when there *was* a soft thing I was doubly defensive of it. Willing to fight for it. Hard and often.

Willing to pull that stupid girl's hair until I ripped great big hunks of it out to make her sorry for pointing it out.

I looked down at my hands. I was still holding some of the long blonde strands, and I hadn't even known it.

Glancing around, I gathered it all into a ball and slipped it behind my chair.

Like it mattered, at this point. I'd already been busted.

And I wasn't sorry. The little brat had deserved it.

But boy was I in for it this time. My grandma would make me sorry I'd lost my temper again, there was no doubt.

"Were you fightin' again, too?" I asked Dante.

We rarely spoke to each other. I had mixed feelings

about him. My grandma worked for his mom and he'd always been standoffish to me and, well, everyone.

His family had more money than anyone else around. I figured maybe he thought we were all beneath him.

I was pretty sure he was probably a snob.

He grunted in answer.

"Why?" I continued. I felt a rare burst of friendliness towards him. This wasn't the first time I'd seen him get busted for fighting.

It made me like him, maybe even respect him a little bit. I got caught fighting a lot too. So much so I was almost positive I'd get kicked out of school for it this time.

He shrugged, not looking at me.

"Were they makin' fun of you for bein' rich again?" I asked him, watching his face.

He shrugged.

"Were they makin' fun of your nice hair again?" I tried, making my voice soft so he knew I wasn't trying to knock him.

He finally looked at me. The rage in his bright eyes made something swell in my chest.

I was pretty sure he was mad at me for saying that, but that look, those eyes, the way it made me feel, was thrilling. Magical. Like I'd just discovered something to do. Some bright new adventure. Some task that gave me purpose.

I smiled at him. "I *like* your hair. I think it looks really nice. Those little shits," I was proud of myself for pulling out a good curse word for him, "just wish they had your hair. Wish they had *anything* of yours."

His jaw clenched, and I thought how handsome he was. No one else looked like him. His solemn face was without flaw.

"Nothin' they say should get to you," I continued. "You're better than them."

"Same to you," he finally spoke back. "Nothing they say should get to you, either."

I was straight up beaming at him. I'd never felt my face move like that, like it couldn't smile big enough.

"I like your gram," I said, and it was true. She always gave me candy and told me I was pretty. She was the nicest grownup I'd ever met.

"Gram likes you, too," he returned. His voice wasn't how I'd heard it before. Usually he was yelling at people. Now, when he was talking softly, it was really nice. I decided I liked it. A lot.

"Wanna know why I was fightin'?" I asked him. I wanted to tell him the story. I wanted it to impress him.

But the fact was, it didn't take much to get me fighting.

Grandma always said I was a prickly little thing. She was not one for kind words, but even I knew that was the nicest way you could put it.

I was a mean little ball of hate.

He shook his head. "I know why you were. As far as I'm concerned," he said, speaking in that way he had, like he only knew how to talk to grownups, "you had every right to do that."

My heart swelled with pride. Not once, in my entire wretched life, had anyone ever offered me encouragement like that, let alone for doing something that even I knew was naughty.

I really, really liked him when he talked to me like that.

I opened my mouth to tell him something, I don't know what, but it would have been something good, something encouraging, to try to make him feel how he'd just made me feel.

That was when his mom showed up.

I instantly closed my mouth and looked away. She intimidated me, and I didn't want to call attention to myself.

I needn't have worried. She didn't even see me, her disapproving glare was all for her troublemaking son.

"Don't start with me; I don't wanna hear it," he muttered at her before she could even speak.

I gaped. In my world, grownups were scary and you didn't talk back unless you wanted to get slapped so hard your ears would ring. Other kids were the only ones you could stand up to.

But she didn't slap him. She just kept staring at him for a few beats, then her lip started to tremble and she turned away.

I gaped harder. I hadn't thought I could like him anymore today, but he'd gone and done it.

He was a bona fide badass, and I loved it.

He shot me one quick glance as the vice principal ushered him and his mom into her office.

His mouth had shaped into a small, conspiratorial smile.

I was hooked. I really couldn't think of anyone that impressed me more in that moment. I wanted to follow him around, learn his secrets.

How had he not gotten slapped for talking to his mom like that? How had he instead made her cry?

Badass.

The vice principal, Ms. Colby, didn't bother to shut the door, I guess because it was just unimportant me out there, but whatever the reason, I got to eavesdrop unabashedly as his mother and our mean as a snake vice principal attempted to reprimand him.

"Ms. Colby," his mother began the conversation with a stern voice. The tears were gone, in their place disdain. "I'm not sure you want to do this. Why is my child in this office for fighting? He's *in trouble* and this other boy, this *miscreant* suffers no consequences at all? Do you have any inkling how much our family contributes to this school?"

"The other boy, Arnold, did not fight back." Mean Ms. Colby could barely choke out the words, she was so close to losing her temper. I knew the tone well. I caused her to use it often. "Dante started it," she continued, "he hurt Arnold *badly*, and did you know that your son refuses to apologize? How am I supposed to work with that? He was violent, and he won't even promise not to do it again!"

Dante's mom made a big show of reassuring Ms. Colby that no, of course it wouldn't happen again, and yes, of course Dante was sorry.

She sounded very convincing right up until the part where she asked her son, "Right, Dante? Promise Ms. Colby that this won't happen again. It's simple. Say you're sorry and we can put this behind us."

I was in a full-on bratty pout by then. It sucked. He'd apologize and get off scot-free, but not me. My punishment would begin soon and end never. Also, Dante was losing all of his badass cred in my eyes the more I listened to his overprotective mother.

"No!" Dante snarled back. "That little shit deserved it, and I'd do it again!"

I grinned, ear to ear, all of my doubts in him put to rest.

"What did that boy do to you, son?" his mother asked, sounding riled. She was grasping at any reason to put less blame on her child.

"It's the way he talks. It's the way all of them talk. The teachers hear and don't care, and they get away with it, with being *total shitbags*, and I'm sick of it! I'm not sorry, and I'll do it again!"

"Darling, what did he say to you?" his mother asked him in a pathetic, baby talk voice.

That same voice turned hard as nails, and I knew she was addressing Ms. Colby. "Words can be assault too, you know! I won't have my son *bullied*. He has a right to stand up for himself!"

Ms. Colby's voice was beyond disgusted when she asked, "What are you implying was said to you, Dante?"

"Not to me. I just overheard. And so did two teachers. And instead of calling the little shits out, they *laughed*! You *all suck*! What kind of a school is this? The teachers are as bad as the bullies!"

Ms. Colby's sigh was loud enough to be heard two rooms away. "And what did you overhear?"

"*You* know," Dante shouted back at her. "You're as bad as them. You know how the other kids treat her, and you look the other way. Well, I don't. I'll do it again. You mark my words."

Bad. Ass.

But who was he talking about? Who was *her*?

"What is he talking about, Ms. Colby?"

Another loud sigh. I really hated her sighs. I had to listen to them a lot.

"I can't be sure," Ms. Colby hedged, but even in another room I thought she sounded like a liar.

"Liar," Dante said to her. To a teacher. The vice principal, no less.

Bad. Ass.

"I need someone to explain this to me!" Dante's mother exclaimed.

"They were picking on Scarlett again," he said, voice pitched low now, so low I had to move closer to the room to hear him. "They always do. They call her trashcan girl. It's messed up. And nobody does anything about it! Not the teachers. Not the *vice principal.* You all suck!"

His mother sounded like she might be choking on something and then she spit out, "You got into a fight over *her?* Are you *kidding* me?"

I felt sick with mortification and light with joy all at once.

He'd gotten into a fight for *me.*

But then, the *pity* in his voice.

Trashcan girl. Even he knew me as that.

It was the exact same reason I'd gotten into *my* fight. It always started with a mean singsong *Hey, trashcan girl* and ended with me hitting someone, or kicking them, or pulling their hair out, or ripping up their homework.

But this was the first time I'd ever heard of anyone else fighting *for* me.

It was something.

No. It was everything. Even enough to overshadow my embarrassment that he knew I was trashcan girl.

Of course he'd known what I was called. I shouldn't have been shocked.

It was his grandmother, after all, that had rescued me.

I'd known the story from the time I could remember. My grandma always said every nasty thing she could think of when she was mad at me, which was a lot, and so it'd come up early and often.

When I was a tiny baby I was abandoned by my parents.

I hadn't been left on the doorstep of an orphanage or church. I wasn't abandoned in some frilly basket by a tearful mother.

Even that was too romantic of a story for me.

I was left in a trashcan. Meant to die, I figured. Or rather, Grandma told me I should figure as much when she was telling me the story.

Even my grandma didn't know who my dad was, but my mom was her daughter, and she explained to me once, after I'd been nagging her for stories about my missing mom, that, "Some women should never be mothers. I'm one of those. And so was my daughter. She won't come back. I guarantee it. You're lucky *I'm* still around. I got nowhere else to go, or I'd be out of here, too."

That was about as sentimental as we got in my family.

And even I knew that my grandma would have never taken me in if her friend from childhood, Dante's gram, hadn't insisted.

I didn't know her well, but I did know that I owed his gram a lot. My grandma told me so all the time. When she got mad, I often earned rants that started with something along the lines of, "You should thank Mrs. Durant every chance you get. She was the one that talked me into taking you in. You can bet your bratty little ass it wasn't my idea."

I'd been found in the trashcan at some point, obviously. No one would tell me how old I was, but I was a baby for sure, a tiny one. Someone had heard me crying, called the cops, and I'd ended up on the news and in the local hospital.

Gram had seen the story on TV, and I don't know all

the details, but she'd put the pieces together and known that Grandma's daughter had recently given birth, so she'd gone and taken a look at me.

One look, Grandma swears, and it was impossible to deny that Renée Theroux was my mother.

I thought that was weird. All babies looked the same to me.

But Gram and Grandma had been sure, Gram had pressed Grandma, and the rest was history.

Grandma had taken me in, made room for me in her tiny trailer. It *did* have an extra room. She liked to bring up how she'd liked that room. She'd enjoyed having an extra bit of space to herself where she could sew and store things. We had many, many conversations like that, where she reminded me of all of the reasons why I was a burden to her.

And I wasn't ungrateful. The place was a dump, but it was a fact that it was better than a trashcan.

Even so, everyone around these parts knew the story, so from my first day of school to present day—I still hadn't lived down the fact that I'd been thrown away like trash.

But that wasn't the worst part. The worst part was, deep down inside, I knew I *was* trash. No one wanted me, that was a fact. What was that if not trash?

Needless to say, it was a sore subject, and it didn't take much to make me lash out when I was teased for it, which was often.

Some days it felt like my life was nothing but one long fight.

But that day was different. That was the day I realized that I just might not be alone in that fight.

When Dante emerged from the office, triumphant

from my perspective, considering all he'd gotten was suspended for fighting and then chewing out the vice principal.

I gave him an ear to ear smile.

He returned it with a small one of his own.

And that was it. He was my very first friend. It was that simple.

I look back on that pivotal encounter of ours often, and I always end up asking myself two questions.

Like most things in my life, they are at odds with each other.

Did that meeting save me?

Or did it ruin my life?

"Love is like war. Easy to begin, but very hard to stop."
~H.L. Menchen

chapter four

PRESENT

Our layover was in San Francisco. It was only for twenty-four hours, just enough time to go out drinking and sleep before we hit the air again.

And boy was I going to drink.

It'd been a doozy of a day, and I was planning to throw one hell of a drunk.

And my girls were with me all the way. Leona knew more about Dante than the others, but Demi and Farrah knew enough to understand that I needed to go out and find some distraction.

San Fran was a bi-weekly stop for our static crew, and we knew just the bar to go to. It had cheap drinks, hot men, and was within staggering distance of our hotel.

The pilots insisted on going with us. They always did. Flight attendants were pilot catnip, and every girl on our crew was hot, so we were catnip times four.

Also, and much to my disappointment, Leona was dating the first officer.

She was young, only twenty-six, but just a little over two years ago she'd been through a really ugly divorce.

I'd gone through it with her.

And now she was finally dating again, but it was a fucking pilot.

Said pilot was with the captain buying us all a third round at the bar while we lounged on a long, red couch and blatantly scoped out the room.

It was packed with men, and even though we were in San Francisco, at this particular bar most of the men were usually straight.

"Never date a pilot," I told Leona, for maybe the thousandth time, as I watched her not quite boyfriend smile at the female bartender.

"He's a nice guy," she defended. "I think it's going well."

"He's totally into Leona," Demi added.

"Of course he is," I agreed. "Look at her. But it's not about her or how he feels about her. He's a pilot."

Leona waved me off. "Time will tell. They can't *all* be bad. There are exceptions to every rule."

I decided to drop it. She wasn't budging, and much as I hated it, she might just have to learn this one the hard way.

I nodded my head at a hipster dude at the bar. He'd gone so full-on hipster that he was borderline lumberjack. "I might give that one the time of day."

Leona's delicate nose scrunched up. It was pretty dang cute. Everything she did was cute. Normally I hated cute girls, but with Leona, it was just part of her charm. "You don't like beards. You always say how they smell bad, how they've done tests on men with beards like that, and they always find shit in them. Literal shit."

I giggled. "You said literal shit."

"I did. That guy is not your type."

"Who cares," I shrugged. "He keeps staring at me. I like it."

"He's not the only guy staring at you. Why him?"

"Because tequila."

Demi giggled. "That's the best toast ever. We're all getting shots of Patrón. Because tequila! This is happening."

I nodded. The more the better. Leona thought that I was impaired and it was affecting my judgement, but the sad truth was that I wasn't even close to being drunk

I needed to remedy that and quick.

Demi had just brought us all limes and shot glasses over brimming with tequila when Leona said quietly, her eyes aimed right over my shoulder, "Bastard at six o'clock."

Fuck.

"Because tequila!" we all chanted the toast.

I did the shot and chased it with a deep gulp of my cocktail.

I'd won the last round. Dante was supposed to disappear after a defeat like that.

What was his fucking problem?

And I wasn't even drunk. I downed the rest of my cocktail and still didn't get there.

What a fucking lousy day.

I was so annoyed by that that when I turned to watch Dante approaching, I already had a few bullets in the chamber.

I began to stride toward him, deciding to meet him halfway.

"You're back," I said when I got close.

"I'm back," he agreed. His suit was wrinkled, his hair mussed, but otherwise he'd recovered rather miraculously. In fact, if I was masochistically honest with myself, he looked edible.

"You sobered up fast," I drawled out grudgingly.

He shrugged. "Mostly. If it makes you feel better, I'm still a little drunk." It did, barely. "Can we go somewhere quiet to talk?"

As he spoke his eyes moved over me.

I'd dressed cute, at least. Cute maybe wasn't the word.

With the small possibility I'd see him again, I'd suited up for the night like I was putting on armor. Sex appeal as a weapon.

My light gray dress was edgy and sexy, with a sculptured bodice that hugged tight to my ribs and waist, a harness strap built-in bra that teased as much as it showed off, and a hi-low peplum skirt over a sleek mini dress.

My legs were bare, tan, and sky-high in a pair of cheerful yellow platform stilettos.

My look was hot and right on trend. It was a cheap as hell knockoff of a designer look, though only a discerning eye could tell it wasn't name brand.

I hated that he'd been raised with just such an eye, and there was no way he wouldn't spot the difference.

"How's Tiffany?" I asked him, tone pleasant as could be considering that it was shaping the name I despised more than any other in the world.

He smirked. "She's fine. She still hates you."

"Oh?" I couldn't keep the delight out of my voice or expression.

"Every woman I've ever tried to have any kind of a relationship with has good reason to hate you."

"Good. The feeling is mutual."

"That sounds like jealousy, tiger."

I rolled my eyes, trying not to wince at his use of my other nickname. "How cute that you want to think so," I bit back, "but you know me better. It's a more simple hate I have for those stupid women. You know I never could tolerate idiots."

"And you're saying *every* woman I've dated is an idiot?"

"Every one of them that settled for my leftovers, yes."

"Well, now, that's all of them."

"You're a quick one. How's your mother?"

That had us both smirking, though mine died as soon as I saw his.

His mother was a crazy harpy, so much so we'd always just naturally united against her. Well, back in the day we had.

Nowadays there wasn't a cause on earth righteous enough to unite us.

"Same as ever," he replied. "Crazy as shit, and evil as Satan."

I didn't ask about his gram. I didn't need to. We still talked every week. She was the only reminder I had of him that was worth keeping in my life.

Everything else I'd left behind.

"How's that director you were seeing?" he asked me, his mouth shaping into a grin that made me want to slap him.

He was mocking me, yet again. I had been seeing a director, no one terribly famous, but one that was successful enough. It'd been more of a friendship behind the scenes, holding hands for the camera sort of thing.

He'd just come out of the closet publicly.

To say that I was not happy to know that it'd amused Dante was a vast understatement.

What I hated, more than *anything*, was to be the butt of someone's joke. Especially his.

I have a terrible temper. Even I am scared of it. And that famously destructive temper came out to *play*.

It was just as well.

The more I hurt Dante now, the better chance I had of getting rid of him.

I didn't know why he'd come, and I didn't want to.

No reason was good enough to drudge up all of these old, filthy feelings.

What I wanted to do—what I needed to do—was scare him off.

I smiled at him. My most vicious smile.

The one that cut him deep enough that we were both covered in the blood.

Saturated and dripping with it.

"How's Nate doing?" I asked him, the words doled out slowly for better effect.

A wise person once said that in a relationship you should keep the fights clean and the sex dirty.

I don't do that. Neither does Dante. We never have.

We do *everything* dirty. And I'd just taken the dirtiest jab of all.

Left hook. I felt it right in my own gut. That's how I knew it was a solid hit.

He stopped smiling, stopped looking at me, his head dropping, eyes aimed down at his feet. "Are you even sorry for what happened with him?" The question came out of him with excruciating restraint. Softly and slowly, each word drawn out.

I was. Wrenchingly so. Kept me awake at night sorry.

Have you ever chewed up someone's heart and then spit it out?

Doesn't sound too bad? Maybe thinking this person is your worst enemy?

But what if it wasn't? What if it was one of your dearest friends? Someone who worshipped the ground you walked on unconditionally.

I'd always had a gift for the irrevocable, and what I'd done to Dante's best friend, Nate, had been just that.

But I'd die before I admitted it to *him*.

"Does he miss me?" I asked instead.

God, that one was so bitchy even I felt the sting of it.

Dante took a very deep breath and straightened. He squared his jaw and stared me down. "Can we call a truce for the night? We really do need to talk. And not here. Somewhere private."

"I've heard that one before," I drawled back. "This wouldn't be the most elaborate thing you've ever tried just to get me into bed."

His face turned hard with disdain. "Trust me, that is *not* why I'm here."

Another, even stronger, flash of temper curled through me, urging me towards destruction.

It was almost funny how we could set each other off with just a few words, the wrong look, the incorrect tone.

We were landmines for each other, and he'd just stepped squarely onto one of mine.

Any show of indifference from him, be it fraudulent or fair, was *unbearable* to me.

Boom. Explosion.

I felt moved by two overwhelming urges in equal parts.

I wanted to slap him silly and fuck him blind.

I restrained myself from doing the first with no small effort.

But I actually considered doing the second. Only for the most twisted reasons, of course.

I was gaging things, trying to decide which action on my part would be more hurtful to him.

Because I wanted to hurt him.

As usual, I wanted to make him *bleed*.

And of all the things you could say about us, about how he felt about me, and how I felt about him, each of us knew that going to bed together again would hurt us both.

A double-edged sword.

I'd take my licks, I decided. It'd be worth it to inflict a bit on him.

It was a sad, tragic fact that I'd take three times my share of the damage just to give him his third of it.

"Fine," I said curtly, barely looking at him. "Let's go somewhere. Where are you staying? Take me to your hotel room."

He nodded jerkily. "That works."

"Let me say goodbye to my friends. You stay here."

"You aren't going to introduce me?" he asked my back.

"Fuck you," I said casually, and strode away.

"You're going somewhere with The Bastard?" Demi asked, sounding scandalized. She didn't know the whole story, but she knew enough. "But I thought you *hated* him."

"Oh I do."

"Are you sure you want to do that?" Leona asked, her eyes on Dante.

"I'm a big girl. I got this."

None of them tried to stop me. They all knew me too

well to even think of getting in my way when I was in this mood.

"Text me when you're in safe for the night!" Leona called to my back.

I waved a hand at her that I would, and left with The Bastard.

"Temptation is a woman's weapon and man's excuse."
H. L. Mencken

chapter five

I couldn't help but mock Dante as he flagged down a cab. "Aw. Look at you, taking a taxi like a normal person. The poor little rich boy's still in denial? Still think you're just like the rest of us?"

He ignored me, though going by his stiffened posture, it was clearly still a sore spot for him.

He was born filthy rich, but he'd always struggled with it.

I was born stinking poor, so his struggle always pissed me the hell off because it was an affront to my own.

We sat as far apart as two people could get in the back of the cab.

I'd decided to fuck him tonight. That didn't mean I had any desire to be near him.

It was a quick ride to the fairly modest establishment where he was staying. I say fairly modest only in comparison to what he could afford. He always did things like this, lived below his means whenever he could.

He was an asshole like that.

I made him walk ahead of me from the car into the building and then down the hallway to his suite. I knew if he was behind me he'd try to take my arm or lead me with his hand on the small of my back, both things I couldn't stomach, because they were too familiar.

Everything about him was too familiar.

I felt a few flutters of misgiving right about the time he opened the door of his room and waved me in.

I ignored them, striding inside.

I can handle this, I told myself. He was the one that should have been worried.

"I don't know how to tell you this," he began but trailed off when he saw that I'd walked straight to the bed.

I perched on the edge, parted my legs, and started to inch my skirt up. It was short, so there wasn't far to go.

"What? Are you going to say now that you didn't bring me here to fuck?"

His throat worked as he swallowed hard, his eyes darting around, avoiding me suddenly. Just the mention of it had him looking like a junkie desperate for a fix.

He took a deep breath then expelled it. He knew what I was up to. In a great many ways, he knew me better than anyone else. "I actually didn't. I swear it."

I laughed, a seductively bitter laugh. Candy dipped in poison.

Eat it up, you bastard.

The sound of it made him wince, which made me happy. "Are you saying that you're actually going to turn me down?"

His eyes latched onto me as he tugged his tie loose impatiently, then tore at the collar of his shirt. My eyes darted away when he exposed the chain he always wore around his neck.

God, why did he still wear that thing? Bile rose in my throat just at the sight of it.

"I'm saying that we really do need to talk," he said.

With a sigh, I stood. This was an unusual amount of resistance from him.

He was easily led in matters of the flesh.

He'd never told me no before. I wondered if this would be a first.

Not fucking likely, I decided, reaching up into my skirt and tugging my panties off with a few impatient movements. I tossed them to the floor at his feet and turned my back on him.

I could hear his breathing change as I contorted my arms behind me and unzipped my dress. I tugged it down my hips as I strutted across the room toward a tall antique dresser. I gripped the edge of it and shot him a look over my shoulder.

I was nude by then, wearing nothing but stilettos and a bad attitude. "Go ahead," I told him. "Talk."

I wouldn't admit this aloud under heavy torture, but as I watched him approach me, I began to tremble. In fear. Trepidation. Horror.

Anticipation. Pleasure. Delight.

When he got close, I turned my face away.

His hands, those big, beautiful, terrible hands of his, brushed my hair over my shoulder an instant before his lips touched my nape.

Head to toe, I shivered.

"I don't have all night," I told him, making my voice hard to compensate for the fact that my insides had gone utterly soft. "You don't have to do your hours long foreplay with me."

He chuckled into my skin. "It's your fault, you know.

You're the reason I'm obsessed with foreplay. Remember when we were teenagers? When we made out for *hours*? God, you made me wait *forever*."

His voice was so full of sweet nostalgia that I had to make light of it.

Had. To.

"If you cry while we fuck I'm putting it online," I quipped.

He laughed and tried to turn my face toward his.

Going in for a kiss, I knew.

I hated his kisses.

Hated. Them.

Hated. Hated. Hated.

I wrenched my chin out of his hand and pressed my body back until my ass was flush to his crotch. He was hard as a rock, bulging through his slacks.

I rubbed against him, teasing him into action.

With a groan, he started kissing my neck again, both hands going to grip my breasts.

I circled my hips, working against him shamelessly. I knew what it did to him, knew he was a hair trigger the first time we made any contact after a long parting. I didn't care. If I got him to embarrass himself before he'd even taken off his pants, all the better.

Humiliating him was a bonus, as far as I was concerned.

No such luck. He knew all my tricks.

He wrenched away suddenly, breaking contact. His hands went to my hips and he tried to turn me around.

"No," I said firmly. "Like this. I want it just like this."

The Bastard wasn't having it. And he was much, much bigger than me, the fucker.

He picked me up like I weighed nothing and carried me straight to bed.

I let out an embarrassing little squeak as he tossed me on the mattress, then followed me down before I could scramble away.

Still fully clothed, he wedged himself between my naked thighs, pinning me.

Slowly, eyes watching me all the while, he cupped my face in both hands.

"I don't think I have to tell you this. You already know it, but—I miss you. Even your bad attitude, I miss." His voice was clear, vulnerable, and succinct.

Shut up, I wanted to snap at him. But it would reveal too much about what his words did to me.

"The feeling is not mutual, you fucking stalker," I told him, voice fraudulently collected.

He just smiled and pressed his mouth to mine.

I turned my head away, gasping, "Don't kiss me!"

He gripped my chin in his hard hand and turned my face back. His defiant gaze bored into mine as he melded our lips back together.

A feeling of raw, violent need quaked through me.

"Fuck you," I snarled into his mouth.

"Yes. That, too," he breathed back. "But first—kiss me, angel. Please."

It was the please that did it. Dirty fighting bastard that he was, he knew how to use that word in the most devastating way—absolutely effective in its rarity.

With a moan, I gave in.

Kissing him ruined me. He knew it.

Apparently I wasn't the only one out for blood here.

His lips were my own personal hell.

They were either his biggest lie, or his greatest betrayer. Every kiss he'd ever given me, when we were in love or in hate, told me how he cared. Told me how he longed.

Craved. Pined. Mourned. Despaired. Told me he was as desperate for me as ever.

I hated him for it, and I couldn't get enough, my hands driving into his hair, nails scoring against his scalp, tongue diving in to taste his liquor sweet breath, clashing with his as unwanted whimpers escaped my throat.

I let it go on for way too fucking long. I have no defense for myself there.

It was too good. Too sweet. Too bitter. Too pleasurable and too painful.

I lost myself so completely that at one point, I even let my hand pull at the chain around his neck, fingering the cursed object that it held, which was a complete slip-up. As soon as I realized I was doing it, I jerked my hand away.

Finally, it was my sex drive that put an end to that torture. I was throbbing from the inside out and addictive as it was, kissing him was *not* enough to physically satisfy me.

It was one of the few times in my life where I could say that my libido worked in my favor.

I started tearing at his shirt, wrenching at the front until buttons flew, shoving it off his shoulders, then pushing impatiently at his chest when it caught on his elbows.

He wouldn't budge, still kissing me like I was the air he needed to breathe.

I'd almost forgotten. Dante always turned fucking into making love. Even when he was drunk. Even when it was rushed, hurried, hard, angry, or desperate. You name it, he turned it all into something more.

I didn't want any of that.

I wasn't here to make love.

I was here to make war.

I bit his tongue hard enough that he recoiled with a curse.

I smiled at him, a hostile baring of teeth, and pointed at his pants. "Clothes off. I didn't come here to make out with you all night."

He was too far gone to tell me no, thank God.

His eyes were glazed over, his breath short as he started to unbutton his slacks.

I rolled over onto my belly and began to crawl across the bed.

If he could resist *that* view, I'd lost my touch.

I didn't want him to have control of any part of this, and I didn't plan to let him kiss me again.

My ploy worked.

He was on my back before I could make it to the other side.

He covered me, lips on my shoulder, hands cupping my breasts right as I felt him lining his thick tip up at my entrance.

He paused too long there.

"Do it," I bit out.

I hid it better, but I was as far gone as he. I needed this. Needed it like the possessed need an exorcism.

"Ask for it," he spoke into my skin.

There he was. The Bastard I knew and loathed.

"Go die in a fire," I gritted out, pushing back against him.

"Ask me *nicely*," he added. "Say, please, Dante."

"Please go die in a fire, Dante," I spat out right as my elbow connected sharply with his ribs. He grunted in pain, and I made a break for it.

He caught me just as my second foot hit the floor and had me flipped around and straddling his lap at the edge of the bed.

He looked up at me with a conciliatory smile and said, "I take it back. Old habits, ya know? But I take it back and I'm sorry. I meant it about the truce tonight."

A please and a sorry from him all in one night?

It was a miracle.

Or the apocalypse.

One thing was for sure, it wasn't fucking normal. Or right. Or even okay. I could count on one hand the number of times he'd said both words combined in the last five years.

And for this he was sorry?

He had plenty to be sorry for, grievances much worse than anything he'd done in the last five minutes.

I was once again torn between wanting to slap him, choke him, or fuck him blind.

I settled for a compromise, my fingers sliding around his throat and squeezing lightly as he pulled my head down to his and started kissing me again, almost clumsy now in his drunken passion.

His pants were opened, his thick cock jutting out, and I shifted my hips, poising myself over him. I gripped his neck and shifted until his tip pushed into me. With a groan, I tried to impale myself on him.

His stubborn hands on my hips halted my progress.

This was how it was with us. A never ending struggle for dominance.

Usually he won the bedroom portion of that struggle, but I always told myself I let him do it for the simple fact that it got me off harder.

He could dominate me physically, so long as I always had the last word.

I thought mine was the better deal, in general, but at that moment it was pissing me off to no end.

I pulled back to ask him what his problem was, but lost the breath to do so as just then he flipped me smack onto my back.

He stood, impatiently shedding the rest of his clothing while I watched. My wide eyes sucked up each luscious inch of tanned, muscled skin he unveiled.

I parted my legs wide and raised my knees up until my heels were digging hard into the mattress. Fuel to his fire.

It worked well enough. He was naked and on top of me between one gasping breath and the next.

"Scarlett," he breathed his sweet liquor breath against my mouth right as he started to push into me.

Even his drunk breath I hated. Even that held bittersweet memories that reminded me inevitably of our love and our losses.

My eyes were shut tight as I breathed back, "Don't talk. Your voice ruins it for me."

"Scarlett," he repeated, this time with a smile in his voice.

"Shh. I'm trying to pretend you're someone else. Every time you speak it ruins the illusion."

"It's been too long, angel," he murmured, then took my mouth and shoved in hard.

I was ready. Beyond ready.

I was wet, throbbing, aching, hungry, desperate for him.

I hated myself for it, but I hated myself for a lot of things. At least *this* thing brought me as much pleasure as pain, or rather this part of it did.

It felt so good when he started moving that I found my nails clawing into his back every time he started to pull out, then clamping into him with every rough shove in, until, as he began to move faster, I was scoring with gusto into the abused skin over his shoulder blades.

He wasn't complaining, and I couldn't seem to stop myself.

It was quick. It always was the first time.

"I can't hold it back," he moaned. "I'm coming."

"Selfish prick," I taunted into his ear.

Of course he took that as a challenge. I'd meant it as such. Either it'd motivate him to get me off faster, or it would make him feel inadequate. Both counted as a win for me.

He chose the former, one of his big hands snaking between our bodies, his familiar fingers going unerringly for my clit, working at it with a precision that made my eyes roll up in my head, my overactive mind gone blank for one glorious, regrettable moment.

Tears stung the back of my eyelids as I came. He followed me with a low groan, taking my mouth as he rooted deep and let himself go, emptying inside of me.

It was the sweetest torture, the most delightful torment, to let the man that had ruined me for joy bring it back into my body for one brief instant.

The full-on drunk I'd tricked him into earlier must have still been affecting him. He was usually good for more than one short round. A lot more.

But this time, after a soft kiss on my cheek (a second before I shoved him off me) he rolled onto his stomach and passed out cold.

With one last sneer at him I got up and started gathering my clothes.

I was just zipping my dress when my eyes caught on his shoulders. Or rather, what I'd done to them.

I'd scratched his back bloody. Literally. A few of the deep scores were bleeding.

He'd be wearing evidence of me for weeks, and though it hadn't been as deliberate as he would no doubt assume, I wasn't sorry.

I paused when I was dressed and ready to go.

I couldn't help myself when he was sleeping like this. I moved closer to the bed, my eyes on his downcast, peaceful face in slumber.

I let myself watch him for a time, my mind worlds away and years ago, recalling a time when his beautiful face had been beloved to me.

This was the problem. Even with all the hate I had built up against him, being in his proximity brought back those other feelings, the ones that had nothing to do with hate.

To counteract such poignant, debilitating regret I felt like I should do something else, make some statement that he'd see in the morning that would further cement my victory here.

I thought about ways to humiliate him while he slept. Throw some dollar bills on him, draw a penis on his forehead, get creative, have some fun with it.

But alas, I was short on cash and I didn't have a Sharpie handy.

I settled for leaving a short message written in lipstick on the bathroom mirror.

Nice talk.
Don't call me, and stay off my flights.

I figured between that and the scratches, he'd understand that I knew I'd won this one.

I had to take this round for myself, but not for the reasons you might think.

Not to win. Not even to conquer. But to endure. It was imperative.

Because even when I won with Dante, I was defeated.

Because, *to this day*, I had a hard time walking away from him.

Something inside of me—some *insidious* thing, deep down in the dregs of my soul raged against every step that took me in the opposite direction of him.

Even after all this time, it *raged*.

"Proud people breed sad sorrows for themselves."
~Emily Brontë

chapter

six

I don't sleep well. I never have.

My subconscious hates me. It exploits me at my weakest moments. When I can't control my own mind, it conjures up new and old nightmares to taunt me—ruthlessly and consistently.

My dreams like to trap me. Take me back to places I badly want to leave. Back to feelings I desperately wanted to forget.

That night my sleep was particularly wretched, as I dreamed about Dante and the way it used to be. The could haves and the what ifs were my own personal hell and had been for a very long time.

I liked to blame Dante for everything that went wrong between us, and when I was in my right mind, I did. But my subconscious had other ideas. How much of our end had been my fault? And worse, how much of it had been preventable? He'd started the avalanche that ended us forever, but it was a fact that I'd fed that disaster once it had started rolling.

If I was brutally honest with myself, I'd even helped to start it. Not deliberately, but I'd always just been so insecure.

When I was a child, I thought that no one would ever love me. For the longest time, I was certain of this. It was me against the world, and the world was cruel.

But then.

Then.

Dante.

He loved me so deep and so hard that I was blinded by it.

I thought it was a miracle. I was so young, so impressionable, so infatuated.

So stupid. For years and years, all I had the sense to do was bask in it.

I let our love rule my life. It was everything to me. He was. I became possessive of every part of him. And it didn't take much for that possessive streak to turn ugly. My jealous rages were infamously brutal on us both.

How much had that desperate insecurity contributed to pushing him away? If I'd been less difficult, less needy, less fundamentally fucked in the head, would things be different?

I tossed and turned all night with those impossible questions tormenting my overactive mind. I'd have been better off just staying up all night, but I was paralyzed, frozen to the hard hotel mattress until my alarm freed me.

I reported for work in a hell of a mood.

"I take it things didn't go well," Leona finally asked me as we strode through the terminal, headed for our plane. I hadn't said a word to anyone on the ride from the hotel to the airport. Not so much as a good morning for a one of them.

I didn't look at her as I answered. "Everything went according to plan. I won, he lost. He shouldn't bother me for a while." My tone was curt. It was my leave me alone voice, and she knew to do just that. It was one of the reasons we could hang.

I was a loner by nature, and she was a nice, friendly, sociable girl that never seemed to have a bad day. When I'd first met her, that had annoyed the *hell* out of me. But over time, when I'd realized it wasn't an act, that she was just somehow inherently *good*, the girl couldn't help it if she tried, she'd started to grow on me. And over time, as I'd given her a shot, and found that she didn't expect me to be like her, I'd become dangerously attached. More so than I usually allowed myself. It was her tolerance that got me, when I normally had no problem staying aloof.

If she saw a storm brewing in me, as it inevitably did, she had the sense to give me space. I'd never been a girls' girl. I didn't keep female friends for long, before Leona. She was the first girl-friend I'd ever had that did that, that took the time to understand me enough to just back off sometimes.

As though taking her cue, Demi and Farrah did the same. They didn't know me or my situation with Dante like Leona did, but they knew enough.

My mood improved a bit as we started to work. Keeping busy was distracting enough that my mind began to clear from the fog of my dreams.

Still, I was looking over my shoulder constantly, some part of me sure that he'd show up again.

But he didn't. To say I was glad to shut the doors on my flight without a Dante in my cabin the next day was a vast understatement.

I was so grateful that I didn't have to deal with him

again I was thanking God, my knees weak with relief at the respite.

It was done. I'd warded him off for the foreseeable future. It was enough.

"Love isn't something you find. Love is something that finds you."
~Loretta Young

chapter seven

PAST

I was waiting outside the vice principal's office again. For fighting. Again.

I'd actually been doing pretty well lately, so this was now a rare occurrence.

There had been some major changes in my life.

After that day when I found out Dante was fighting for me, we were near inseparable.

We just fit together, he and I. Not necessarily in a sweet or romantic way. We were both thick skinned and sharp tongued. A tad too jaded, a touch too sarcastic. Hotheaded and stubborn to an extreme.

Dante was just as prickly as I, just as jaded, more sarcastic, more hotheaded, but thankfully, not as stubborn.

Which meant that when we clashed, as we invariably did, I won more.

I *needed* more wins.

We both knew it, and he was kind enough to let me have it. It was one of many reasons why we fit so well together. Despite all of his flaws, his sullen moods, his tempers and rages, he showed me an enduring compassion that no one else ever had.

We were in our early teens. It was that age where the sexes had separated to a polarizing degree. Boys hung out with boys. Girls played with girls. Those were the rules. There was some general flirtatious banter, some note passing, and lots of brief, teasing interactions but other than that, there was a clear segregation of the sexes.

We didn't care. We ignored that rule completely. We were each other's only friends, and I wouldn't have had it any other way.

We spent a good amount of time over at his gram's house. Her huge mansion of a place was a five-minute walk up the hill from my grandma's trailer, a walk I hadn't known I was welcome to take before, but now, like magic, I was. She'd told me I could come over any time I wanted, and since my grandma was gone a lot, I took her up on the offer almost every day. And Dante, who lived on a huge property between, almost always met me on the way and went over with me.

Now I didn't have to be alone so much. It was the best thing that had ever happened to me.

Things were so much better, in fact, that I wasn't as angry anymore. Wasn't fighting every kid over every insult they sent my way, and, miracle of miracles, there even seemed to be less insults these days.

No one was much intimidated by a little skinny girl like me, even a vicious one, but plenty of the kids had learned to be wary of Dante.

He fought like a demon, and word had spread that he'd pound anyone that messed with me.

It was wonderful.

But it was not absolute. Today was a case in point.

This time it'd been a boy I'd been fighting with. I'd decked the asshole right in the chin, and when he'd decked me back, I'd kicked him so hard in the balls that he'd fallen to the ground and cried like a baby.

The rest of our class had watched the whole thing with varying degrees of disgust, exasperation, and horror, but of course none of them had tried to step in or help.

I was used to all of it.

I'd always been the indisputable outcast. Other kids were very comfortable uniting against me.

Flu going around? Trashcan girl.

Lice outbreak? Trashcan girl.

Even though neither of those had been pinned on me for sure.

Lucy Hargrove, who had four brothers and two sisters and lived in a dump of a house no better than mine had started at least one of them.

Still, Lucy was sweet. Lucy had friends. Lucy didn't make a good target because other kids *liked* her.

So Scarlett it was.

And today it was: *Does something smell bad?* Trashcan girl.

That one was maybe true in the past, but since Gram had taken me under her wing, I'd learned how important it was to bathe and how to do it properly. I didn't smell bad now, I was sure of it, but it didn't matter. I'd never live down the stink of the dumpster I'd been left in.

And even though the dynamic had changed and things had shifted a bit in my favor, I was still the butt of many jokes, and I still took strong exception to it. It was just that usually now kids had the sense to make the jokes *behind* my back.

Not today, apparently.

I'd been minding my own business, which was actually what I usually *tried* to do, when Tommy Mann had started in on me.

The teacher was out of the room and we were supposed to be working on an assignment.

I was not a good student by any stretch of the imagination but I *had* been trying to stay on task.

And here came asshole Tommy with his, "Does something smell bad?" right into my ear.

I gritted my teeth and still tried to ignore him. It hadn't been a big enough insult to be worth dealing with my grandma if I made her angry again.

"Does anyone else in here smell something bad?" Tommy asked loudly. "Something that reminds them of garbage?"

There were some loud snickers around the room, but no one outright answered him.

Like a coward I wished, for at least the thousandth time, that Dante and I had been placed in the same class. We never were. He was across the hallway, but at moments like these, it may as well have been a world away.

"Shut up," I muttered at him darkly.

I didn't even see it coming. He was behind me, and though I heard some rustling, some movement, I had no idea what he was doing until the classroom's full trashcan was being dumped over my head.

It didn't have much other than paper in it, but it didn't matter. It was more than enough to bring my temper out to play.

I threw the trashcan off my head, shook away all of the papers, and went after him.

I only stopped when he was a crying ball on the floor.

And of course that was when the teacher walked back into the room.

And now there I was, waiting for the vice principal to call me in.

Tommy was still in class. He hadn't even been reprimanded.

I hated this part. It wasn't even that I cared what they punished me with. Getting kicked out of school was a gleeful fantasy of mine on days like this.

I just didn't want to deal with how my grandma would react.

Also, I hated verbal confrontations. I fought exclusively with my fists for one very important reason.

My voice was a coward.

Ms. Colby made me wait a good hour before she called me in. I'd known she would.

It wasn't an exaggeration on my part to say she didn't like me. More so than any kid in this school, I did nothing but make her job harder, but it felt to me like it went beyond that. She almost seemed to get a strange kick out of putting me in my place.

She was a thin, middle-aged woman with steel gray hair that she kept so short that a lot of the kids had taken to calling her Mr. Colby. At least that's why I thought they called her that. I wasn't friendly enough with most of the other kids to ask if that was the reason for it, so I just assumed.

"As usual, your grandmother couldn't be reached," she began with. "And knowing her, it doesn't matter. She hasn't shown her face here once, no matter what you've been up to. So your punishment for this is, clearly, going to be at my discretion. Before I begin, do you have anything to say for yourself?"

"I-I-I—, h-h-he—" was all I could get out. I never got much farther, especially with Ms. Colby. My stutter was particularly vicious with me when it came to her. The injustice of it, the fact that I could never voice my side of things out loud, only seemed to make the problem worse.

"There's nothing you can say that will excuse what you've done. You can save your pathetic, stuttering breath today, Scarlett."

My shoulders hunched up, eyes pointed at the ground. The pathetic comment really got to me, but it was more or less in line with the things she usually said to me after I'd gotten into trouble.

I resigned to just stand there and take it. It usually lasted awhile. She'd basically find several interesting ways to tell me I was troublesome, worthless, and a nuisance to the school.

And with any luck, she'd kick me out.

But something happened. Something pretty amazing. Before she could get any further, a furious Dante came storming into the office.

He went off on her and it was a glorious thing. He was foul-mouthed and surly when provoked, and he was plenty provoked just then.

"What the hell is *wrong* with you?" Dante raged at her. "A boy attacks her, she defends herself, and she's the one that ends up in your office getting reamed out? Are you even kidding me?"

He was the opposite of me. I stuttered hopelessly, and he seemed to have a talent for saying what would make everyone around him shut up and wait in stunned silence until he was finished.

Ms. Colby seemed to be no exception. She was just staring at him. I didn't think she could believe what she was hearing. Kids did not talk to her this way.

"He threw a trashcan on her head!" Dante screamed. "He's twice as big as her and he punched her in the face! What the hell is wrong with this school that she's the one in trouble for that?"

I watched him without blinking; my heart so full, I felt it would burst.

The entire terrible day had been worth it for this moment.

Without looking at me he grabbed my hand and started to tug me out of the room. "You know what?" he snarled at a still mute Ms. Colby. "We're *done* here. I'm fed up with this *shit*. This school is *out of control.* Whatever you're going to try to pin on Scarlett, you can just go ahead and take it up with my gram."

Something moved on Ms. Colby's stunned face. Something that I liked. Dante had clearly struck a nerve.

Dante saw it too, and he smiled unpleasantly at her. "Don't like that, huh? Well, like I said, you can take it up with my gram. I just called her from the reception desk and let her know what happened. She'll be here in fifteen minutes. Good luck."

He gave her a mocking little wave and tugged me out of the room, then the building.

"Where are we going?" I asked him when we'd crossed off school grounds and had moved into the forest. I was pretty sure I knew. This was a familiar path.

"Home," he replied. He stopped suddenly, turning to me.

I was looking way, way up at him, thinking that he was the most beautiful boy in the world, and it was only as he touched my cheekbone that I remembered I'd been punched pretty hard earlier.

"Are you okay? Does it hurt?" he asked.

"It's fine. I was so pissed off I barely felt it. And I *did* punch him first."

"Yes, I know, tiger, but he *attacked* you first."

"Who told you about it?"

"Nate Becker. He got a hall pass and got himself into trouble flagging me down in the middle of Mr. Jameson's history lesson."

I tried to keep my face impassive. Nate seemed like a nice enough kid, but I was savagely territorial where Dante was concerned, and I *hated* the idea that he might be making a friend aside from me.

"And then you got yourself into trouble storming Ms. Colby's office," I said, smiling up at him, my heart in my eyes.

"Well, yeah, but that was after."

I blinked a few times. "After what?"

"After I stormed into your classroom and gave Tommy Mann the pounding he deserved."

My jaw dropped. "We're both going to get expelled," I breathed, but not like I was sad about it.

He shrugged. "Either we will, or Gram will take care of it. My money's on Gram."

I squinted at him. "She's the sweetest woman on earth. Ms. Colby's going to chew her up and spit her out."

He threw his head back and laughed and laughed. "Oh, you haven't seen her when she's mad, Scarlett. And you know she has influence over the school board. She donates a lot of money, money they won't want to lose.

Just you watch. There's finally going to be some justice at this stupid school."

He grew serious again, his eyes, then his fingers going to trace softly over my injured cheek. "We need to get you home and put some ice on this."

I made a face. "It's nothing. Stop making a big deal of it."

But he didn't listen. Instead he leaned forward and pressed a soft, chaste kiss on the tender flesh.

When he straightened, I took a deep breath. I'd been struggling not to say anything sappy to him, but I just couldn't hold it in.

I squeezed his hand really hard, looked down at my feet, and said, "I love you," for the very first time in my life.

He squeezed my hand back. "Love you, too." His voice was quiet, but he hadn't hesitated.

I swear I didn't stop smiling for three entire days.

"Unless life also gives you water and sugar, your lemonade will suck."
~A realist

chapter eight

PRESENT

We arrived at LAX before noon, with four days off looming ahead of us. I was the only one on our crew that wasn't happy about that.

The day was sunny and fresh to an unwholesome degree when combined with my mood. I didn't need a nice day. I longed for a dark and dreary one. I wanted to crawl into a hole and stay there. A hole dark enough to wipe my mind clean of the night before.

Why had I done that to myself?

Why did I *always* do that to myself?

Because Dante. The Bastard.

We got home early enough that it gave us only two choices. Take a nap, or keep going. Any activity that consisted of sitting would wipe you out after a full day of work finished at eleven in the morning.

The four of us shared a sprawling apartment in a

somewhat affordable area of town (if you had enough roommates) that had just converted some old warehouses into decent living spaces. We each had our own bedrooms, spaced far enough apart that none of us felt stifled, but shared a living area that was big enough for a hell of a party when the mood hit us, and it often did.

We'd been roomies for nearly a year, and surprisingly I had very little complaints on the arrangement. I'd thought for sure at the beginning that it was a horrible idea. It had all been Leona's idea, and I'd gone along with it because it would save me money. She'd met these two young sweet girls in her flight attendant class and they'd hit it off.

Like us, and what felt like most of the women in L.A., they were aspiring model/actresses.

I saw it as points against them. Stubborn woman that I am, I'd refused to even meet them at first. Leona was one of my first truly close female friends, and to be honest, I felt possessive of her. What if she found some new friend she liked more? What if I didn't like these women, and she chose them over me?

But it was around that time Leona had found this apartment, and we needed two more to make the rent, and so she'd talked me into giving them a shot. The first time I met them, I disliked them on principle. They were too young, too gorgeous, too bright-eyed and optimistic. Too sweet and undamaged.

But, like Leona, they'd grown on me.

I'd been conflicted about it in the beginning. They were literally my direct competition. We'd be auditioning for some of the same roles. It was inevitable.

In spite of myself though, over time I'd gotten over it. For one simple reason. I liked them. They became my friends.

Even now, a year later, I tried to picture how I'd feel if one of them got a part I wanted. Any of them. Demi, Farrah, or even Leona. I'd hate their guts, I told myself. I'd feel betrayed, I reasoned. I'd been working for this longer. I wanted it more. There were no friends in show business, I told myself sternly.

But if I were being honest with myself there was a good chance I'd be happy for them. I might even be *thrilled* for them. Because I'd come to care for them and wanted great things for them. Because they were my friends.

What the hell had these damn girls done to me? When had I gone soft?

I'd surrounded myself with nice people. Apparently the condition was contagious.

Fuck me. I'd always been taught that kindness was a close cousin to weakness, so it didn't settle easy on me. I doubted I'd ever let it.

I told myself they were the exception. I was otherwise still hard as nails.

Leona went out with her new 'boyfriend' for the day. I tried not to roll my eyes when she referred to him as such. They'd been dating a very short time, and she didn't know him well enough to give him that title, and also he was a pilot, and therefore untrustworthy, but I kept that to myself. She seemed happy, and I did enough of my own bubble bursting. I didn't need to do the same to her. Not everyone had to be as miserable as I was. Maybe she'd found herself the one faithful pilot on the planet. My cynical mind couldn't fathom it, but I hoped for her sake that I was wrong and she was right.

Demi decided to crash for the day, and Farrah took off shopping with some friends.

Normally I was down to shop in a big way, but my mood was too dark even for retail therapy. I was not fit company for anyone today, let alone someone I actually liked. I might inflict this extra sharp version of myself on my worst enemy if I were forced to, but certainly not a friend.

I did the only thing post-therapy me could do when fuming with impotent rage.

There was no real way to vent it. No way to make it actually go away.

The best I could do was try to push it somewhere to the back of my mind, or at least not at the forefront.

So I baked. And drank. A lot of both.

Baking cupcakes and drinking scotch. Ardently courting comfort and oblivion.

Oblivion was particularly elusive when I was at this level of keyed up, so I settled for getting buzzed and keeping busy with mindless chores.

I don't bake often, but I do it well, even out of practice. Sweet carbs rarely find their way into the apartment of four actresses, but I knew no one could resist my cupcakes, even if they'd all be cursing me for it later.

I told myself, to appease the sharper half of my personality, that if I made my competition gain a few pounds it was an added bonus, but it rang hollow, more like a humorless joke than anything else.

Our hideous dog, Amos, kept me company, nudging my legs and licking my toes as I worked, the damned mutt.

He was the ugliest dog in the world. His fur was half kinky curly, half sticking straight up in the air and the color was a mix of different shades of poo brown. He had one light blue eye, one dark one, and his muzzle was long and homely, his teeth sticking out of his mouth at odd angles. He was hideous. Some kind of a mix that apparently nobody but me had wanted.

Well, I wouldn't say I'd wanted him.

So why did I have a dog I'd never wanted?

Ten months ago I'd found him in a dumpster down the street. Someone had thrown him away.

I sympathized with the poor guy.

I tolerated him. He was a sweet thing. Slobbery and ugly as hell. And affectionate to a fault.

But I didn't even like dogs. I was a cat person.

I loved cats. Everything about them. I loved that they could be vicious and adorable in equal parts. The way they loved you more if you ignored them. How they did whatever the hell they wanted and with outright defiance. They soothed me with their sleek bodies, soft fur, loud purrs, contrary ways and bad attitudes.

I loved cats, but I had a dog.

Story of my life. I was a conflicted person. Never at peace with myself. Hard to please. A malcontent.

I refused to be happy about any part of it, even something as simple as having a pet.

I collected eccentric and funny cat T-shirts. I liked to wear them around the house, sigh at Amos, and occasionally lecture him about how disappointing he was to me.

He'd always just wag his tail, gaze at me with absolute adoration, and wait for any affection I might have to give him.

Damn dogs, with their unconditional love and unfalteringly bad breath. Who could deal with either of those things?

I knew I should have just gotten a cat, but it seemed

wrong somehow, to get a frivolous thing like a second pet when we all traveled as much as we did. Our neighbor took in Amos when we were out of town, but we could hardly ask him to take in still another pet part-time.

Also, some part of me had a really big problem with openly seeking out something that might bring me joy. Like, with all the things I'd done that were *actually* sins, looking for a bit of happiness in my life was the real transgression.

"Give a girl the right shoes, and she can conquer the world."
~Marilyn Monroe

chapter

nine

For all intents and purposes, I had the apartment to myself for the majority of the day.

It was for the best. I had a lot of baking and drinking to do before I was even close to fit for company.

I was frosting my fifth batch of cupcakes (these red velvet) when the doorbell rang.

My eyes narrowed, and my first instinct was to ignore it. I just had a bad feeling. Nothing I could put into words, just a need to avoid that could be for any number of reasons, not the least of which that I was working on getting stupid, sloppy drunk, and the condition was eluding me.

Nope, I decided. Not answering.

The doorbell rang again, and this time a sleepy Demi came out of her room, gave me a good morning/afternoon wave, and went to open it herself before I could stop her.

I went back to frosting and didn't look up again until she plopped a large red box on the kitchen counter scant inches from my growing horde of cupcakes. I'd made three flavors—German chocolate, vanilla cream, and red velvet.

"Oh my God," she said slowly, her big blue eyes wide. "What are all these cupcakes for?"

I looked at her. She was a gorgeous little thing with big, bright blue eyes, masses of dark hair, pale skin, and a rosebud mouth. She was petite but curvy in all the right places. She basically looked and was the Hollywood version of Snow White. "You. Help yourself."

"You bitch!" she shot back, making me smile for the first time all day. Her calling me a bitch to my face was 100% my influence on her, and I loved it. "You know I have an audition in two days! And red velvet is my absolute favorite!"

I had known that. The whole point of my baking was never to make something for myself. I despised cupcakes. I had the opposite of a sweet tooth. I had a bitter one.

I nodded at the red box. "What's that?"

"Something for you. Some sort of special delivery from a guy in a suit."

I froze, my insides coiling up tight. "Not . . . Dante, right?"

"No, not him. I'd have recognized him. It was some guy I've never seen before, but he insisted I give the box directly to you and said it should be opened immediately."

I felt no better. This reeked of Dante, even it that hadn't been him at the door, though I was still thanking God for that.

"That's odd," I noted, my tone deceptively casual.

"The whole thing was bizarre," she agreed.

I finished frosting the cupcakes, taking my time, smiling when Demi gave in and started eating one, then moaned and raved about how divine it was, but all the while, my mind was on the damned package.

"Is there a return address on that thing?" I finally asked her, avoiding it myself, like that would somehow help.

"Nope. There's nothing. I checked. No postage. That guy just brought it here. You got a new stalker or something?"

My mouth twisted. "Not a *new* one."

"Are you going to open it or you want me to?"

I almost told her to do it, but that felt too cowardly, and realizing that I *wanted* to be a coward was what finally spurred me into action. I had many, many bad qualities, but I'd be *damned* before I'd let cowardice become one of them.

With a curse, I reached for the box, tearing it open.

Inside were red shoes in exactly the same style as the ones I'd been wearing yesterday.

But these were Louboutins.

I read the note tucked in beside the shoes before I could think better of it, and immediately wished I hadn't.

Scarlett,
I know you have a weakness for expensive shoe porn.
And you know i love to exploit your weaknesses.
Enjoy.
Thanks for everything,
D, aka the love of your life
p.s. we still need to talk.

I nearly threw the shoes out of the closest window. I had them free of the box, had moved from the kitchen and across the living room, opened a window, but as I stared at them I just couldn't do it.

They were so gorgeous. How could I throw away something so perfect?

Shoe porn, indeed.

I hated that I loved it. The note. The shoes. Everything about it tailored perfectly to appeal to my senses and tear out pieces of me in precisely equal measures.

We were over, had been for years, but it didn't matter. If he had his way, he'd keep me tied to him forever. He was cruel like that.

The shoes, and particularly the note, was an attack disguised as a white flag, and it worked, did exactly what he intended—got to me. Enraged and weakened me both.

He knew me that fucking well.

No one on earth should know a person that well.

Lovers should have secrets.

In fact, they need them.

Some part of you should stay a mystery in every relationship. Enough mystery to keep some distance and a bit of perspective.

Dante and I had gotten together too young for any of that. I'd given him *everything*, been too smitten and naive to hold back even one selfish part of myself.

Even one essential part of myself.

Never relinquish the keys to your soul to someone else. It gives them too much power.

That kind of power in the hands of a ruthless man like Dante, well, needless to say, it'd taken its toll on me.

I was standing, hands clenched at my sides, glaring at the shoes when my phone started chiming a text at me from the kitchen.

I set the shoes down carefully on the coffee table and stalked to check it.

The text was from an unfamiliar number and read:

Wear them and think of me.

Predictably, it set me off.

And even so, I couldn't throw away the shoes.

I settled for spending a ridiculous amount of time making it look like I had.

Demi was still the only one home, but she was game to assist me in setting it up. She was a sweet young thing. It constantly surprised me how much she liked to help out with any random plot I was hatching on a daily basis just for the sake of sisterhood, just because her first inclination was to be nice, even after I'd made her cupcakes that I knew weren't on her diet.

I'd never been sweet, but ironically some of my closest friends these days were. I was finding that my particular flavor of bitter was sometimes best complemented with a bit of saccharine. Go figure.

I recorded a short video on my phone that showed me tossing the shoes out of my bedroom window, one by one with two short flicks of my wrist.

Our place was on the first floor, so it was fairly simple. Demi was outside, crouched low to the ground, out of the shot, a pillow in her arms.

"Are they okay?" I called out as soon as I stopped recording.

"Caught them both with the pillow!" she called back cheerily. "Your ungodly expensive shoes are unharmed!"

I grinned and sent the video off to my new contact,

which I'd named: Bastard/Stalker/Liar/Cheater/Ex/
TheDevil.

Me: I thought of you while I was doing this. Lose my number.

The smile died on my face at his near immediate
response.

**Bastard/Stalker/Liar/Cheater/Ex/TheDevil: No worries. I'm almost
to your place. I'll rescue them for you.**

I was so caught off guard, not sure if he was messing
with me but rattled with even the possibility of having to
face him again, that I wasn't sure how to respond.

I focused on the most immediate concern—hiding
the Louboutins.

I intercepted Demi right as she was bringing the
shoes back to the front door. I grabbed them from her,
throwing out a, "Thank you," as I hurried back to my
bedroom. I stuffed them in the corner of my closet, threw
some clothes on top, and rushed into the bathroom.

I glared at my reflection. Why today of all days had I
made no effort at all? I'd showered and scrubbed my face
clean of makeup the second we'd gotten home from our trip.
I'd washed my hair, but then let it dry as is, which meant it
was basically a slightly damp rat's nest at this point.

And my outfit could only be described as quirky. In
reality, quirky was kind. I was wearing yoga pants and an
oversized cat T-shirt.

At least it was a somewhat combative cat shirt. The
cat was sweet looking enough, a big, fluffy white thing
surrounded by pink and blue flowers but at the bottom it
read in clear black print: **I WILL END YOU.**

It was really kind of perfect if I thought about it, so I kept the shirt on, switched the pants out for some tiny shorts that showed off my legs, and focused on my hair, dragging a brush through it and doing a quick blow dry, just enough to make it look tousled instead of messy.

I'd just applied the bare minimum of makeup when the doorbell rang again.

I knew it was him. I could feel it in my flesh, just like I could feel my temper bubbling up under my skin, ready for any excuse to ignite.

I was irate that he had the nerve to clash with me again so soon. He'd lost the last round. It had been a clear knockout win for me.

He should have the decency to *stay down.*

I waited in my room, wondering if he'd go away if I just didn't answer.

But I wasn't so lucky, and Demi had the blasted habit of answering the front door.

It was her tentative knock outside my bedroom that jarred me into action. That and her kind voice calling through, "Um, Scarlett, I'm sorry, but, uh, Dante, I mean, The Bastard, is at the front door and refuses to leave. Should I call the cops on him or something?"

"Sic Amos on him," I called back. It was a lovely thought, but unfortunately, our mutt was incapable of violence. He thought every creature in the world was his friend.

Stupid dog. He should have been a bitter ball of hate. He had, after all, been thrown in a dumpster by some neglectful son of a bitch. Didn't he know that the world was out to get him?

"I doubt that will work," she countered through the door. "You know Amos isn't likely to cooperate. We could just ignore him until he leaves."

I sighed. It was tempting, but I was not in the habit of taking the coward's way. Also, Dante was a stubborn son of a bitch. I doubted he'd just go away after coming all the way here.

I'd face him, if only to rub my win from last night in his lying, manipulative, evil, shoe-buying face.

I opened my bedroom door and met Demi's worried eyes. "I'll handle him. Don't worry about it. And eat as many cupcakes as you want. *All* of the red velvet ones are for you."

She cursed me for that (even her curses came across sweet, and dammit, even cute) and left me to it.

I didn't rush to meet him. I didn't have a problem making him wait. In all our time together, I rarely had.

Of course, I didn't much dawdle, either. Wasting his time was one thing, but it wouldn't do to give him the impression that I dreaded seeing him as much as I actually did.

I applied one last precise bit of nude lip-gloss like it was war paint and went to answer the door.

I braced myself for the sight of him, taking one deep breath before I faced him again.

"What the hell are you doing here?" I asked the moment our gazes clashed.

He looked like hell, wearing the same suit he had the previous day, his golden hair unkempt, his normally precise, perpetual stubble turned to outright scruff.

He looked exhausted and hungover, but also, good enough to eat.

His eyes were taking in the front of my shirt, a smirk forming on his lips as he read it when he replied, "Love the shirt, tiger. Very appropriate. Would you believe me if I said I was in the neighborhood?"

"No. You hate L.A. with a passion. Why are you here?"

"To see you, of course. Can I come in?"

"I'm surprised you recovered and made it here this quick. Must be nice to have a private jet."

His smirk died and his jaw set. "Do you know how wasteful it is for one man to use a private jet to get around? I'm not my dad. I flew commercial. The only thing wasted was my money on a last minute airline ticket."

I rolled my eyes. Oh Lord. If I had a private jet, I wouldn't fly commercial on a bet, in fact, I'd probably fly to New York for pizza on a whim, but then Dante had always seen his wealth as a sort of a hindrance, something to feel guilty about, a bigger weight on his shoulders than it was worth.

Again, that had always pissed me the hell off. As a twenty-seven year old that still lived paycheck to paycheck, it was more infuriating than ever. "If I see you driving around in a Prius, I'm seriously going to barf. Right before I key the hell out of it."

He grinned. "Can I come in?" he repeated, tone polite, conciliatory even.

"What do you want?" My tone was rude. I was determined that his charm was not going to make me any less hostile. On the contrary.

Because, obviously, I was contrary.

"Same thing I wanted last night," he replied, face and voice gone very solemn.

"Not likely, stud," I drawled out, though some part of me quickened at the thought. Or at least at the picture his words brought up for me, a flash of the two of us writhing naked in bed. "Not in the mood. And even if

I was, you weren't exactly impressive enough for another round. One lackluster performance from you was plenty to last me for quite some time, thank you. You aren't what you used to be, if you know what I mean. Or hell, maybe I've just grown accustomed to having *better*."

He flinched just the slightest bit, tried to catch himself, smoothed his features into blandness in a blink, but I caught the slip. "I still want to talk, is what I was trying to say," he added, voice gone stiff and formal now.

I could tell I'd struck the nerve I'd been going for. *There we go.* Point for me.

I flashed my teeth at him in a snarl thinly disguised as a grin. "Care for a *drink*?"

Perverse creature that he was, that made his smile reappear. "I don't think so. Not falling for that again. Not today. That was a dirty trick, you know, but I suppose it was my fault. And as for last night, I'd like to defend myself; obviously I had *way* too much to drink."

I eyed him top to bottom, the regard deliberate and insulting. "That's what every guy says when he's past his prime."

"I had *a lot* to drink. *You know* because you served it to me."

"Excuses, excuses."

"Want me to prove it to you?" His smile was way too self-assured.

"Don't make me slam this door in your face and call the cops if you don't leave."

"Sorry. That last one just slipped out. I really meant it about the truce."

"A truce?" I tasted the word in my mouth, and it tasted as wrong as it *felt*. "You call that note you just sent me a truce?"

"The shoes were for the truce. The note was for that cheap shot you took at me last night," he tried, smiling again, back to his charm routine. "But now that I got it out of my system, I'm back to just wanting a truce."

"I don't like you coming to my home," I pointed out. He knew as much, but it never hurt to point out boundaries when it came to Dante. There was a time we'd been boundary-less, and the results had been disastrous for us both.

"I know. That's why I tried to catch you the first time at work."

"Work is *not* better."

"Okay. Well. Noted. Now we need to talk. It's important. Can I come in?"

I thought about it for a while. "I'll give you five minutes, but then you need to leave me the hell alone."

"It's important," he reiterated, face gone solemn again in a way that made me start to panic.

I hid it well; I am an actress after all.

I gave him a long suffering sigh and, knowing it was a terrible idea, knowing I'd regret it now and later, I let in the man that had broken my heart in so many ways that it would never heal again.

"Fortune knocks but once, but misfortune has much more patience."
~Laurence J. Peter

chapter ten

"Oh God," Dante breathed out as I closed the door behind him. "You've been *baking*? It's like you knew I was coming." He made a beeline for the kitchen.

"Oh yeah," I drawled to his back, trailing him slowly. "I made all those cupcakes just for you, you narcissistic ass."

"Are those German chocolate?" he asked. "Like you used to make?"

"Not quite the same recipe. I tweaked it a bit. Spoiler alert: The secret ingredient now is hate."

He laughed, shooting me a sideways look out of his devastating eyes that made my traitorous knees go weak. "So you *did* make them for me."

I gritted my teeth as he helped himself, but the truth was, though I hadn't been expecting him, and emphatically did not want him here, I did want him to eat one. He had a surprisingly sweet tooth for a man with a rock hard body, and he'd always loved it when I'd baked for him. He and his sweet tooth was actually the whole reason I'd ever learned to bake.

I wanted him to taste and be reminded of one of the many things he'd thrown away when he'd ruined things with me.

Demi was hovering near the hallway that led to her and Leona's rooms, looking back and forth between the two of us like she didn't know what to do.

Dante waved at her, mouth full of food.

She glared at him. Or tried to. It was a baby lamb glare. She looked like she meant it, but it came across like a Disney princess trying to make a mean face for the very first time.

It was adorable and ridiculous. She was a soft-hearted girl, and she had my back, would muster up every meager ounce of hostility inside of her for the sake of me and protecting my notoriously hard heart, and I loved her for it.

"I'm good," I told her. "I can handle him."

"I know you can," she reassured me, still aiming her princess glare Dante's way. "I'll give you privacy, but you holler if you need anything, Scarlett dear."

I bit my lip to keep from outright smiling, because who wouldn't smile at a twenty-two-year-old who called them dear? God, I liked her. I'd tried to fight it, but Demi was an irresistible sweetheart, damn her. "Thanks, hun," I told her.

She left with one last adorable sneer at Dante.

"She seems nice. I like her," Dante said when we were alone.

"She hates *you*," I assured him.

His cupcake eating face was not one ounce offended by that. "I'd imagine she does. It boggles the mind, the things she must've heard about me. I assume everyone living in this apartment hates my guts?"

"Everyone," I agreed blandly and unpleasantly.

He finished his first cupcake, grabbed a glass from the cupboard, rummaging around in my kitchen without a qualm, and downed a large cup of water with a few big swallows. "God, that was amazing. You haven't lost your touch. And by the way, I'm glad to hear I must still be on your mind if your roommates know that much about me."

I cursed him—a long, fluid tirade.

He didn't so much as blink. "That was a lot of vowels," he stated serenely when I'd finally finished.

His calm made my hellish temper boil up at an excessive and alarming rate. I looked away from him and tried to tamp it down. As I've said, I have a very healthy fear of my own temper. It has made me do some terrible things.

In my peripheral, Dante continued to watch me as he took a long swig from the bottle of scotch I'd been working on, grimaced briefly (his rich, entitled ass hates cheap scotch), and reached for another cupcake.

"What do you want?" I asked him, yet again.

He took his time answering, finishing off another cupcake, taking another long drink of my subpar scotch before saying, "Just give me a minute to enjoy this, will you? Do you know how long it's been since I had one of your cupcakes?"

I did, of course. I opened my mouth to answer him when I saw him shrug his shoulders slightly and wince.

He was at an angle to me, and involuntarily, my eyes shot to his back, covered in a suit now, but I still knew what was under there.

He craned his head trying to follow my gaze.

I gave him an insouciant smile. "How's your back?"

"Scratched me up good, didn't you?"

I shrugged, still smiling.

"I'm flattered you still have that urge."

My smile died a short, violent death.

"What urge?" I asked through my teeth, mood plummeting to dark with a few careless words from him.

"I think you know the answer to that. You marked me up rather impressively, considering that I didn't even feel it at the time. Your claws are as sharp as ever."

I shrugged again. "Oopsies. It was an accident," I told him, knowing he'd never believe it even if it was the truth.

His mouth twisted into a self-deprecating smile that I *despised*. "I didn't mind. To tell you the truth, it was enlightening. I didn't think you still saw me as your territory to *mark*."

Point for Dante.

"Enough with the useless banter," I gritted out. "Tell me what you came here to say and then *leave*."

His smile died its own short, slightly less violent death, his whole face going somber again. "We should sit down for this," he told me solemnly. "And go somewhere more private. Your room, I guess."

I stared at him incredulously. Even now, knowing him as I did, the sheer nerve of him threw me off balance. So much so, I found myself leading him to my room, letting the devil even deeper into my sanctuary without much of a fight.

He made himself right at home, perching on the edge of my bed without asking, his eyes solemn and probing on my face in a way I couldn't stand.

"What do you want? Just spit it out." I shut the door behind me as I spoke, hovering in front of it, in case I needed a quick escape.

There was always such familiarity, such an unspeakable intimacy between us when we were alone. Distance and time had never dulled it. Even my outright hostility could not kill it, and I had tried my best.

"It's not that simple," he said in a bracing way that did indeed make me want to brace. "I don't know how to tell you this. I don't *want* to have to tell you this."

"Enough with the fucking dramatic suspense. Just spit it out," I repeated, less and less certain by the second that he was just messing with me because every note in his voice, every line in his body was telling me to worry. Something was very wrong. My rage at him, my enduring spite had let me overlook it since my first sighting of him yesterday, but it'd been there all along. He'd not been acting like himself because something was wrong.

"What is it?" I asked, voice softer now, tentative with a dread I could no longer deny.

He couldn't look at me, and I took a step back involuntarily as I saw the light hit his eye and noticed a sheen there.

He was *crying?*

Oh God. Something was *wrong*. My hand went to my chest, gripped my shirt over my pounding heart as my mind flew to the only thing we both still shared.

The only person.

Oh no. Not that. Not—

"Gram is dead."

Denial was my first reaction. "That's not possible. Bullshit. I call *bullshit.*"

"You think I'd lie—"

"Yes. Yes, I think you're a lying bastard." I did believe that. I needed to believe it. It was a firm part of the very foundation that kept me going.

His damp eyes glared at me. "You think I'd lie about *that*?"

I didn't. Dante's gram was Switzerland. She was neutral territory. Sacred ground. Even with us.

"I just spoke to her a few days ago," I explained to him, as though it would make him change his mind. "She sounded fine."

"It was very sudden. A fatal stroke. No one expected it."

It all made sense suddenly. He hadn't been himself for this little fucked up reunion. Not by a long shot. He was usually more of a bastard. When I took a swipe at him, he took two back, but this time he'd been reticent, talking about truces, letting volatile subjects drop.

No. Not Gram. Any loss but her I'd have taken with a stoic face and a hard heart.

But I had no hardness in me, no protection on my heart, superficial or otherwise, when it came to Gram. In my less than happy childhood, Dante's grandmother had been the stuff of fairy tales. I'd always felt, and still felt, that she'd saved me in a lot of ways.

She'd been the only thing connected to Dante that I couldn't let go of as an adult. She was too essential to me.

And she was gone.

I staggered where I stood, and Dante, predictably, wretchedly, was there to catch me.

I tried to shove him away, but he wouldn't let me, pulling me to him, my face to his warm, familiar chest, where I gasped in and out, in and out, trying to fight back hated tears.

Breaking down in front of my worst enemy was not something I would ever give in to easily. It went against every ingredient that made up the sum of who I was.

Which just goes to show how weakened I felt at that moment, because I found myself clutching at his shirt, digging my cheekbone hard into the firm, plump pad of his pectoral.

Melting against him, I let myself cry.

"A quick temper will make a fool of you soon enough."
~Bruce Lee

chapter eleven

"Let it out, Scarlett," he uttered, a deep rumble that came wetly out of his throat as he tried to hold back his own tears. "I know it hurts. Believe me, I know."

Gram was in her eighties, so this should not have come as *such a shock*.

Of course I knew she wasn't immortal, but something about her, her spirit I supposed, had always seemed, always *felt* so indestructible to me.

"I know it hurts," Dante murmured into the top of my shaking head. "Believe me, I know," he repeated.

I went from shaking to seizing up, body going stiff as a board.

God, I was an inconsiderate bitch. Of course it hurt. And not just me.

I hated Dante like aspiring actresses hate cupcakes, but Gram was *Dante's* grandmother and not my own, and here I was forcing *him* to comfort *me*.

"I'm s-s-s-so s-s-s-sorry, D-d-d-dante," I stammered out.

My eyes shut in horror, eyes burning as the hot lids made contact with each other. I felt my skin flushing. I didn't have to look to know I was red with shame. Worse than crying even, my dreaded stutter from childhood had emerged.

A little noise escaped from his throat, a little pained, distressed mewl that I knew was a direct reaction to the re-emergence of my despised stutter.

Great, now he was feeling sorry for me, which was the thing I hated the most.

I tried to pull myself together, shifting away slightly to look up at him.

My eyes darted quickly away at what I saw. I couldn't take his unguarded expression.

Could not handle what it did to the traitorous organ that was trying to pound its way out of my chest.

"Why didn't you tell me yesterday?" My voice came out small and faint, but far steadier than I felt.

"You think it was easy to tell you? You think I *wanted* to? You were determined to distract me, and I was just as determined to let you. I didn't think I'd pass out like that when we were . . . finished."

"You were drunk."

"Well, yes. My drunk brain didn't realize it was doing drunk things, but as you well know, sober or senseless, I wasn't about to turn *that* down."

My only excuse was that his unguarded expression had taken down some of my own defenses, but at his words, I felt myself *blush*. It was inexcusable, even under the circumstances.

I pushed away from him, and he let me, going back to perch on the edge of my bed, facing me. I could feel his eyes on my face. Mine stayed on his shoes.

"Was she by herself when she had the stroke?" I asked him, voice trembling, body trembling. I couldn't bear the thought of that, of her dying alone.

"Yes. Staff found her after she'd already passed."

I took deep breaths, still fighting the good fight against hated tears. "When is the funeral?"

"Day after tomorrow. I already booked your flight home." If I could have found the composure or the breath, I'd have pointed out that that dreaded little town was *not* my home, but I couldn't find either.

"I took care of everything, actually," he continued. "I'll email you the info. Sit down, Scarlett, before you fall down.

I tried again to look at him, glancing up briefly, eyes again darting quickly away at what I saw.

That face. Those eyes that saw everything I wanted to hide. No, I still couldn't take it. Not at all. Not even close.

A fierce whisper escaped him, one that carried across the room and hit me straight in the gut, *"Come here."*

Every clenched part of me seemed to break at once, and I didn't even feel myself move, didn't even will it, but one moment I was standing several feet away from him, and the next I was in his arms, sobbing like the broken child that Gram had always tried so hard to fix.

I cried for what felt like hours, until my soul felt scraped raw, and he was there with me, arms around me, face in my hair, legs tangled with mine.

We had melded ourselves so close together in our mourning that it felt like there was only one of us.

After a time, a whisper came out of him, one that ached, and I ached with it, "I couldn't believe it at first either. Didn't want to. Still don't."

I opened my mouth to say something, what I wasn't even sure, but the sound of the doorbell ringing again distracted me.

"You expecting anybody?" Dante murmured into my hair.

I sighed. "No. I'm sure it's for Demi. She's a social creature. Makes friends everywhere. Has people over constantly." As I spoke, I realized I was babbling into his chest, and I straightened. Having a weak moment was one thing. Lingering at it was another.

I stood, turned my back on him, and took two decisive, necessary steps away. I didn't know what to say to him, what to do with myself, but I knew I couldn't wallow in his arms for another fragile second.

We were both silent for a solid minute and then another. I stared at the wall, my shoulders hunched, fists clenched.

Finally, I couldn't take it anymore, and I turned around to look at him again.

His gaze was so warm on me—tender—and I didn't know what to do with how that made me feel. He hadn't had that warmth in his eyes for me in *years*. I'd made sure he had no reason to. Gone to drastic measures to make sure.

Why was he looking at me like that *now*? Shared grief? Rekindled feeling?

"Stop looking at me like that," I told him slowly, reproach in every syllable of every word.

"Like what?"

"You know."

"You think I can help it?" he countered softly. "When could I *ever* help it?"

I lost my breath. No, he'd knocked it out of me.

This was the problem with fighting Dante. I got in my jabs, loudly and often, but it only took one good hit from him and I was stripped of my defenses. A few sentences out of his gorgeous, manipulative mouth and I lost the whole fucking round.

K.O. Done.

He needed to leave *now*.

I opened my mouth to tell him so, but just then there was a soft knock at my bedroom door.

"Scar dear, your boyfriend is here," Demi's concerned voice called.

My eyes were still on Dante's, so I saw the moment when the warmth left them, watched unblinking as all tenderness was sucked out and replaced by something else.

Something cold and dark and all too familiar.

I told myself I was relieved at the change. I almost believed it.

"Boyfriend?" he uttered softly, his voice rumbling and low, a distant clap of thunder, the way it got when he was on the edge of losing his temper.

Oh yes, he had a famous temper like me, though his was harder to provoke.

My own temper was quick to ignite and could be indiscriminately destructive but his was just as terrible of a thing to behold when things went south.

A small but powerful thrill moved through me.

Our eyes were still locked as I called back to Demi, "I'll be out in just a second, hun."

"Boyfriend?" he repeated quietly, punching it out in a dangerous clip, the thunder closer to the surface now, eyes going black as he began in earnest to lose the battle with the storm inside of himself.

I firmed my jaw and squared off against him. It was almost easy for me to deal with him angry. Familiar, safe ground. Enjoyable, even. A much needed distraction. "You should go, Dante."

"Does he know I fucked you last night?" He did not say this quietly. He said it loud enough to be heard, and not just by me.

I felt my nipples tighten, a slow, familiar throb starting up between my thighs.

I was a perverse creature and his jealous rages had always turned me on.

My mouth twisted in something not quite a smile.

Predictably, it set him off. "Does your *boyfriend* know I rode you *bareback* last night?" He said this even less quietly, voice pitched to be heard across the large apartment.

It was an effort to keep from showing any reaction to his increasing hostility. "Your jealousy is showing," I pointed out evenly.

He shook his head, lip curling as he spoke, "It wasn't a rhetorical question. *Does he know* what happened between us last night?"

"Does it matter?"

A shudder moved through his big, agitated body.

I tried not to shudder at the sight of it. I was in a state.

"I can't believe you," he gritted out.

"Can't you?" I countered, voice steady, pulse not so much.

He stood abruptly. "I'm leaving. As I said before, I'll email you the details of your travel arrangements."

He hadn't had to do that, arrange it all for me, but I couldn't bring myself to thank him. "When do I leave?"

"The day after tomorrow. Early."

"Fine."

His lip curled. "Fine," he clipped back and strode from the room.

"When I'm good, I'm very good. But when I'm bad I'm better."
~Mae West

chapter twelve

PAST

Gram was old but that didn't make her any less glamorous. I'd never seen her without a face full of perfect makeup, expertly coiffed hair, and a flattering designer dress wrapped around her still trim figure.

She lived in a nowhere town now, and it *was* the town she'd been raised in, but she hadn't *always* lived here and it showed in every sophisticated flick of her wrist.

In her heyday, as she'd say, she'd been an actress on the silver screen. For nearly a decade, she'd reigned supreme as the undisputed Queen of Hollywood.

She'd lived a life that people had written books about. Many, many books.

I read every one I could get my hands on. Every time I'd finish one, I'd start badgering her about what was true and what wasn't.

It tickled her when I did this. She was a passionate

storyteller, and she loved to reminisce about the good old days.

The books never got it right. There were always some important pieces of her many escapades that they left out, and the way they portrayed her was always off. They liked to make her into either a ruthless femme fatale or a clueless starlet, a caricature of a woman, when she was not that. Gram was complex, her personality rich in delightful contradictions.

I worshipped her.

I'd just finished the latest biography on her glory years, and I had a million questions for her.

This one had been much different from the others I'd read. Instead of focusing on her movie career or the set dramas she'd been involved in, this one was all about her love life.

We were in one of the sitting rooms in her fancy mansion of a house. She was serving me tea, a habit she said she'd picked up when she was shooting a film in England decades ago because it added structure to her day.

I studied her. I'd read a lot of things, but I hadn't quite believed them and it was an embarrassing subject to bring up, so I'd never asked. "You had boyfriends before you met Grandpa?" I asked it as if he had been *my* grandfather. I'd taken to doing this because Gram seemed to expect it of me, but I only did it with Gram and Dante. The rest of their family was much less welcoming.

She threw back her head and laughed.

I smiled with her. She had one of those of laughs, it was a tinkling, delightful thing, and it brought joy to a room.

"Oh yes, dear girl, I had boyfriends before I met Grandpa."

My eyes widened. I hadn't quite believed it when I'd read it. "H-how many boyfriends did you have?"

She laughed some more. "I was a wicked, wicked woman," she drawled.

"Gram!" Dante protested.

She nudged me playfully and nodded her head toward her grandson. I glanced at him. He was across the room, sprawled out on a couch, eyes closed, but he wasn't sleeping. He was listening to us, and occasionally he'd add something into the conversation.

"Look at the power you have over him, Scarlett," said Gram conspiratorially, but loud enough for him to hear. "He's heard all of my stories a hundred times, but he'll listen to them all again if it means being in the same room with you. Not even fourteen and you've already brought him to heel."

"Gram! Gram!" We both protested.

"And look at her, dear boy," she called out to him. "Here is a girl that will adore you the way you deserve to be adored," she told him. "Treat that like the precious thing it is."

She looked back and forth between our blushing faces. "Don't fight it, my lovely children. It's a beautiful thing. Love will make your life worthwhile. It's the most powerful force on earth. Let it *rule you* and you won't be sorry."

Dante was sitting up now, eyes open and trained on his wicked grandmother.

She smiled at him fondly. "Your grandfather's love saved my soul. All I want is for you to love and be loved in the way you deserve, and I'm *green* with envy that you found it so early in your life."

"What happened to Grandfather?" I asked her, changing the subject, but I was curious. I'd never been told how he'd died. I'd always wondered but they never talked about it.

"Cancer, dear. Dreadful thing. I didn't have enough time with him, but then a lifetime wouldn't have been enough, I think."

She looked sad for a long moment, heart-wrenchingly so, but then seemed to shake it off. "You should try acting, my dear. Your face was made to be onscreen."

"Really? You think so?" I was highly flattered. The way Gram talked about acting, in reverent loving tones, I could tell it was a sacred thing to her. That she thought I was worthy was *everything* to me.

"Oh yes. You have a face that doesn't come along often. Once in a generation, if that. So expressive but so lovely."

I eyed her doubtfully. I didn't spend a ton of time looking in the mirror, and the only family I had was my grandma (and to say she was homely was putting it kindly), so I'd never had any reason to think I might be pretty, let alone beautiful. If I had to come up with one word to describe my looks, I'd have picked wild, or messy.

She smiled at me, then sent a meaningful look toward Dante, who'd taken to lying down and listening to us again. "You don't believe me, but you will. You don't favor your grandmother, obviously, but your mother was a stunning girl. Breathtaking. Like you. But if you really have your doubts, if somehow you don't see your beauty when you look in the mirror, just try to notice how other people react to you, how they stare. Don't you ever wonder why they stare?"

"Because I'm the trashcan girl," I said simply. Out of

the corner of my eye, I saw Dante shoot up again, and I knew I'd agitated him. He hated when anyone called me that. Even me.

"No, my dear. The people who call you that are being cruel and jealous. It says more about them than you, and it's much easier to hate someone that they *envy*."

I was still more than a little skeptical, but she shrugged and went on. "And you'd enjoy the escape of stepping into someone else's shoes, I'll bet. Life hasn't been easy on you, but when you act, you can live any life you want. There's nothing like it. Please at least consider giving it a try. If for no other reason than to humor me, okay?"

I didn't hesitate. "I'll definitely try it, Gram. I'll give it my best. For you."

"Love is a fire. But whether it is going to warm your hearth or burn down your house, you can never tell."
~Joan Crawford

chapter thirteen

PRESENT

I took my shaking self to the bathroom the instant Dante had left my room. I gripped the counter and told myself to breathe, my trembling limbs barely holding me up.

I told myself that the shaking was relief at his absence.

When it passed, I went into the living room. I smiled in spite of myself when I caught sight of the mystery man.

Ah. Anton. I should've guessed.

"Hopefully Demi didn't get you punched in the moneymaker with her little stunt back there," I said in greeting.

The tall man that lounged comfortably on our oversized sectional rose at my entrance, his rueful grin a familiar, endearing sight. "It was a close thing, I think, but despite her best efforts, I seem to be unharmed.

I hugged him briefly, air-kissing both of his cheeks while he bent down far enough to real-kiss mine.

"So that was the guy, huh?" he said, his trained actor's voice steady, his knowing eyes something else.

I shrugged dismally. I hated to give Dante that much credit, whether he'd earned it or not. "He was *a* guy, one I prefer not to talk about."

I fingered his beard. He was growing it out for a role as a scruffy biker, complete with long brown hair that he kept tied back in a neat little bun. I'd hated the change in his look when he'd first gotten the part, but lately it was really growing on me.

Anton was Hollywood good-looking, versatile, and ever changing but polished to gleaming, with perfect teeth, handsome features, and total control over every muscle in his face.

We'd met two years ago shooting a doomed pilot. The show had never made it on air, but at least I'd gotten Anton out of the deal.

We were so much alike that it scared me sometimes. He was basically a male version of me.

We'd dated for about five minutes, and I'd even been about one drink from sleeping with him, but then I'd realized that I actually liked him, so friends it was.

He grinned. "You're starting to like this biker vibe I have going, aren't you?"

"Fat chance, beardo," I told him, making a face at him as I moved to take a barstool at the counter.

"Dante has a temper," Demi pointed out from the kitchen, where she was staring at the cupcakes forlornly.

"Yes," I said succinctly.

"But he's not what I was expecting," she added.

My lip curled. "He can be charming—"

"It's not that. I figured he'd be charming."

"What then?"

"I don't know. I knew you hated him, and I guess I just figured he hated you back. But he definitely doesn't *hate* you."

I waved my hand in the air as though warding off the notion. "It's complicated. He's as hostile as I am, he just hides it better, but don't let him fool you—he's a fucking beast when it comes to breaking hearts.

She nodded, her eyes so solemn that I had to look away. "That I gathered. I'm sorry I said Anton was your boyfriend. I thought I was helping, but I made things worse, didn't I?"

"On the contrary," I assured her. "Your interruption couldn't have come at a better time, so thank you."

She smiled cheekily, shrugging, "Anytime."

"What was he doing here?" Anton asked from the sofa.

I looked down at my hands, bracing myself for the pain of saying it aloud. "Gram died."

They both gasped.

"Oh no," Demi uttered softly.

"Not Gram," Anton muttered, followed by a steady and vehement string of cursing.

Just like anyone important in my life invariably knew at least something about Dante, they also knew about Gram. She was the only person I considered family and talked about as such.

"What happened?"

"A fatal stroke. That's why he was chasing me around. I guess he didn't want to tell me over the phone."

"But he didn't tell you last night?" Demi asked.

Anton coughed and I glared at him.

"He didn't." I knew they'd heard what he'd said back in my room, or at least enough to suspect, but I had no intention of hashing it out.

"What can I do?" Demi asked, sounding so sincere and concerned that I could hardly stand to hear it.

I nodded at the open bottle of scotch I'd left in the kitchen earlier. "Hand me that, will you?"

There was only one thing to be done. Because crying in my room alone held no appeal, and crying in front of other people was even worse—I was throwing one hell of a drunk.

I was hoping this one was more successful than the last attempt.

Or, at the very least, less disastrous.

Demi and Anton didn't hesitate to join me.

I stopped drinking out of the bottle (because we had company now) and made myself an oversized tumbler of scotch.

Anton and Demi did the same. Demi despised scotch, so I knew she was just being a good sport.

"I hope you can stomach this stuff," I told Anton as he took a long swallow. "It was way too low class for Dante the Bastard."

"I think it's fantastic," he told me, toasting the air.

"You don't have to drink scotch for me, Demi," I told her.

She shrugged and toasted at me. "It's for your gram," she said and took a long, painful-looking swallow.

We got good stinking drunk and watched reruns of our favorite reality show, *Kink and Ink*.

I nodded at the screen at some point after drink number three. "I'd go lesbian for a day for her," I told an extremely drunk Demi and a fascinated Anton.

"I'd suffer through some pretty terrible things to see that happen," Anton said.

Demi shook her head. "She's pretty and I like her, but uh uh. Only boys for me."

"What about this? There are only three people left in the world. You," I nodded at Demi, "Frankie," I nodded at the hot lesbian tattoo artist on TV, "and Justin Bieber. You have five seconds to pick."

She didn't hesitate, blurting out "Frankie!" before I'd even finished talking.

We couldn't stop laughing after that, giggling our asses off.

"I vote that when we sober up we drive to Vegas to get tattoos at her shop," Demi said at some point.

"It's only a five-hour drive," Anton pointed out. "Four if I'm driving. What kind of a tattoo do you want, Demi?"

She flushed when he said her name, and it was only in my drunken state that I realized for the first time that sweet Demi had a huge crush on jaded Anton.

Oh no.

I wanted to tell her to run in the other direction. He was too much like me. He'd had his heart ravaged by some sadist years ago and what was left of him ate little girls like Demi for breakfast.

I made a note to tell her such when I'd sobered up enough to be taken seriously.

"I don't know," she finally answered. "I'd have to brainstorm about it on the drive. Something pretty. With color."

"What about you, Scar?" he asked me.

I nodded at the TV where someone was currently getting a heart with initials in the middle of their back.

"I'd get the opposite of that. There are too many love tattoos. I'd get an anti-love one."

Anton's rueful grin came out to play. When I was in this state, it was really hard to remember why I'd never slept with him. He was way too good-looking for his own good, beardo, man-bun, and all. "Yes, yes, we know, Scarlett. You don't believe in love. You've said it many times."

For some reason, that set me off. I blame the scotch.

"I never said I don't believe in love," I said heatedly. "Trust me, I believe in it. I know love. It lives in me still. Like a cancer, it *thrives* under my skin, *metabolizes* in spite of all of my attempts to eradicate it." I had to take a few breaths I was talking so quickly and passionately. "What I said was that if you feel yourself falling, you should *run like hell*. Avoid it. If it tries to set its hooks in you, rip them out. If it tries to shackle you, break the chain." I was waving my hands around to illustrate my point. "Love is never satisfied with *half*-measures. It won't take parts of you. It will own all of you, every single, longing piece.

"Love will make you its slave," I stated venomously. "It will ruin you. Grind you under its heel until you don't recognize what's left.

"Love will take your soul." I looked pointedly at Demi. "If you're very unlucky, it might even turn you into someone like me.

"I *do* believe in love," I reiterated. "I believe it's the most destructive force on earth."

When I finished my impassioned rant, they were both just staring at me.

Demi looked like she might cry. She was hugging Amos, her eyes huge with pity and sorrow. "Oh, Scarlett," she whispered. "I'm *so sorry*. Dante is such a *bastard*."

Even Anton didn't look right. His mouth was twisted bitterly, eyes boring into me, something powerful moving behind them. "That *fucker*," he said succinctly. "Excuse me." He got up and left the room.

Getting his rage in hand, I knew. He was another one with a wicked temper. *So* my type.

Why hadn't I slept with him again?

"You'll find love again," Demi told me tremulously, sounding like she really believed it. "Just when you least expect it I bet you'll run into some wonderful man that makes your heart *race* again."

I knew better, but I kept my piece. Demi could stay sweetly naive, her soul light and beautiful. I didn't want to take that from her.

But she couldn't have been more wrong.

There is only one heart in this universe that calls to mine, and it does call. Constantly, relentlessly, it sings out to me in a captivating, resonating voice.

Day after day, year after year, it calls to me.

But I won't listen to it. It belongs to a liar.

When Anton returned, he seemed more or less back to normal, and we didn't comment on his absence.

We were still huddled on the couch watching people get tattoos, and he rejoined us without a word.

"There's like a six month waitlist to get ink in her parlor," I pointed out in true buzz-killer style. I liked crushing dreams. It was a hobby of mine. "And from Frankie herself? Who knows. Probably years. You'd probably have to know somebody."

"Well, poo," Demi said.

Anton and I shared a smile. She was way too adorable for her own good.

Meanwhile on Kink and Ink, someone was crying as they described the reason for their angel tattoo.

"I hate it when this show gets emotional," Anton said, rising from the sofa to refill our glasses.

"Why does the term emotional have such a negative connotation?" Demi asked him, sounding riled. "Humans are emotional creatures. I'm emotional but that doesn't mean I run around *crying* all the time. I'm more likely to laugh and love harder *because* I'm emotional."

I blinked at her after she'd finished her own little rant. I liked this sassy side of her.

I sent Anton a sideways glare because he seemed to like it too by the way he was looking at her. I made a note to have a talk with him at some point. He was not allowed to mess around with Demi. She was too innocent for him.

At some hazy point Leona came home. I was pretty numb by then and so it didn't hurt quite as bad to tell her about Gram.

"Oh Scarlett," she said, coming to sit beside me, taking one of my hands into both of hers. "What can I do? Do you want to talk about it?"

I thought about that. "I do not. The scotch is helping. This show is fucking awesome, so that helps, too. You drinking with us?"

She bit her lip and nodded.

Even later than Leona, Farrah showed up and joined us in over-toasting my gram.

At some point I was so sloppy drunk that I even confessed to Leona, "I slept with him last night."

Her eyes widened and I could see by how horrified she was that she was far from as drunk as I was. I was at the drunken stage that was incapable of horror.

"You *what*?"

I nodded, giving her what I imagined was a thoughtful look. "What indeed, my friend. What indeed."

I thought she was going to drop the subject, and I thought that was odd, but eventually she came back with a stunned, "You *slept* with him?"

How to explain? I thought about it and, "It's complicated."

"Clearly," Anton drawled.

"Are you guys in a better place, then?" Leona asked.

"Not fucking likely. It's complicated."

"Sounds that way," Leona said, still giving me worried eyes.

"We have history." What a light, little sentence that was to hold such clenched, fathomless, unabated pain inside of it.

"I still can't believe you slept with him," Demi added.

I shrugged. It was hard to articulate sober, harder now. "Have you ever done something that hurts you just because you know it hurts the other person, too?"

They were all just staring at me. I shrugged again. "I hate his lying, conniving guts, but sex with him can be a religious experience. He remembers things about my body that even *I* forgot."

"Ah."

"Oh."

"I see."

That they seemed to get. The universal understanding of phenomenal sex. Go figure.

"Love is a trap. When it appears, we see only its light, not its shadows."
~Paulo Coelho

chapter fourteen

The morning of the funeral arrived too quickly. I packed light and went with dread to the airport, making it to my flight with mere minutes to spare.

Leona dropped me off, her best friend eyes worried on me as we said goodbye. Though she never voiced her concerns, she didn't have to. She knew this was an unpleasant trip for me, unhealthy for my state of mind, but it was unavoidable.

"I'll be fine," I told her chidingly, avoiding eye contact.

That was the closest I'd get to voicing my trepidation of the ordeal to come: Acknowledging the fact that there was something I might not be fine with.

"I know you will," she assured me.

We kissed cheeks and said goodbye.

And off I went. Heading back into hell for the sake of Gram.

Oh the irony. She'd been one of the few people in my life that'd actively tried to keep me out of it.

I wasn't even mildly surprised when I found myself in a first class seat for the flight from LAX to Seattle. It was so Dante. The nonchalantly rich bastard.

I'd been conditioned to stay awake on airplanes, so I didn't sleep a wink for that entire leg of the trip. I'd brought a book, and it was a good one, but I couldn't focus on it for shit.

Instead, I stared out the window and drove myself crazy.

Why did I still feel so much for Dante? What would it *take* to make me *numb*?

I'd have paid a heavy price for numbness, felt I'd already paid it in the attempt to seek it out.

And for the price, nothing. All of my efforts had been futile. Every furious, vengeful, masochistic thing I'd ever done to get over him had left me at ground zero.

I still felt. Too much. With just the slightest provocation, I was wrapped up in him again, in the good and the bad. He got to me, was so deep under my skin that even now, years after the end of us, it was a fight with myself not to let the bitterness of it consume my waking hours.

At SeaTac I switched to a tiny commuter jet for the short flight to the small town I'd been raised in.

That flight was shorter but worse for my peace of mind. I hadn't been back in years, and when I'd left, I'd been ecstatic to be done with the place.

I hadn't planned to come back *ever*, and the reason for it . . . *fuck my life*.

One small relief was that Dante didn't pick me up himself when I arrived. I'd been almost certain that he would.

Instead it was an unfamiliar middle-aged man wearing

a comfortable looking T-shirt and jeans and holding a small sign that said SCARLET.

Despite the spelling of the name, I figured it was meant for me. *Who else?*

He was the only one in the tiny airport holding a sign, so it was a bit laughable, but I walked up to him with a straight face.

"You Scarlett?" he asked me, looking bored out of his mind.

I nodded and held out my hand. "And you are?"

"Eugene. I'm, er was, Mrs. D's gardener. Dante, er, Mr. Durant asked me to pick you up and take you to your, erm, lodgings."

"Lead on," I told him wryly. It was a random welcoming committee Dante had sent, but frankly, it was a warmer reception than I'd expected from the town of my nightmares.

He took my one rolling suitcase without another word and started to walk.

I followed silently.

The town was a small one by city standards, but not tiny. At about a hundred thousand residents, last I checked, it had a whopping three high schools, and more importantly, four Walmarts.

I couldn't remember how many hotels it had, and didn't particularly care which one I was staying at, so I didn't ask. Anything would do, because whatever it was, I was used to worse.

Eugene didn't open the door for me, and I didn't take exception to that. I just got in the car, which happened to be an old beat-up truck, and stared out the window while Eugene steered us wordlessly through my despised hometown.

Time hadn't been kind to the little hellhole. I'd read a few years ago that it'd become the drug capital of Washington, the entry point for cartel distribution into the northwest, and the signs were apparent nearly everywhere I looked.

I took in every change I saw with a stoic face. It was dirtier than I remembered, with more dead behind the eyes pedestrians loitering aimlessly in the busier parts of town.

It was as though every negative thought I'd ever channeled into this little slice of purgatory had taken root and poisoned each dark corner of the place while I was absent.

It gave me an unwilling and brief spiteful thrill. The way I'd been treated here, it felt almost like justice, like it'd finally gotten the reckoning it deserved.

But all of that was stupid, emotional drivel. It was only a place. A spot on the map.

It was the people here that deserved a reckoning. Not all, but many. Too many hostile faces and names for me to recall that had helped to shape me into the bitter, little ball of hate I was today.

We were nearly to our destination before I shook myself out of my memories enough to realize just where we were going.

"I'd like to go straight to my hotel. I need to freshen up and change before the funeral, since I still have a few hours," I told Eugene, voice firm. "Thank you."

He shot me a glance, cleared his throat, and kept driving.

"Did you hear me?" I asked him when he didn't respond.

"I did. You'll have to take that up with Mr. Durant.

He didn't tell me anything about a hotel. He just said to bring you to Miss D's house."

My jaw clenching in agitation, I pulled out my phone, sending off a hasty text.

Me: Which hotel am I staying at?
Bastard/Stalker/Liar/Cheater/Ex/TheDevil: You're almost to the house, right? We'll talk when you get here.

I shot Eugene a hostile look. He'd officially reached collaborator status in my book.

I punched out another furious text.

Me: I hope you don't think I'm staying at that house.

He didn't respond, which was just as well, as we were pulling into the long drive that led to Gram's large estate.

As usual, manipulative bastard that he was, Dante had orchestrated everything before I saw the trap that had closed around me.

There were several cars in the drive, and I assessed a few of them with an eye for whom they might belong.

A few nondescript sedans: whoever had been hired to prepare the huge house for refreshments after the funeral.

Silver Rolls Royce: Dante's father, Leo.

White Mercedes: Unknown but worrisome. Any sign of money pointed to either Dante's family or someone even worse.

Black Audi: Dante, because he always freaking loved Audis.

I didn't even want to get out of the truck, in fact, I sat there for a few awkward minutes, Eugene holding my door open for me, just staring at the house before Eugene muttered, "Well, shoot. I can take you to a hotel."

Sure, I thought scathingly, *now* he was offering, right as Dante emerged from the house.

With a heavy sigh, I got out of the car.

He was wearing jeans and a black T-shirt. I hadn't seen him wearing anything but a suit or, well, nothing, for ages, and the sight struck me, reminded me of when we were teenagers.

Already off to a horrible start, I noted. As bad as I'd dreaded it would be.

"I'm not staying here," I told him as he approached.

He didn't respond, didn't even aim his stern eyes my way, just took my bag from Eugene and started heading back to the front door.

"What are you doing?" I asked his back, following him with a quick, furious stride. "I need to go to a hotel to get ready."

He paused at the door and finally looked at me. I could tell he was angry with me, some remnant of the temper he'd last left me in still present. "Your room is untouched. Gram kept it for you from the time you left."

This got to me. The sentiment of it. In my last year of high school my grandma had decided she was done dealing with my shit and kicked me out. I hadn't had to go far. Just that five-minute walk uphill from my grandma's trailer, and I'd been welcomed here with open arms. It had meant the world to me. Still did.

"The house will likely be sold by whoever inherits it," Dante continued, "so I assumed you'd want to go through your old things yourself before all of that happens. If I assumed wrong, Eugene will take you to a hotel, but in case you forgot, there isn't one close. You're looking at a forty-five minute drive each way. The funeral is in two hours, so you won't have much time, but if that's what you want to do, by all means, be my guest."

I glared at him, temper boiling up. "I should have seen this coming. I should've guessed you'd pull something like this."

"What did you expect? Did you think I was going to put you up at the shitty hotel over on Main Street?"

"I'm used to shitty hotels."

"You know what?" His voice was unsteady suddenly, volume going up with every word, "I don't give a *fuck* what you're used to." By the unholy light in his eyes, I could tell he wasn't talking about hotels anymore.

Perversely but predictably, his apparent fury calmed my own. I leveled a serene look on him, one meant to either stir him up or stop him cold. "Okay, fine, it's hardly worth arguing over. I'll stay here and I'll go through my old room, though I can't imagine I left anything behind that I wanted to keep."

His jaw was clenched, eyes still flashing hotly at me. Stir him up it was. "You might surprise yourself," he told me softly.

That made my eyes narrow, serenity gone. It was amazing the landmines we set for each other with the most innocuous phrases, and I wasn't interested in walking over even one of his, particularly not at the start of what was bound to be a trying few days.

"I'm quite certain," I enunciated slowly, "that there is not one thing I left behind in this town that I have *any* interest in now."

He seemed to deflate at that, eyes darting away, shoulders slumping, and without another word, I walked into the house.

Point for me, though I wasn't sure it counted. It certainly didn't *feel* like a victory.

"Heaven has no rage like love to hatred turned,
Nor hell a fury like a woman scorned."
~William Congreve

chapter fifteen

I went straight to my old room, leaving the bag for Dante to handle.

It was a huge old house, with ten bedrooms and several living spaces, but while I heard people working (cooking, cleaning, preparing) somewhere in the house, the kitchen and dining room I assumed, I didn't pass by one soul as I made my way through, which was a relief. I wanted a brief respite before I went straight into battle again, especially here, where every unchanged thing I saw brought back bittersweet memories. From the entryway to the old den where we used to spend hours our senior year of high school watching movies.

All of it was bad, but my old bedroom was the worst. The second I walked in the door, I had an almost overwhelming urge to flee.

I shouldn't be here, I thought to myself, staring at the dresser that remained exactly as I'd left it, covered in sweet, little knickknacks, almost all of which had been gifts from either Gram or Dante. Every one of those things had meant something to me once upon a time. Years' worth of Valentines, birthday, and Christmas gifts from the boy that had broken my heart and the woman who had tried to save it.

No matter the circumstances, I should not be subjecting myself to this, I thought, eyes fixated on a small silver key strung across the corner of the mirror.

"Uncanny, isn't it?" Dante's voice came from the doorway, mere inches behind me. "She didn't move one thing. Ten years later, and she was keeping it for you exactly how you'd left it."

"Like a tomb," I murmured.

"Or a shrine," he returned, moving past me, brushing against me like it was nothing, and setting my suitcase onto a large ottoman at the foot of a comfy armchair in the corner by my old bay window.

He didn't look at me on his way out, but he did stop at the door, clearing his throat, his back to me. "If I were you, I'd search that dresser before my mom gets to it. She's going to clean this place out fast, mark my words, and everything in this room is yours by right, so claim it now if you want it."

I waved my hand, dismissing the notion. "She can have whatever she wants. I won't be taking *any* of it with me."

Only his head turned as he leveled me with a hard stare. "You're going to want to double check that dresser, just to be sure. Trust me."

I didn't trust him. Never would again, but I nodded at him that I understood and as soon as he left, closing the door behind him, I went to the dresser and began to shuffle through it.

I knew, or at least some part of me did, what I was looking for. I don't think I really *believed* it would be there, but it was a thought somewhere in my mind.

Still, when I found the small, white velvet case I staggered a bit where I stood.

And, as I opened it, I had to sit down at what I found. *How? Why?*

He must not have known what was in this dresser, I told myself. He couldn't have.

And, while I could be a spiteful bitch, I was not a thief, so the first thing I did was track him down to give it back.

I heard his voice before I saw him, but no one else's, and so I stumbled into them without any time to brace myself.

Blindly I reached one hand out, holding myself up with the wall, the other gripping the small, white box hard enough to imbed an imprint into my palm.

She was facing Dante, her back to me.

He saw me right away, and whatever he was saying trailed away, his attention properly caught at my presence.

At least I had that. No matter what he'd done, how he'd betrayed me, at least when I was there, he couldn't look away from me.

Not even for *her.*

She caught on quickly that they were no longer alone, but I had enough time to recover before she turned and saw me.

I hated her like every creature since the dawn of time has hated its natural enemy.

Blind, fear-induced, debilitating hatred that never let me see past the moment to the big picture.

She was a threat, my gut told me now.

My gut had been telling me this since I was fourteen.

She needed to be eliminated—was all my mind could ever seem to process when it came to her, because one undeniable truth had always resonated through me—her existence meant the end of mine.

The end of everything I cared about. The end of the *only* thing I used to care about.

Still, I'd been so shocked when I'd been proven right.

A part of me, some pathetic thing deep down in my soul, still couldn't believe it.

I gave her a lie of a smile. "Tiffany," I said in greeting, my voice fake friendly.

"Scarlett," she returned; her soft voice even and unaffected. She must have known I was at the house. She'd had warning.

I hadn't been given the same courtesy. It was an effort not to glare at Dante for that.

"How've you been?" she asked, sounding like she actually cared.

Perhaps she did. If I was doing terribly, I knew she'd love to hear about it.

I studied her for a time, not answering. I hadn't seen her in years, but she hadn't changed much. She was still beautiful. It was an icy blonde, wintry blue-eyed beauty that appealed to men with a taste for the unattainable.

She was slight, rail thin, and petite, but somehow all the more intimidating for it, a delicate princess of a woman.

She, like Dante, was raised with money, and it had always been apparent in the way she dressed, wearing designer clothes even as a teenager. It was no different now. Her elegant black dress undoubtedly cost a small fortune, and her lavender stilettos were on point.

I hated her for it. And I hated that I was still wearing the comfortable, torn-up, old jeans, plain white tank, and worn to death gray Toms I'd traveled in.

I hated that her hair and makeup were done so heavily and precisely that I knew she'd had a stylist do it for the occasion.

I hated that my hair was a messy mane down my back, and my makeup was minimal and what there was likely smeared from travel.

Basically when it came to Tiffany, there was no end to things I found to hate. About her and myself.

The most toxic relationships in life are defined by the way they make us feel about ourselves. She and I were the worst of that. Whatever I was, always felt diminished by what she was.

"Just peachy," I finally answered. "You?"

She smiled wistfully, like the question brought her joy, and turned to glance up, up, up at a much taller Dante.

Seeing them next to each other, especially standing so close, made me want to wretch.

It brought out the worst in me, seeing him with the woman he'd thrown me away for.

It made me feel, yet again—*story of my life*—like trash.

"I can't complain, can I, Dante?" she asked him.

My eyes shot to him. I didn't bother to hide the hate in them from him.

He was still staring at me. As far as I could tell, he hadn't so much as twitched since he saw me enter the room.

I almost smiled, not a happy smile, more of a *you made your bed now die in it, you fucker* smile, because this had to be even more uncomfortable for him than it was for us, and that didn't make me sad for him.

I almost felt a twinge of pity for him though.

Imagine the burden of being the only person that hateful little me had ever trusted.

Now imagine betraying that trust in all the ways that would hurt me the most.

Hell hath no fury.

Every hard thing inside of me turned harder still against him. Went from steel to diamond hard.

"I need a word," I told him coldly, turned on my heel, and walked away.

He could follow me or not, but I couldn't take even one more second in a room with the two of them. I'd do something violent if I had to endure any more.

He chose to follow, though I didn't acknowledge him until I was back in my room, door closed behind us.

I held up the little white box. "*This* was in the dresser," I spoke quietly. God only knew who was eavesdropping.

Not a muscle moved in his face. "Yes, I know. I'd put it somewhere safe before my mother shows up here if I were you."

I just stared at him.

He shrugged. "It's yours. Gram wanted you to have it. That much she made clear to me. It was hers to give. So take it. Like I said, keep it safe if you don't want my mother to take it from you."

I was shaking my head, but I said, "I can't believe your mom didn't already take it. It wasn't even *hidden*."

"Yes, I know. I put it in there right before you showed up. I'm well aware of how my mother operates. She no doubt ransacked the place before they'd even taken Gram's body away."

I took a few deep, bracing breaths and thrust the small object at him. "I don't want it. You take it. I have no right to it now."

He took a weighty step back, one so impactful I swayed where I stood. "You're the only one with any right to it," he said, tone dull, lifeless. "Whether you want it or not, I won't take it. Either you keep it, or my mother will. I'll let you decide."

Without another word, he left.

I sat heavily on the bed, staring fixedly at the tiny thing.

I didn't have a clue what to do with it, but one thing was for sure—I'd never be letting Dante's mother have it, not if I got to have a say.

If for no other reason than pure spite, I'd keep it at least from her.

I began to unpack, hanging the few clothes I'd brought in the near empty closet.

I knew Dante had meant it literally about his mother ransacking the place, that even my luggage wasn't safe from her grasping hands.

Luckily I'd packed a bit of jewelry for the trip. I found a small gold chain that ironically, but not surprisingly, Gram had given me, looped the object through it, and strung the thing around my neck, tucking it into my cleavage. The dress I was wearing would cover even the chain.

I hid the box in one of my shoes. If his mother found that much, it wouldn't be good, but at least all she'd be getting was an empty box.

I began getting ready for the funeral almost right away. Nothing made a girl want to look her best more than facing a room full of her most despised enemies.

I spent nearly an hour on makeup, going full out— smoky eyes, red lips, the works. I looked my best when polished to killing sharpness.

My hair was easier. I left it down. It was long and thick, a wavy, streaky brown mane down my back that needed only a bit of taming to look like I'd just come from a rather graceful tumble between the sheets, which suited me just fine.

I wore a form fitting black dress with a high collar. It was polyester made to look like silk, and it almost succeeded. What the dress did succeed in was accentuating every single one of my outrageous curves, the skirt hitting just above my knees.

I wore the red Louboutins Dante had given me (damn him) though it had been a struggle with myself to do so.

It was a testament to how much I hated the other people that would be attending the funeral that I'd let Dante see I hadn't thrown them away, to let him see me wearing a gift he'd given me.

But desperate times called for desperate measures, and nothing made me feel more confident than a killer pair of shoes.

"Jealousy is always born with love but it does not die with it."
~Francois de La Rochefoucauld

chapter sixteen

PAST

When the teenage years hit, what Dante and I had just sort of turned, shifted a bit. It was an unspoken rule that we belonged to each other in a new and more possessive way.

We just made sense. Something naive inside of me couldn't imagine anything else.

Neither of us could have tolerated someone soft.

I'd chew up and spit out a soft boy, a fact I'd since then proven many times.

Dante would eat a soft girl for breakfast.

We fit together, and it wasn't until I was nearly fourteen that it even occurred to me that anyone or anything could come between us.

We were at Dante's house, which was rare. His mother didn't work, and she hardly ever went anywhere, so being at his house was pretty much a guarantee of running into her, not to mention the fact that my grandma worked there and she'd kill me if she knew how much time I spent with Dante and that we were close enough he'd bring me to his home.

Dante had forgotten his backpack, though, and he was just running upstairs real quick to grab it.

He wasn't quick enough.

His mother terrified me, but she was the kind of woman where you knew you shouldn't let her see it.

But some things you just couldn't hide.

I tried my best, but she was a shark and I was perpetually bleeding. There was no way she didn't notice.

Usually I had a tough skin. I liked to think I had a tough everything, but I did have one weakness.

One. In my entire child/woman body, and we both knew it.

Dante. He was the chink in my armor. My soft underbelly.

She didn't single me out often, but every time she did, it was memorable.

And terrible.

I'd grown several inches over the summer and I was awkward with it. Most of my clothes were ill-fitting. Gram helped some with it, well, she helped what little Grandma would let her. She wasn't allowed to buy me anything nice or even anything new, but Gram still took an interest, making sure I went shopping a few times a year for the basics on consignment, but even she couldn't keep up with how my body was growing.

I'd always been rail thin, skinny looking to the point of unhealthy, but all of a sudden, I had sprouted, and as I'd gone up, parts of me had started to grow out.

My legs had grown longer than was proportionate

with my body, and I did not own one pair of pants that made it to my ankles, or one set of shorts that weren't embarrassingly high, exposing way more of my upper thighs and butt than I was comfortable with. And nothing in the world fit comfortably over my shapely hips.

My shirts were too tight, my dresses small to the point of obscene, and on top of all of that, I kept having growth spurts, so I felt less coordinated by the day.

And my breasts—which were the bane of my existence, had grown too large to hide.

I couldn't talk to a boy and have him look me in the eye anymore.

Except for Dante. He was good at being my exception.

Even when he pissed me off, he rarely disappointed me.

I knew he noticed my changing figure, but he never mentioned it, never teased me for it when we usually teased each other about *everything*. He seemed to sense it was a sensitive subject for me.

I was waiting for Dante in the intimidating entryway of their mansion when she approached me wearing her usual unpleasant smile.

"Scarlett," she said, eyeing me with cold eyes. "Just look at you. Growing up so fast." Each word was dripping in disdain.

I swallowed hard, my throat so dry the motion stung like sandpaper going down, and greeted her, keeping my most stoic mask firmly over my face.

"Come this way," she ordered, turning her back on me to stride down the hallway to her wing of the house.

She just expected me to obey. She was a bitch like that.

I wished more than anything that I had the nerve to call her one to her face.

I hated that I followed her without a word.

As much as I rebelled against the very idea, she intimidated me, and some insecure part of me always ached for her approval.

She led me to her study, and my entire body clenched tightly in dread when she locked the door behind us.

I stayed where I was by the exit not moving a muscle as she glided with her smooth stride to her antique desk and retrieved something.

A picture, I realized as she brought it close.

It was of a girl, maybe my age or a bit older. She was beautiful, with pale blonde hair and wintry blue eyes. She was slender and elegant, and even in the picture I could tell she'd never had an awkward moment in her life.

She was dressed in the kind of clothes you never saw real teenagers wearing. The latest expensive trends, head to toe.

"Do you know who this is?" Dante's mother asked me.

"A model?" I guessed. She fit the bill.

"She should be one, but no. This is Tiffany Vanderkamp. Have you heard the name?"

I shook my head. I knew this was headed somewhere bad, somewhere that would be disastrous to me, but I wasn't quite sure which direction the disaster would come from.

"Dante hasn't told you about her?"

I shook my head again.

She tutted, her face placing itself into something resembling sympathy. I knew it was a lie, but she still had me half convinced with her perfectly arranged expression. She was evil like that.

"Tiffany, or Fanny as we affectionately call her, is the young woman that Dante is going to marry when he graduates from college."

Ah. There it was.

She was a dirty fighter, so of course she'd gone straight for my soft spot.

I felt my stoic mask slipping off, being replaced by something akin to dismay. I recovered it, but not quite quickly enough.

"Oh dear, I can see that he hasn't been upfront with you about this, the boor."

"I-i-i-i—" Oh God, the stutter was here. I'd known it wasn't gone forever; it still came out to play at the most dreaded moments.

She smiled at me, looking delighted. "You're upset, aren't you? Did he lie to you? Did he say you were special to him? Naughty, naughty boy, just like his father. Are you two having sex yet?"

I was shocked. Completely. We hadn't even *kissed* yet. "N-n-n-n—"

She threw back her head and laughed, the first time I'd ever seen her actually look happy. Apparently all it took was making someone else miserable.

"You are," she incorrectly guessed. "Of course you are, you little slut. No wonder he thinks he's in love with you, but that will all wear off soon enough. And of course you're in love with him. He's a beautiful boy, but he's not for you, do you understand?

I did not. I set my jaw and shook my head at her, done with attempting to speak.

She was so wrong about so many things I wished I could have voiced it.

We had not done any of the things she seemed to assume, but she was right about one thing.

I was in love with her son.

But she was so wrong about the rest. I owned him. He was mine, and I was his. She was underestimating us both if she thought she could change that.

Mutely I tried to hand the picture back to her but she waved it away.

"You keep that. It's yours. And go ahead, continue doing what you're doing. Have your fun. Enjoy it all while you can. Be my son's little plaything while he's young and stupid. Just never forget that you aren't his future. If he ever tries to put a ring on your finger, I'm cutting him off."

Just then Dante began to pound on the door.

"Put that away," she snarled at me.

I stuffed the picture in my bag. It was embarrassing how relieved I was that Dante was rescuing me from his malevolent mother.

It's not like she was beating me. Her only weapons were words.

But they were lethal.

I didn't bring up the incident or that girl to him for a long time. I was embarrassed to.

And what if he told me it was none of my business?

I'd be crushed.

So I sat on it for a long time, letting it simmer inside of me like an infected wound.

"Never back down from her, okay?" Dante told me when we were free of his house. "If she ever senses she can intimidate you, she'll make your life hell."

"Hell is empty and all the devils are here."
~William Shakespeare

chapter seventeen

PRESENT

I was just stepping into my shoes when someone knocked on my door.

It was Dante. He'd changed into a dark, dark suit that set off his golden hair and skin to an unfair degree.

This was the look that suited him best; he was born to be a villain in black.

My shallow, superficial self was devastated by the sight of him.

It should have been against the law for him to go out in public like that. It did indecent things to me.

"Are you ready?" he asked me, eyes on my feet, though he didn't comment on the shoes. "It's almost time to go."

"I won't share a car with her," I said quietly and vehemently.

I hadn't even realized I was thinking the words. They'd flown out of my mouth completely of their own accord.

But I meant them. I would not, could not share a car with Tiffany. I refused to share *anything* with her for the rest of my life. I had shared enough.

He nodded solemnly. "Of course not." He held out his arm. "Let's go?"

"Is Eugene driving me?" I asked.

He went from looking stoic to annoyed, which had been my intent. "No. I'm taking you. Are you ready?"

"Is it . . . just us driving together?" I wanted to know what I was in for. The dreadful possibilities were endless, and it was telling that being alone with him was far from the worst option.

"Yes, if you're all right with that," he bit out the words. I could tell he'd misunderstood the reason for my question, and it was almost a relief to realize that sometimes he could completely misread me.

"Fine," I said. I grabbed my small purse out of the room, taking his arm but giving him nothing, letting him stew on the misunderstanding. "Let's go."

He led me out of the house without another word.

Moving with him, the way we walked together, how he opened every door and handed me into his car like it was his personal duty, all of it was painfully familiar. If I let myself, I could forget for a moment, two, three, four, that we were years away from the time when we'd belonged so desperately to each other.

I tried to distract myself from it on the drive by antagonizing him. "Is *she* staying at Gram's?"

He glanced at me, then back at the road, tugging at his collar. "I've no clue. I assume she's staying either at my mother's house or with her parents. I didn't ask."

"I won't stay under the same roof as her."

He started chewing his lip so intently, a nervous tell of

his, that I had to look away. "The only accommodations I arranged were yours and mine. I honestly have no clue what anyone else is planning. Well, besides my father. He's staying at Gram's, as well."

That didn't surprise me one bit, and I couldn't have cared less. Still, it was a sore spot for Dante, so I did a bit of picking at it.

"Did he bring his mistress?" I prodded.

His mouth twisted bitterly and the look he shot me was not hostile so much as wounded. "No."

"Don't you find it ironic how much you resent his mistress, all things considered?"

Oh, ho. Big point for me. That one was a doozy. The black look he sent me for that had my heart beating faster and had me fighting not to smile.

"Apple doesn't fall far from the tree," I hummed under my breath.

He hit the brakes, stopping the car so fast that I had to brace myself against the dashboard.

"Oh my God. Really?" he ground out. "Is there any low fucking blow you won't resort to, on today of all days? Can't you save it for even *one* fucking day? On *this* fucking day, when we bury Gram?"

My high at riling him went instantly to a low, and I had to look away, flushing with shame. "I'm sorry," I said quietly. Not even *I* was this big of a bitch, not even to *him*. "I was just trying to distract myself by antagonizing you," I admitted to the window.

"I'm well aware, but can you give it a rest for a few hours? Please."

I nodded, stunned at how freely the P word seemed to roll off his tongue lately.

He began to drive again and the car fell quiet for a time.

Without even the distraction of messing with him, my thoughts went dark, to Gram, to the past, to how long it'd been since I saw her last, and how that was all my fucking fault.

"I still spoke to her every week," I told him. "She'd call me like clockwork, and I always made sure I was available to talk to her for at least an hour." It was a small bit of comfort for him, and I offered it up as a defensive apology.

"I know. I know," he said with jaw clenching stiffness. Clearly, he was still upset.

That had been my whole repertoire on trying to make him feel better, so I gave up after that.

I couldn't even make myself feel better. How on earth would I know how to fix him?

My talent lay in making him feel *worse*, and if that was off the table, I figured I should just shut up.

It was a bit of a drive to the funeral parlor, I vaguely remembered, though I'd only been there a few times my whole life.

We were maybe halfway there when Dante put his hand on my leg. His warm grip squeezed the spot just above my knee.

It was so familiar, something he'd done hundreds of times at least, that at first I just stared, my sensory memory at war with my current perception.

It took me a minute, but finally I managed to get out a quiet but firm, "Stop touching me."

"It calms me, you know that," he returned, his deep voice still rough with the storm of his temper. "I need to get a handle on myself before we get to the funeral home, okay? *Need* to."

Who could argue with that? Apparently not even me.

But a few minutes later I was glaring at him again. His hand just kept inching higher. Now it was at mid-thigh, my skirt going up with it, and I knew he was doing it deliberately.

"Knock it off," I told him, tone as scathing as I could manage.

With a smile, he took his hand away. Apparently it'd worked. He was in a markedly better mood.

"Did you want to speak at the service?" he asked me. "I'll be getting up to say a few words."

"No, thank you," I replied. I didn't even have to think about it. I couldn't do it, couldn't speak about Gram to a roomful of hostile faces. Oftentimes I flourished under the heavy weight of that contempt, but this was so personal. I couldn't speak about her and not share too much about myself and in the sharing, expose my too raw emotions. Also, this was just the sort of thing that brought my stutter back. I couldn't bear the humiliation if that happened.

Gram wouldn't have asked that of me. It would have been enough for her that I was there, that I'd come home for her.

Dante didn't pursue it any further.

"Who else is speaking?" I asked him.

"My dad, me, Father Frederick. We're keeping it brief. You know how she hated funerals."

I was relieved to hear his mother wasn't speaking. She'd hated Gram, her mother-in-law, but she rarely turned down an opportunity to be the center of attention.

"There'll be a short viewing," he continued, "then the service, followed by a reception at her house."

I'd figured as much, with all of the prep going on at the estate.

A short, tense length of time passed and suddenly we were there, parking, Dante handing me out of the car, giving me his thick arm to hold, heading inside, passing by countless, faceless black clad people.

I didn't look at any of them. I tried to look only at the ground, determined to get through this without breaking down.

She lived a good life, I told myself. A long life, full of joy and surrounded by people who loved her.

But I already missed her. I wasn't ready to let her go.

The viewing was unpleasant, seeing her for the first time like that, her face so still in death.

I wanted to remember her smiling and animated, her eyes open, and filled with mischief or delight.

Still, it was like I felt her there. I spoke to her coffin as though she could hear me. "It won't surprise you that I'm not too keen about being back here," I told her quietly. "Only *you* could get me into a room with these people, Gram."

Of course there was no response, and the loss of her hit me anew, because there was so much I wanted to tell her from just the last few days alone, the last hours, things I'd only ever vent about to her. She'd been my shoulder to cry on for so many years, held so many of the secrets that I couldn't tell *anyone* else, not even my closest friends, and it struck me then that I would never again have anyone who I could talk to in just that way, as a child does to a parent. She was the only adult figure in my life that had ever given a *damn*, and now she was gone, and I felt more alone than I ever had.

In a moment of utter weakness, I closed my eyes and set my shaking hand on her casket. "What am I going to do, Gram?" I asked her quietly. "I feel so alone in this world without you."

Dante, who'd been a silent presence at my back, spoke then, "You're not alone," he said, his voice emotional. Intense.

I acted as if I had not heard, as if he had not spoken. Those words meant *nothing* to me, particularly coming from him.

"You were wrong, Gram," I said softly, tone emotionless because I was resigned to the awful, lonely truth of it. "Love doesn't save our souls. It kills them."

I could hear Dante literally grinding his teeth behind me.

For some strange reason, Dante sat me next to him in the front row for the service. I didn't have the energy to fight him on it, so I took my seat, glancing surreptitiously around at all of the familiar faces and the significance of where they were sitting and whom they were sitting with.

Predictably, I clocked Tiffany's location first, but she'd placed herself so close to us, directly behind Dante in fact, that it was hard not to.

I almost moved when she first sat down, almost got up and made a scene, but something kind of wonderful happened to stop me.

As she sat, mere moments after we had, she perched herself on the edge of her seat, putting both of her delicate hands on Dante's shoulders.

I had my head craned around to stare daggers at her. She was opening her mouth to say something, I'll never know what, because we were all distracted by what Dante did next.

Without looking at her, without so much as acknowledging her, he pulled his shoulders out of her hands, leaning far forward to avoid her touch completely.

As he did this he glanced at me, his hand cupping the spot on my leg that had so soothed him earlier.

I allowed it to stay there purely for spite and turned my head again to meet her eyes, letting her see what was in mine.

You might have had him for a bit, my triumphant gaze told her, *but it was all you'll get.*

You're nothing to him. Insignificant.

Whether he's with me or not, it won't help you. He's done with you.

Whether I was the love or hate of his life, nothing and no one would ever overshadow me.

I swallowed the memory of every woman he had ever known.

Swallowed it whole.

I covered his hand with my own, still staring at her until, finally, her face drawn tight, eyes flashing at me, she looked away.

The victory was short lived, however.

I took my hand away from Dante's when I saw who was taking the seat beside Tiffany.

I faced forward right as his hand fell away from my knee.

He hadn't turned around, but I could tell he knew that his mother was behind him.

Dante never touched me when she was near. It had been this way for as long as I could remember.

I used to have a problem with it, used to be sensitive about it, but just then it suited me fine. The less he touched me the better.

His mother, Adelaide, made a big show of greeting Tiffany. Kissing both of her cheeks, telling her how wonderful she looked, complimenting everything about her, from the top of her head to the tips of her toes.

She didn't acknowledge me, nor I her. This was not the place for it.

There wasn't a civil word to be had between the two of us. There never had been.

I thought she was evil, and she thought I was trash. Neither of us would ever change our minds.

I was surprised, though, that there was no greeting between her and Dante. He didn't turn around, and she didn't take exception to it.

That was a new and interesting development, to be sure, one that I didn't mind at all.

Adelaide's lifelong friend and Tiffany's mother, Leann, soon joined them. Again there was not a word or gesture of greeting between the first row and the second, and for the same reason.

Adelaide by herself was an evil force to be reckoned with. Add in her best friend, and any sane person would run in the other direction. Two more manipulative women I had never met. They were a team made in hell, and if they were ignoring me, all the better.

"If a thing loves, it is infinite."
~William Blake

chapter eighteen

Dante's father Leo sat on the row with us, but not close. Father and son did not speak. Husband and wife, one mere feet in front of the other, did not exchange greetings of any kind.

That was the normal way of things in the Durant family.

The sight of the father had me doing another surreptitious glance around the room, clocking at least four of his other sons, all by different women.

I wasn't sure if somehow Leo had only sired boys or if he just never acknowledged the daughters. With what I knew of Leo, if I had to guess, it'd be the latter.

None of the siblings were sitting together, none of them so much as acknowledging each other.

Only one of them ventured into our row. It was Bastian, Leo's second oldest son, his first child with mistress number one, born mere months after Dante.

Bastian sat on the far side of Leo, exchanging a brief but civil greeting with his father.

Dante was Leo's only legitimate child, but he was far from his favorite. If I had to guess which one was, it'd be Bastian.

Dante stared straight ahead, not acknowledging his half-brother. Again, expected, but I sent Bastian a little nod of a greeting that he returned solemnly.

I'd never had a problem with Bastian. Despite getting along too well with his bastard of a father, he wasn't a bad sort, which was not something you could say about all of Dante's half-brothers.

I made another scan of the swiftly filling room. It would be standing room only soon it'd gotten so crowded, but still most seemed loath to take the front row seats, which were traditionally reserved for family.

My eyes stopped dead on a familiar face.

I nodded at my grandmother.

Her tightly drawn mouth drawing tighter at the sight of me, she nodded back.

I hadn't seen her in almost ten years, but I was still shocked at how much she'd aged, how haggard her homely face appeared.

I knew Gram's death couldn't have been easy on her. I had never been sure if my grandmother loved me, but I was certain of her love for Gram, and losing her must have hit her hard.

After that I faced forward and looked neither left nor right. I'd seen enough familiar faces for the moment.

The service was brief but emotional. Even Leo's speech had me struggling not to lose my composure. Leo was a shitty human being and a worse father, but he had loved his mother and didn't even try to hide his grief at her passing.

For Dante's speech, I had to put on the dark sunglasses

I'd stowed away in my bag and look down at my hands while Dante spoke of his grandmother and all that she'd meant to him.

His words were sparse but worthy of her.

The shades hid my eyes, but they couldn't hide the tears that ran under them and down my face.

When he finished and came back to sit beside me, I covered his hand with my own for a few brief moments, Adelaide and my grudges be damned.

We were at the front of the procession that flowed out of the funeral home, into cars, and along the short drive to her gravesite.

She'd been allotted a beautiful spot in the sprawling cemetery, right next to her long deceased, much beloved husband.

I stood stiffly beside Dante as Father Frederick recited Gram's favorite poem and it made me cry all over again.

By that point I wanted nothing so much as to lock myself away somewhere, curl up into a ball, and cry until the tears ran out. That was the irony of funerals, of gathering to grieve when no one who was *really* grieving wanted anything to do with company. I was worn out, and we still had the reception to get through.

I almost (almost) considered escaping to my room for that ordeal, just running from it all, but I knew I couldn't do it.

I was a lot of terrible things, but I was not a coward.

I would, however, be getting the hell out of dodge in all due haste.

"My flight home is tomorrow, right?" I asked Dante as we began to walk away from the gravesite.

"Hmm," he responded, and I could tell just with that

noise that I was about to be manipulated. "I'll have to double check. Didn't you get all of the info yourself in that email I sent you?"

"No," I answered, knowing full well that he'd asked a question he already knew the answer to. "You only sent me half of the itinerary."

"Oh, I see. An oversight. I'll look into it and have it sent to you as soon as I can."

I kept my narrowed eyes on him. The problem was, I knew him too well. I could tell when he was planning something, even if I couldn't have said what precisely it was.

I decided not to push it here. It didn't matter what he planned, besides. I'd be out of here come morning, that was a fact.

Unfortunately we ran directly into my grandmother on our way back to Dante's car.

I wasn't going to say anything to her, we'd never had much to say to each other, but she had other plans.

"Hello, Scarlett," she sneered at me. Not a good sign.

I nodded at her, making cursory eye contact. "Hello, Glenda."

I tried to walk right by her, but she moved into my path, her small frame squaring off in front of me. "Did you really have to wear red shoes to a *funeral*?" She made the dig quietly but with effect. My grandmother had never had to raise her voice. Her vicious tongue was just as damaging with or without being loud. "And could your dress be any tighter? You look like a Hollywood *whore*. Is that what you've been doing down in California? Whoring for old directors, trying to sleep your way to the top? Must not be working."

I gave her an unpleasant smile. She hadn't changed a

bit. I hadn't expected her to, but my old resentment for her flared anew.

Just my luck it was the nice one that had died.

Everyone has a little voice in their head, holding them back from showing enthusiasm, forcing them into pessimism.

Oftentimes that voice takes the shape of someone we know. Sometimes it's a snarky friend, a cynical parent.

In my case, especially back when I was a kid, it was my grandma. Every happy urge I ever had she tried to talk me out of and a lot of the time she succeeded.

When she'd kicked me out at seventeen, I'd left and never looked back. In fact, it'd been a relief because after that I got to live with Gram.

Though I shared no blood with Gram, in a lot of ways, most ways, she'd always felt more like family to me than my own grandma, and unlike my complete adoration for Gram, my feelings for my own grandmother could only be described as complicated.

She resented me because I was a burden she'd been forced to shoulder but never felt she'd owned.

And I resented her because I was really, really good at it.

Also, she was mean. Deep down to her core mean. She was cold, stubborn as a mule, and vindictive to a terrible degree and with very little provocation. There was no give in her, and if you caught her in the wrong mood, she would absolutely cut off her nose to spite her face. She could self-destruct like nobody's business if it meant taking someone else out with her.

Her entire wretched life was pretty much a testament to that.

Obviously, I'd taken after her with at least a few of

those undesirable traits. The irony was not lost on me. But in my defense, I do believe that many of the toxins that resided inside of me had been set into motion quite early on and a good number of them had been planted by her.

But then again, sometimes it just feels better to have someone to blame, and my grandmother had always made herself into a very convenient target. It was one of the few nice things I could say about her.

I opened my mouth to give my obligatory scathing retort, but Dante beat me to it.

"Have a little respect," Dante told her, voice low and mean. "What would my grandmother think about you talking like that at her funeral? For shame. And the red shoes are *perfect*. You of all people should remember how much Gram loved red."

I lowered my head and started wringing my hands. The day had gone from bad to worse.

Dante defending me was perhaps the most cruel thing he could do. More than anything else, it made me remember why I'd been so devoted to him for most of my life. Reminded me of a time when I had absolute faith in him.

Made me almost forgot that all of that had only set me up for a more brutal fall.

"Oh, well," Grandma derisively bit back, "you're carrying on with *this* one again? Didn't he dump you?" she asked me. "Like trash," she added. "Didn't you marry Leann's girl?" she asked Dante. "I always told you he'd break your heart," she told me.

This was typical. She lobbed out hurtful things like steady grenades until one hit its mark, and she never stopped before something vital was damaged.

Story of my childhood.

I began to walk away as Dante answered. "No and no. And I know what you're doing, Glenda. You're lashing out because she cut off all contact with you. Maybe if you'd try to be less awful to her, she'd give you a ring every once in a while."

I didn't hear my grandmother's response because I'd picked up my pace.

chapter nineteen

PAST

"I *hate* my name," I complained one day to Gram when I was over for tea. My name was just one thing on a very long list that the kids at school teased me about, but I'd decided to take particular exception to it because that day I'd overheard some girls chanting *Scarlett harlot* when they thought I couldn't hear.

So I'd come to rant about it to Gram. She was the only grownup I knew that I could say anything to, tell anything to, and she took it all in stride.

This though for some reason seemed to take her aback.

Her hand went to her chest and she blinked at me several times before responding, "You do?"

I looked away. I couldn't maintain eye contact with her when she appeared so . . . wounded.

I shrugged, not so sure about my outburst now. "I guess so," I muttered.

"Want to know something absolutely fascinating about your name?"

My eyes went back to her as I nodded.

"A very famous woman named you that. She named you that because scarlet is a brilliant, brave, and daring color. You see, she knew you'd have an interesting life where those qualities would serve you well."

"*You* named me?" I breathed.

She smiled and nodded. "I did. Glenda was . . . overwhelmed when she first got you and so I took over for a while. I named you because I felt strongly about it, and she didn't mind. I always had a talent for naming, if I do say so myself. Do you want to know who else I named?" she glanced over at Dante as she asked the question, and I found my eyes following hers.

He was in his usual spot on the sofa across the room, just lying there listening to us, occasionally piping in to add to or argue with what we were saying. He sat up now and looked at Gram.

"Who?" I asked, though I saw what she was hinting at.

"Dante. Don't those names sound just wonderful together? Scarlett and Dante. They have a romantic ring when you combine them, don't they?"

Dante and I were just looking at each other.

"Did you know that she named us?" I asked him.

He smiled and laid back down. "I did, but I thought you'd enjoy the story more coming from her."

"A man's kiss is his signature."
~May West

chapter twenty

PRESENT

I was striding across the cemetery, had nearly made it to the car when Dante caught up to me.

"Don't," I told him when he fell in beside me. "Don't involve yourself in my issues. Just. Don't. It's not your job to defend me."

"Since when?"

I shuddered. *Hello, temper.* "Since you dumped me."

"I didn't dump you." He sounded upset, which upset me.

"I didn't *dump* you," he repeated when I didn't respond.

"Are you trying to pick a fight?" I asked him pointedly. He had, after all, been the one to declare this a day of peace between the two of us.

He set his jaw and fell quiet. Good.

I thought and hoped that he'd just stay quiet, but about halfway back to the house he pulled the car over onto the shoulder suddenly, putting the car in park.

He gripped the steering wheel with both hands and lay his forehead against it.

"God, I don't want to do this," he spoke quietly, not turning his head. "I don't want to deal with those people being in her home, talking about her, pretending to care, most of them just waiting to see what she left them in the will."

What he'd said didn't need a response. He knew how I felt about those people.

"And if one of them says an insulting word to you, so help me, God—"

"Let's just get home and get it over with," I cut in, speaking to the window. "And besides, the sooner we get there the sooner I can have a drink."

One plus for the day—liquor. It would be flowing freely for this ill-fated gathering, I had no doubt.

"Yeah, okay," he said dejectedly. "Just give me a minute. I need to get a grip."

I was fine with that, because I thought he meant to just leave him to his thoughts for a minute.

He didn't mean that, it was quickly clear.

He started tugging on my arm, and I looked at him. He wasn't leaning on the steering wheel anymore. Now he was leaning toward *me*.

"What are you doing?" I asked him warily.

His answer was to keep tugging me to him, not stopping until my resistant head was pressed to his faithless chest.

Still without speaking, he started stroking my hair.

"Stop it," I demanded.

He kissed the top of my head and kept stroking, a soothing, familiar motion, his heavy hand moving with just the perfect amount of pressure from my temple to the ends of my long hair.

Perfect because he'd done it a thousand times. More. This used to be how he'd soothe me down from a temper.

"Stop it," I repeated faintly.

Just like the bastard to declare a truce and then launch an attack.

And somehow it was working. I was leaning into him, relaxing into his familiar embrace.

I caught myself and tried to push away.

He wouldn't let me. And he was stronger than me, the bastard.

I struggled harder, then harder. It did me not one bit of good. He held me to him easily, both of my wrists captured in one of his hands.

He knew me, knew how I fought. The first thing he'd done was restrain my hands, or more specifically, my vicious nails.

"Why are you doing this?" I panted at him. I was still struggling, but not as hard now. I'd quickly worn myself out.

"Why won't you let me comfort you?" he said, the words mumbled into the top of my head.

I don't know how, I thought. *Even if I wanted that, wanted to pretend with you long enough to feel better, I don't know how.*

But I said none of it. Instead I kept on struggling in his hold.

Finally he let me go, and I turned away from him to stare back out the window.

"You were always like this." His tone was fond, damn him. "Even when you were just a scrappy little kid. Always so extreme. You take things either with a stoic face or you lose your mind. Never any middle ground. I miss that, you know. You always challenged me."

I had nothing to say to that.

"But today," he continued, voice going softer with a tender emotion that he had no right to, "give me some middle ground. Let me comfort you, or at least, comfort me."

"Please," he said, closer now. "Comfort *me*."

I blame the please. Hearing that word coming from those lips was hopelessly disarming to me, so when he pulled me to him again, I didn't fight him. I laid my head over his black, traitorous heart, and let the tears fall.

I was weary of trying to suppress them, and they came out freely for a time as I quietly sobbed against my enemy's chest.

How could you find comfort in the soul that had shattered you?

I didn't know, but perversely, I found it anyway.

Eventually I pulled back, not looking up at him, eyes trained on the wet spot I'd left on his beautiful suit jacket.

My hands went to my face, feeling at my cheeks as I realized that my makeup was in ruins.

"I'll need to go upstairs and redo my makeup when we get back," I said blankly. My mind was worrying about something small in an effort to avoid thinking about something big.

"Well, there's no hurry. The bloodsuckers will be there all day I'm sure," he murmured, and not so much the words but his proximity had me stiffening.

His face was moving closer to mine, then closer. His hands cupped my face, angling it up to his.

I kept my gaze pointed down, but it didn't matter. He wasn't concerned with my eyes. He wanted my lips.

He took them unrepentantly, passionately, devouring me like he always did, as though he'd never have enough.

And I let him have them, the fight gone out of me. I'd

always had a weakness for his kisses. That's why I hated them so vehemently.

I started shifting, falling against my seat back, though there wasn't far to go.

It was the damnedest thing. Every time he kissed me, all I wanted to do was lie down flat on my back. That urge was quickly followed by one to open my arms, and then my legs.

It was a natural inclination. Instinctual and all the more powerful for it.

"*I have to remind myself to breathe—almost remind my heart to beat!*"
Emily Brontë

chapter twenty-one

PAST

"Let's ditch school," I told Dante.

"And do what?"

"Go watch movies at my grandma's house." She wouldn't be there. She was gone from seven a.m. to seven p.m. every single working day like clockwork.

And Dante never said no to movies at my house. It had become our thing lately.

In fact, it had become my favorite thing in the world.

He shrugged. "Fine. Whatever. I'm not in the mood for school anyway."

We walked back toward my place leisurely, side by side as we strolled, so close that our arms and hands kept brushing against each other.

The third time it happened, he took my hand and laced our fingers together.

A thrill ran through my entire body, and I couldn't hold back a smile.

Neither of us said a word about it. He'd been doing it more and more lately when we were alone, but we never talked about it.

We'd been doing lots of things when we were alone together that we never talked about.

Nothing like what his mom had suggested, in fact all of it could be called more or less innocent, just physical contact that kept progressing, lingering until we couldn't seem to stop.

But he'd never even kissed me. I was starting to worry about it. From what I heard other girls talking about concerning boys, it seemed like if he wanted to he should have tried to by now.

It didn't take us long to walk to my grandma's house. Okay, house was a generous term. It was a rundown two-bedroom trailer on a plot of land that belonged to Dante's family.

Still, it was the only place we had where we could be alone.

I let him pick out the movie.

He chose *Gladiator* even though we'd already seen it like five times. But neither of us actually cared what we watched. The movie was not why we'd started spending all of our free time doing this.

I turned it on and Dante sprawled out on the couch, his big body taking up most of it.

As much as I complained about how fast I was growing, he was growing much faster. He towered over me, and his lean body had started to develop muscles I couldn't help but notice.

And as fast as he was growing, he was still as graceful,

as comfortable in his own skin as he'd always been. I hadn't seen him suffer through one awkward faze yet.

It was infuriating.

I shot him a pointed look at his spot on the couch and moved to sit on my grandma's ancient recliner.

This was another game we played. I wouldn't sit with him until he asked me.

No. *Cajoled* me into it. I resisted every time. I knew I couldn't make anything too easy for him. Grandma had slapped that bit of wisdom deep into my skull.

"Psst," he called to me.

I ignored him, eyes glued to the screen.

"Scarlett," he tried. "You don't have to sit on your grandma's nasty old chair."

"That couch is just as nasty," I pointed out. Everything in the place was nasty. Old and cheap and dirty. I lived here and even I thought so.

"Well, you don't have to sit alone over there."

"You've taken up the whole couch. Where would I sit?" As I said it, I shot him an arch look.

He grinned at me. He was sprawled out, long arms perched at the top corner of the sofa. He kicked one knee up, throwing the other on the ground, and patted his thighs. "You can sit right here."

I eyed him warily. This was new and a little intimidating. "I'm hungry. Do you want a snack?"

"Do you *have* snacks?"

Of course not. We never did. It was a wonder I grew so much with the lack of food available when I was at home. Then again, I got free lunch at school and had dinner at Gram's more often than not.

"No," I said, sorry I'd asked. But I was *hungry*.

"You should let me give you money for food," he added, his tone careful and blank.

This was a very old and very sore subject. And he knew it.

I glared at him. "I won't take any more of your charity. It's bad enough your Gram buys me clothes for school and feeds me dinner almost every night."

His jaw set stubbornly, and I was pissed and bummed. If we got into a fight, it would ruin the rest of the day.

But then he sighed and looked away, breaking the tension.

Sometimes when we locked eyes, it was like predators having a standoff. One wrong move and—blood.

On the flip side, if one backed down then—peace.

He'd backed down for this one, thank God, because I never could have.

He paused the movie.

"Well, I need food," he said. "Is it all right if I order myself a pizza?"

"All right."

"I can't eat a whole one myself. I'll only order it if you promise to eat some, too."

That was a compromise I could live with, and he knew it. It didn't feel so much like charity if he was feeding himself and I was just sharing.

I grabbed the phone and brought it to him. While he dialed, I sat down carefully between his thighs.

We'd never done this before. Usually he just put his arm around me and we'd progress through varying degrees of touching each other tentatively. I'd lay my head on his chest, sometimes, if he was extra bold, he'd rub my knee with his hand.

Once we'd even spooned, my back to his front both of us turned to the TV. That had happened two weeks ago and it'd been the most exciting moment of my life.

But sitting between his thighs felt like a decidedly bigger step.

Tentatively I leaned back into his chest while he dialed up the pizza place.

"Any toppings you prefer?" he asked me

I was having a hard time finding my breath. "Whatever. You pick. You're paying."

I always said this and never meant it. We got the same thing every time. It was my favorite. I couldn't even have said if Dante particularly liked it, but he always got it.

"Yeah," he said into the phone, his free arm moving to drape over my shoulder. "I'll take a large pie, thin crust with jalapeños, chicken, and sausage. Extra sauce."

When he hung up I pushed play on the movie again.

We sat stiffly like that for a few minutes before I felt him put pressure on my shoulders, pulling me back more firmly against him.

"Relax," he said into my hair. "I won't bite. Just lay on me."

I tried, but it was impossible to relax like that. He wasn't relaxed either though, to be fair. I could feel the tension coiled in him like a spring about to bust.

I wiggled my hips, pushing closer to him. He jerked like I'd hurt him, and I stopped. And that's when I felt it, that hardness poking into me from behind, through our clothes.

I swallowed and spoke, my voice like a croak, "Is this comfortable? Should I move?"

He didn't answer, but he was breathing hard into my ear.

I laid back, putting the weight of my shoulders more firmly to his chest. I wasn't any more relaxed, but I didn't really care. This felt better than relaxed, like something important was happening, and I didn't want it to stop.

His arm around me moved suddenly, went up, gripping the top of the sofa above us, his knuckles white with the pressure of it.

I started to sit up to look at him, but he stopped me with a touch from his free hand to my belly.

I stilled, my eyes glued to that hand and the way it kept moving, stroking my stomach, pushing me harder into him.

I didn't stop him, and he just kept rubbing. I started to move my hips, rubbing against that foreign hardness at my back. He didn't stop me.

This went on for some time. Not progressing, but not stopping, which seemed like enough for a while.

Until it wasn't. Eventually I craved more contact. I wasn't sure what. It was a tangible desire for something intangible.

Feeling drugged, my body heavy and aching, I started to turn.

I pushed my chest to his. His eyes were on mine as we breathed each other's air, our lips less than an inch away.

I don't even know how it happened, but he was suddenly sitting up and I was straddling him, my fingers in his hair, his hands on my hips.

He was panting into my mouth, and I didn't know what to do with myself I loved it so much.

He's finally going to kiss me, I thought in wonder.

I'd been waiting for this for what felt like my whole life. And, at last, it was going to happen.

I didn't move to him. I wanted him to make the move. I held perfectly still as he leaned that last inch toward me.

The doorbell rang, breaking the spell.

I scrambled off him, cursing in my head. My first kiss ruined by the fucking pizza man.

I was sullen as I grabbed the two cleanest plates I could find and laid them out on the coffee table.

We ate in silence, the movie playing on. I had two slices, Dante the rest. There wasn't so much as a crumb left by the time he was done. He always ate like that, and it was no surprise with the way he was growing.

He got up, threw the box away, and joined me again on the couch, throwing his arm over my shoulder.

I shrugged it off. I felt my temper suddenly brewing. It felt separate from me at times like this, a storm out of my control. I couldn't have calmed it if I'd wanted to. I only seemed to know how to fuel it. Every bitter pill I'd ever swallowed was lodged somewhere inside of me, just waiting for these moments.

"So that girl you're going to marry," I ground out, voice tight and angry. "Is she nice?" I turned my head to watch his reaction.

He shot me a genuinely baffled look. "What the hell are you talking about?"

"Tiffany. Fanny. Your mom told me all about her."

"What? Who?"

"Tiffany Vanderkamp. Ring a bell?"

He looked no less confused as he said, "That's the daughter of my mom's best friend. I barely know her. What on earth does she have to do with anything?"

My eyes narrowed on him, looking for any signs of deceit. "Your mom told me you were going to marry her after you graduate from college."

His mouth twisted, and he glared back at me, his own temper coming out to play.

It seemed to instantly quiet my own. I acknowledged to myself that some perverse part of me loved to rile him.

"You know my mom is crazy. She was fucking with

your head. It's what she does. I can't believe you let her get to you. You're smarter than that."

My head cleared like I'd been lost in a fog and I was suddenly out of it. He was right. His mother was nuts, and this was just the kind of thing she'd pull whether there was truth to it or not.

"So you know this means she's going to try to get you to marry that girl," I pointed out to him.

He rolled his eyes. "Good fucking luck to her. She tries every day to get me to do things. Ask me how often she succeeds."

I didn't have to ask. I knew. Seldom, and only when he *wanted* to go along with whatever it was.

"You really thought I was planning to marry that girl?" he asked. There was a world of reproach in his voice.

I shrugged. "It's not my business." I turned my face away.

With a hand on my chin he turned it back. "It is your business."

I shook my head.

"It *is* your business, but you of all people know that I don't want to marry some random girl my mother chose. There's only one girl I want."

My heart was pounding so hard I thought both of us could hear it.

Without a word he lifted me onto his lap, turning me sideways, bringing our faces close.

"When are you finally going to let me kiss you, Scarlett?" he whispered to me, both hands cupping my face.

"Now," I whispered back.

With a smile he gave me my first kiss.

I didn't know what to do, but it was still good. I didn't

know how to be passive, so I imitated him, opening my mouth, and when I felt his tongue I mashed my own against it.

So good, even with our unpracticed mouths and unsteady hands. It wasn't long before he shifted me, bringing me to straddle him, our bodies making heavy contact.

Even more than my own pleasure in the kiss, I enjoyed what I was doing to *him*.

He was moaning into my mouth, his hands all over me, touching my neck, my shoulders, my ribs, all along my sides, then down to grab my hips.

It was wonderful.

It escalated too quickly, I later reflected.

I was so drunk on my first taste of him that I let it get out of hand.

He tentatively touched the side of a breast with his palm, the other still on my hip, moving me, urging me to rock against him, and I did, the core of me discovering the hardness of him and exploring it through our clothes. I felt empty, aching, and hot all at once. And I wanted more.

The hand at my chest stayed there for a while, and eventually I realized he was asking for permission.

With a little suck on his tongue, I took my fingers out of his hair and gripped his wrist, pulling his hand over and onto the center of my full breast, right at my nipple.

I gasped and he moaned as he palmed the aching globe. It was quickly not enough, and I found myself lifting my shirt, pulling aside my bra so he could touch skin.

We both groaned.

And that was when my grandma came home, hours and hours earlier than she usually did.

She went into such a rage, and I got into so much trouble that I avoided Dante for a solid week after that, which was not easy. I had to skip a lot of school to do it.

He finally cornered me at my house, climbing into an unlocked window to get to me where I cowered in my bedroom.

"Listen," he said, looming over me where I huddled on my bed, "if we went too far, just say so. I'll back off. Whatever we do, all of that sort of stuff, it's all on you what pace we go, okay? We won't do anything you aren't ready for, not even kissing if you don't want."

"I'm okay with the kissing," I told his feet. "But the rest was going too fast for me, okay?" Grandma's hours of chewing me out had ingrained in me one important fact: I could not give a boy too much or he'd lose interest in me.

He grinned from ear to ear and perched himself on my bed. "But you liked the kissing, right?

I smiled back. "Yeah. But what does it—I mean—are we . . . " I couldn't even finish I was so embarrassed.

His entire gorgeous face was flushing in pleasure. "Yes, Scarlett. Of course. We're together. We've always been together."

I was bright red and I couldn't look at him anymore, but I needed more assurances, something concrete. "S-s-s-so you're my . . . "

"Ah, Scarlett," he said softly and fondly. "I'm your boyfriend. You're my girlfriend. Yes. Is that what you were getting at?"

I shot him a look. "Isn't that something you're supposed to ask a girl, not tell her?"

He got a real kick out of that, in fact I didn't think I'd ever seen him happier. He leaned close, touching our foreheads together. "Not this. Not us. Neither of us have a choice in this. You and I being together is not a question, Scarlett, it's a fact of life."

And he kissed me. And kissed me.

After that we were making out every day. Every chance we could get. We kissed goodbye, we kissed hello, we kissed in the woods on the way home from school. Anywhere we went where we thought no one was watching, but he was true to his word. He didn't take it any further until I was ready.

"Go to Heaven for the climate. Hell for the company."
~Mark Twain

chapter twenty-two

PRESENT

Dante ripped his lips from mine so abruptly that it felt like a Band-Aid coming off.

He was panting into my face. "Tell me you don't miss this," he said emotionally.

This was what made him such a bastard. We were over, had been for years, but it didn't matter. If he had his way, he'd keep me tied to him in so many ways I could never break loose. He was cruel like that.

I subjugated every pathetic thing inside of me that jumped to do his bidding. *I would not feel* what he was trying to make me feel.

"I don't miss this," I managed to get out through my constricted throat.

"Liar," he breathed at me, madness in his eyes.

I shuddered, my own madness coming out to play. "No. No. *No.* I'm not the liar. You know why I don't miss *this*? Because it's a *lie*."

It was his turn to shudder.

"Because it's a lie," I repeated.

He flinched.

"It was always a lie."

"Don't say that."

"It was always a lie," I repeated. "Want to know how I know?"

"Stop."

"I won't stop. I'm not finished. Want to know how I know?"

"Enough. Stop it. You'll say any horrible thing when you're in a temper."

"I will, but that doesn't mean it isn't the truth. What we had *was always a lie.* I *know* because if it was *real* it wouldn't have *ended.* It felt like forever, and forever *was a lie.*"

I'd won the round, I noted numbly as his shaking body withdrew back to his side of the car.

He gripped the steering wheel, staring straight ahead, shoulders hunched.

After a few drawn out minutes of silence he started driving again.

"You're terrible at truces," I said. It was an effort to keep my voice from trembling.

He nodded jerkily. "Ditto, tiger. Peace was never your strength. You were born for battle."

"Look who's talking?"

His mouth twisted. "A match made in hell."

Wasn't that the truth.

The problem with us was that he and I had become deeply attached in our formative years. Young me had become essential to young him and vice versa.

We were too precisely built together, each too

profoundly shaped by the other. Every part of us had been assembled as one piece. Of course we did not function well after the construct had been ripped violently apart.

And of course I would despise the one who had done the ripping.

The car was silent as a tomb until we were nearly at the house, both of us trying to regain some composure, trying to reconcile ourselves to the past and come back to the present.

"Is my dress really too tight?" I asked him as he pulled down the long winding road that led to the house.

Grandma always got her digs in, and they always found a place to fester. I'd known the dress was flattering, provocative even. But was it *trashy*?

Dante cursed. "God, she always could get to you with her venom. No, it's not too tight. You look amazing. Perfect. Gram would be proud."

"Thank you," I said simply.

"Damn," I cursed as I took in the transformation of Gram's large driveway. Parking attendants had apparently been hired to manage the large influx of vehicles for the reception. They were trying their best to valet each one, using the front lawn to fit in as many cars as possible. "Gram would have hated this. She loved to keep her lawn pristine."

Dante cursed. "What in the actual fuck? *Goddamn* my mother. This has her stamp all over it. Keeping up appearances when the fact is these people can walk a few fucking feet instead of ruining Gram's lawn."

He was right. There was a paved road a mile long leading up to the house with plenty of shoulder room, i.e. ample parking.

But Adelaide had always hated Gram and it surprised

me not one bit that she was messing with the property that had once been hopelessly out of her reach.

Dante refused to use the valet, parking on the shoulder just shy of the chaos.

"I'm going in the back entrance," I told him as I opened my door. "I need to freshen up," I added, feeling awkward. "Um, see you around."

I took off.

I carefully redid my makeup and then lingered in my room for a cowardly amount of time.

It was just so unpleasant, the sounds of a large gathering in Gram's house with the woman herself absent. It felt wrong and I didn't want any part of it.

But then I thought about all of the vultures down there circling, all of the blood-sucking opportunists that had come, not for Gram, but to eye up the property she'd left behind, to speculate about who she'd left it to.

I *had* to go down, had to be there to thicken the ranks of those who were genuinely mourning her loss.

It didn't start out well for me. In fact, it couldn't have started worse.

I took the back stairs down to the kitchen, because I knew the place well. I went straight for the liquor in the butler's pantry, pouring myself a liberal tumbler of scotch that I was sure was up to even Dante's standards.

I downed it, then poured another.

Only when I was in two deep and holding a third did I move to venture out into the melee.

Unfortunately I didn't get that far.

This place, these people rattled me and so I was uncharacteristically clumsy.

I'm sure the liquor didn't help make me more coordinated, to be fair.

I moved to open the door that swung out from the kitchen into the formal dining room, but I mistimed it, and one of the many servers that were taking trays around frantically came in right as I was going out.

Half of my glass ended up on my chest.

The server, a young nervous guy, apologized profusely and brought me a stack of napkins.

I set down my glass, took the napkins, and waved him off. I started patting at myself, wondering if I should change.

At least I was wearing black.

The liquid came up easily, but the napkins left little white fuzzies all over my bust.

Fumbling with it, I opened my little clutch, taking out a moist towelette that I kept in it because I was one of those girls that knew the proper purpose of a handbag, which was to be prepared for anything.

It took forever, but I slowly got the front of my dress looking normal again.

I tossed the towelette and napkins into the trash, but somehow ended up bouncing a tube of lipstick out of my open clutch.

It landed right on top of the pile.

I would spend my last twenty dollars on a tube of M.A.C. lipstick. I took that shit seriously, and so I went in after it.

With a curse I bent down, grasping at it, trying to get a hold before it slipped in deeper.

To no avail, it kept falling deeper, through layers of leftover food and used napkins.

I almost left it, in fact had resigned myself to, when I felt the smooth edge of it touch my finger. I grabbed it and straightened, but not before the damage had been done.

That was how they found me. Elbow deep in the garbage.

Fucking typical.

"Trashcan girl is back, and I see that not much has changed," a laughing female voice told my bent back.

The old nickname was familiar and despised, and epitomized everything I hated about this place.

I straightened with my lipstick in hand to face a small group of snickering women. There were three of them, all girls from high school that I recognized instantly as being part of the mean girl pack that had done their best to terrorize me back when I'd been a stuttering mess.

I was not a stuttering mess now.

"I see the bitches still travel in packs around here. And by the way, guests aren't even supposed to come into this part of the house." I told their leader, Mandy, my voice steady, eyes flashing. That had been a strict rule of Gram's. No guests in the kitchen, ever.

Also, I was extra defensive and hostile with the way they had caught me, the sore spot they had rubbed right off the bat.

"Oh, guests aren't welcome, but charity cases are?"

She had a point. Mandy was a bratty little bitch, but even a stopped clock is right twice a day.

Just because Gram had treated me like family didn't make me any less of a charity case. I'd just been too stupid to see it myself back then.

No, I shook off the thought. *No.* Just because Dante had thrown me away didn't mean Gram had.

Gram had really loved me. I was as sure of it as I was of anything.

I smiled unpleasantly at Mandy. She hadn't grown up to be an attractive woman, but then she'd never been an attractive teenager. Looking at it in retrospect, I could see clearly now at least one of the reasons she'd hated me. I may have been trash, but I was beautiful trash, and there was not one beautiful thing about her. Her weasel face was as ugly as ever.

"Well, this charity case is allowed in the kitchen, and you're not." I waved at the door that led to the front part of the house, the section where company was allowed.

Mandy took a threatening step toward me.

I laughed, setting down my clutch. I held my arms out wide. "Please. Is that a threat? Come at me. I dare you. If all three of you attack, it'll be just like old times, right? I remember how you thought the odds of three to one would *help* you."

Of course they backed down. When they went in for the kill, it was usually with words.

Because mean girls don't kill. They dehumanize.

A few times they'd tried their luck with me the other way, but I could see that they still remembered how *that* had gone for them.

That was the moment that Dante walked into the room, and damn him, and me, I was actually happy to see him.

He zeroed in on Mandy and strode right up to her. "I'm only going to say this once," he told her harshly. "It's your first and final warning. If you can't be civil, if you try to pull one of your childish stunts, or I catch you making one snide comment, or even hear that you did, you're out of here. Also, no guests in the kitchen." He pointed to the door.

The pack of bitches left, shooting murder at me over their shoulders.

"God, do you have any idea how you just crushed

her?" I asked him, smiling. "She's had a thing for you since high school, and don't ask me why, but it looks like she still does."

"I give less than zero fucks how she feels. That one is a coward and a bully. I don't even want her in this house. I haven't forgotten how she treated you in high school."

"You haven't?" I asked him.

He looked at me. "I haven't forgotten anything."

I looked away. "Well, this started as badly as it could have. I already got caught digging in the trash and almost got into a fistfight, all before I've even walked into the reception."

"If anyone else gives you any problems, I'm kicking them out, I swear to God."

My eyes flitted to him and then away. "Why are you being so nice to me?"

"It's not hard, Scarlett. In fact, it feels a hell of a lot more natural than what we've *been* doing."

"If I know what love is, it is because of you."
~Herman Hesse

chapter twenty-three

PAST

Something awful had happened when we started going to high school. It wasn't immediate, more of a gradual shift, but nonetheless detrimental to me.

Dante was physical and he always seemed to need an aggressive outlet for it so, much to my chagrin, he was often in some sport or other. Football was his favorite so every fall from the time we were in sixth grade, he had practice. Every year practice seemed to eat up more and more of his time.

I tried to take it well, but I was so jealous of his time and attention that I didn't. But I did try.

I started taking drama after school myself, and it suited me. My stutter still plagued me at the worst of times, so I never got a speaking role in the school plays, but I was happy to fill extra spots and work on the set.

I thought for a while that it would work. We both

had things to do, opposite interests that took up our time.

I'd finish drama and go watch him from the bleachers, sometimes I'd do my homework, sometimes I'd read, sometimes I'd just ogle him, and then we'd either drive or walk home together.

On paper it sounded great, but that's not what happened.

In high school it became apparent that he was quite good at everyone's favorite sport and for some reason it started to matter to people and seemingly overnight he was one of the popular kids.

It was awful for me. I was no more popular than ever. In fact when jealous girls got wind that I was his girlfriend and just how long we'd been an item, and how smitten he was with me, I was more hated than ever, which was saying a lot.

I started getting into fights again. Bad ones. And I was old enough now that I was getting in serious trouble for it. I almost got kicked out of school for one incident with a girl in the locker room (a girl who unfortunately also happened to be the daughter of one of the local sheriffs) that involved her dumping Gatorade on my head and me slamming her face into the locker.

It'd predictably started with the familiar mocking chant of, "Hey, trashcan girl."

I was resigned to the fact that I would never live this down. It was a part of me. It was a thing I had to own that would always make me an outcast.

I was odd. I had been shaped by uncommon, unrelatable things. This I knew.

And since I couldn't get into a fight every time I heard that, even with *my* temper, I ignored the first verbal jab.

We'd just finished gym class. Normally I liked gym.

I didn't talk to any of the girls in my period, but there weren't many kids I talked to. I was good at being a loner. It suited me. The things I heard the girls talk about couldn't have interested me less.

All they seemed to do was complain about things they could easily change or things that were so insignificant they sounded like petty brats for complaining about them.

One didn't like her thighs. One hated her butt. One was too flat-chested, her best friend had huge boobs that she hated.

This one had fat fingers, that one had big feet. One complained for an entire mile that her mom had cut off her credit card when she'd overcharged it. Another couldn't believe her daddy had bought her a used car.

Oh the humanity.

I had no patience for it. I didn't feel like humoring them with their petty, wonderful lives with parents that loved them and normal problems.

Some of us had real problems. Ones that weren't skin deep. A real problem was waking up every day to a world that had cast you aside, a world that had no place for you, with peers that hated you and cards stacked against you.

A real problem was being trash and having everyone around you know it and point it out regularly.

A real problem was being fundamentally unlovable. Struggling everyday not to hate yourself.

So I tried my best to tune them out and apply myself to whatever physical thing they had us doing. Today it had been tennis, which I liked just fine. The smaller the teams the better. I wasn't the best team player.

I was actually in a good mood before she'd said that. I was a terrible student, so P.E. was naturally my favorite class, and it was last period. Now I was changing fast because I got to see Dante for a bit before he went to practice and I went to drama.

But then, "Hey, trashcan girl." The words had me setting my jaw, a familiar feeling moving through me.

My mind flashed to that infamous trashcan, my baby self somewhere inside of it.

I had no real idea what it'd looked like, but I'd obsessed about every little detail of it. I imagined that dumpster, lid closed. I don't know why, but I always imagined that it was only half-full. *How else could my mother have fit a baby into it?*

I imagined my baby self somewhere inside of it. Sometimes I was wrapped in dirty blankets and set neatly on top of the trash. Sometimes I wore only a diaper, was buried halfway down, and they'd had to dig for me when I'd been discovered. I liked to fantasize that some kindly paramedic had picked me up tenderly, maybe even cried for me.

Some of these imaginings came from nightmares, some merely my imagination, but the taunts always brought it all back.

Still, I was going to ignore her. I wouldn't let her waste any of my precious Dante time.

"Did you hear me?" the girl said, her hand shoving lightly at my shoulder.

I shut my locker and turned to level an unpleasant look at her. "Leave me alone," I said simply. It really was that simple. Why couldn't they just leave me the hell alone?

She sneered at me. I tried to place who she even was. Brown hair, medium height, familiar weasel-like features.

Oh Lord, I was oblivious. I'd been going to school with her since third grade.

Mandy, I recalled. Her dad was a sheriff, I remembered too. Cops made me nervous, so of course I'd made a note of that.

She took a long swig of her red Gatorade, wiped her mouth, and asked snottily, "What's your deal? Is Dante really dating *you*?"

"Yes," I said tonelessly. Maybe if I was as boring as possible she'd leave me alone before I lost my temper.

"Since when?" she asked.

I didn't know how to answer that even if I'd wanted to, which I didn't. I'd been devoted to him since that first fateful meeting outside of the vice principal's office.

"Answer me, trashcan girl!"

"No," I snapped back. Hello, temper. If she'd wanted an actual answer, she had a lot to learn about me.

"What the hell does he see in you?" she sneered.

I eyed her, top to bottom, letting her see in my face what I thought of her. Not one attractive thing about her, inside or out. "As opposed to what, *you*? Keep dreaming."

She gasped and dumped the contents of her Gatorade bottle over my head.

Loud giggles echoed in every corner of the locker room. Apparently a lot of the girls had enjoyed that. As I've said, I was far from popular.

I didn't even think, my body just reacted. I grabbed a handful of the hair at her nape and *bam*, slammed her face against the locker.

On the tail of that, only one week later, I almost went to Juvie for an incident with the same girl. Again in the locker room, she (bruises still on her face) and three other girls snuck up behind me, slammed *my* face into the lockers, and dragged me to the toilet, then proceeded to try, with a stress on the word try, to dunk my head into the bowl.

I fought like a wildcat.

Here's the kind of fighter I am: I don't care if you're bigger than me. I don't care if you're so massive you could take me out with one punch. Hell, I don't even care if there are three of you to my one. I will take you on, and I will keep swinging until someone either knocks me out, drags me away, or kills me.

I fought them like a wildcat, and they were *not* fighters. They were little princesses who thought that they knew what revenge was.

When they realized I was going to struggle, that I wasn't going to make it easy on them, they started slapping at me, smacking at my head and face like that was going to do anything but piss me off more.

I clenched my hands into fists and started punching.

It wasn't my first fight or even my tenth, and as far as grappling went, I wrestled with Dante, a boy twice my bodyweight, for fun.

These girls were nothing.

I didn't lash out indiscriminately. I'd learned a long time ago to go for the spots that debilitate.

The first girl I punched hard in the nose. I heard a crunch and blood started spurting everywhere.

One down.

The second girl, Mandy, the sheriff's princess daughter who had freaking started it, I kneed *hard* in the stomach because she was almost on top of me, still trying to get me into the stall that I'd just escaped from.

She doubled over. The third girl was grabbing my hair, trying to pull me away from her friend, but I grabbed the side of Mandy's head and viciously slammed it sideways, right smack into where the stall protruded sharply.

Third girl started backing away when she realized that both of her friends were crying huddles on the floor, but I wasn't having it.

I stalked after her. When she turned to start running away, I grabbed the back of her long black hair and yanked.

She went flying like a rag doll and ended up on her back.

I was raising my foot up to stomp on her when the gym teacher walked in. She was a big, athletic woman, and she had to physically drag me away from the girl before I stopped fighting.

Of course I got blamed for all of it. I'd broken the first girl's nose. Mandy they thought had a concussion, and I assumed she did. I'd smashed her head *hard* into the stall.

The cops were called, three besides the usual on-campus officer, and they took turns threatening me, chewing me out, and trying to scare me.

When I tried to argue that they had started it, I'd been defending myself, and there had been *three* of them, my stutter predictably came out to play.

I almost decked one of them, a large man that kept getting right in my face, close enough that I could feel his spittle and smell his breath, but I managed to control my temper at least that much.

After about an hour of them harassing me behind a closed door (they'd borrowed the principal's office to interrogate me), I heard a commotion outside, someone getting loud. Someone losing their temper.

My chest warmed and I felt instantly safer. I even managed to get out a few sentences through my stutter. "Th-th-they attacked *m-me*! There were three of them.

H-h-h-h-how can you not see that there were th-th-th-three of them?"

One of the cops (the second girl's father!) took a menacing step toward me. "Are you calling my daughter a *liar*?"

Oh no. I was going to lose it. Nothing got my temper going hotter than injustice like that, the supposed mediator in the situation blood related to one of the culprits!

I nodded at him, glaring. "Y-y-y-yes. H-h-h-how can you deny it? Th-th-there were three of them!"

Dante crashed into the room, the principal, a small middle-aged man, right behind him, grabbing at his arm, clearly trying but failing miserably to hold him back.

"Are you fucking kidding me?!" he started shouting the second he cleared the door. "*Four* male officers harassing one teenage girl behind a *closed* door? You can't detain her like this! You need to arrest her or let her go, but just so you know, my lawyer will be here in ten minutes and Vivian Durant will be here in five. You might want to start acting like real cops now."

I ate up every rage-filled inch of him with complete adoration.

I don't know how he made it across the room to me, it wasn't easy, no one wanted to let him, but he made his way to my side, touching my cheek lightly, crouching down beside my chair.

"You okay, tiger?" he asked me softly.

Even with how angry I was that made me smile.

In short order Gram showed and *barely* kept them from taking me into custody.

It was the first time I'd gotten to see her in action. She was a glorious sight to behold. She had a way of declaring a thing and making it so. She was like Dante, the opposite of me, able to articulate exactly what she meant to with absolute, precise effect.

I made a promise to myself right then and there to grow up to be just like her.

"When you trip over love, it is easy to get up. But when you fall in love, it is impossible to stand again."
~Albert Einstein

chapter twenty-four

PRESENT

I thought Dante would head back to the reception, but instead he headed the opposite way, casually grabbing my arm as he walked by, tugging me with him.

"What are you doing?" I asked him.

"Scotch," he answered.

It was a good answer.

He poured us both a full glass and we toasted to Gram.

"How do you like the flight attendant gig?" he asked me.

I fucking hated it. For so many years I'd been so determined to devote my life to being an actress, waiting tables and tending bars to pay the bills. Making a career move that monopolized a huge chunk of my potential auditioning time had felt so much like giving up on my dreams. It still did.

"I fucking hate it. It's not where I saw myself at this

stage of my life. I was so sure I'd have gotten my big break by now."

"You're only twenty-seven. You still have all the time in the world."

I rolled my eyes. He didn't get Hollywood. Every year that I slipped closer to the Botox phase of my life, the less likely it was that I could be the next 'fresh' face. And I wanted to be that. I wanted to be the beautiful young ingénue that all the guys wanted, and all of the girls wanted to be. I craved it more than anything. What better way to shove my success in the face of all of the people that'd ever wronged me?

"I do get a lot of lucrative offers to do porn," I said lightly.

It was supposed to be a joke (though I had gotten some offers), but he definitely didn't laugh. In fact, his expression became so black and he turned so quiet that I had to change the subject.

"You know what my biggest fantasy was when I was a kid?" I asked him.

"What?

"That Gram would adopt me. That she'd take care of me and let me live with her."

"She tried to, you know."

I was shocked. Deep down in my bones shocked. "What?"

"She wanted to. She tried to. Your grandma fought her tooth and nail. The only thing they could settle on was letting Gram buy you school clothes and a few other essentials, but if it'd been up to her she'd have taken you in."

"I had no idea."

"Yes. It's still a hard pill to swallow, that your grandma

wouldn't let you go to Gram, but then she treated you like *that*. What the hell was that about?"

"I could tell you." I understood how my grandma's twisted mind worked, understood it *too* well.

"Please do."

"It was pride. Pride is a terrible thing. She couldn't let someone else take on one of her burdens. My grandma has a lot of awful qualities, but she can't stand the thought that she's not earning her keep."

He let out a disgruntled breath. "How senseless. Making you miserable for all those years just for her pride?"

I didn't comment. I couldn't, really, without being a hypocrite. I'd done some terrible things myself for the sake of pride.

We'd been silently sipping our drinks for a stretch when he leaned in close to me, whispering conspiratorially, "Let's ditch this thing and go check out our old swimming hole? Can you think of a more Gram thing to do?"

I was more distracted by the way he was leaning into me with that old, familiar twinkle in his eyes than his words. I was looking up at him, eyes devouring his face, some part of me so stuck in the past that I couldn't even remember why I was supposed to hate him so wholeheartedly.

But then I remembered.

There was a great pit of despair inside of me, and I felt it flare open, given life by his nearness, fed by his proximity, growing every second I let him close enough to breathe my air.

Just then it felt big enough to lose myself in.

"Excuse me," I told him tersely, and fled *in*to the reception.

The place was packed. The good news about that was I didn't even see a familiar face at first so I was free to move about, ignoring the strangers to my little anti-social heart's content.

I heard noises coming from one of the large parlors and I knew instantly what it was.

The house was old, but they'd still done a halfway decent job converting one of the larger parlors into a makeshift theatre.

On the screen they were playing one of Gram's old movies.

I'd been afraid to watch any of them since I'd heard the news, even though I loved them all. I'd thought it would make me too sad.

But as I saw her beautiful face on screen, so young then, I felt only comfort.

She was immortalized.

And this role in particular suited her. She was playing what she would have called a wicked, wicked woman, and she threw out one sassy line after another in grand Gram style.

It was everything. I took an empty seat toward the back of the room and ate it up.

I don't know how long I sat there before a man sat down in the chair beside me.

I shot him a glance and found him studying me.

"Have we met before?" he asked me.

I gave him a second look. He was an older man with a kindly face. "I don't think so. Were you a friend of Gram's, I mean Vivian's?"

Something slipped into his eyes, some bit of dawning recognition that was odd to me. It hit me in a strange and troubling way.

"Oh," he said very quietly. "I recall now. I treated you once. I'm a doctor."

My brow furrowed. "I don't believe so."

"I-I'm terribly sorry. You're right. Please forget that I ever brought it up."

And with that he stood up and left the room, looking harried and I don't even know what.

As he walked out, Dante walked in. The men saw each other, each briefly pausing, steps faltering before they both nodded and continued on their way.

"Who was that?" I asked Dante when he, predictably, sat down beside me.

His whole face closed off. "Some old friend of Gram's, why?"

"He said he was a doctor and that he'd treated me once," my voice trailed off and I looked away as realization struck. "Never mind," I muttered.

Dante squeezed my hand, and for a second, I let him before pulling away.

I nodded at the screen. "This is my favorite part," I said weakly.

"Mine too."

"I could stay in here all day."

"Let's," he replied.

We didn't do that, but it was tempting.

One of Dante's old football buddies came in shortly, sat down next to him, and started catching up.

I didn't even look at the guy. I hadn't been friends with any of the jock douchebags in high school, and I saw no reason why I should have to waste my time on one now.

Also, just thinking about football put my mind in a dark place.

I got up without a word and left.

I couldn't move without tripping over a server, but I went back through the kitchen and served myself another scotch.

It was starting to do its job and take the edge off. Numbness felt just around the corner.

I lingered at my moment of peace. It was just too pleasant to take a minute alone when the last thing I wanted was company, especially the company that could be found in this house at present.

"Of course you drink scotch," a soft voice said behind me. "That's so you. Always the guys' girl."

I turned to face Tiffany, tipping my glass back to pointedly finish off my drink.

Once again, I eyed her dress. It was perfect, damn her. Flawlessly tailored and obviously designer.

I wore cheap, trendy clothing, and I despised all the people there that knew the difference. She was certainly one of them.

One consolation was that my shoes were up to snuff today, at least as nice as hers, though I still had a mad shoe crush on her lavender stilettos.

We just stared at each other for a pregnant moment, and I, for one, had no clue what was going through *her* head.

It seemed to me that some bond should be made between two women when they've both had their hearts broken by the same man.

But there was no bond here. There was no person on earth I felt less of a kinship with.

It was like we didn't even speak the same language. She was fluent in passive aggressive fake niceties. Darling is what she said as she plunged a knife into your gut.

I'd never understood it, could never relate. Passive

aggressive women were beyond me. Or the passive part of it, at least.

Straight up aggression, that I understood.

I was fluent in liberal doses of painful honesty, well, at least when the subject didn't delve too deeply into how I felt about a certain manipulative bastard.

"No guests in the kitchen," I finally broke the silence with. Rudely.

I was feeling three-scotches-in honest, could not even try to play her fake nice game.

"Actually, I'm staying at the house." She dropped the words on me pleasantly as she moved to the old bar I was leaning against, carelessly tossing her drop-dead gorgeous black and white clutch on it. Damn her and her amazing bag choices. "That grants me the precious kitchen access even according to Gram's rules, right?"

I was floored. Why the hell was she staying here? Unless . . . My mind wanted to draw the worst conclusion, which was likely the truth. Of course she was doing it to get close to Dante. The only question was: How did he feel about it? Did he know? Care? Was he playing the same games with us both, drawing us in, messing with our heads?

"Why wouldn't you stay at your parents' house?" I asked her bluntly.

She started making herself a drink. She didn't answer me until she'd taken a drink that made her nose scrunch up in distaste. "Renovations. Two thirds of the place is under construction. You know how my mother is."

I didn't. I only knew her as Adelaide's evil counterpart. I'd never been to their house and I had no clue about their decorating choices.

"Isn't it like a mansion? They don't have one spare room you can use? A sofa?"

She shrugged. "It's fine. I don't mind staying here. I love this house. Reminds me of the good old days, spending time with Dante here when we were teenagers."

She could have punched me in the stomach and it wouldn't have knocked more of the wind out of me.

She's a manipulative bitch, I told myself. *She hides it better, but she's just like his mother. She's either lying or exaggerating.*

"Did you spend a lot of time here when you were a teenager?" I asked, trying for a bland tone, having no idea if I succeeded.

I knew she'd spent some, I'd been there for most of it, back in the early days of my hatred of her. But the way she said it was the way I thought it, like it had meant more to her than the simple short trips when she'd come to visit.

She eyed me and, seeing something, changed the subject.

Either she couldn't back up what she'd said or she wanted me to think that she was sparing my feelings.

It wasn't hard for me to pick one, and I felt instantly better when I did.

"Did you see that Whitney Holloway is here?"

Well, she was certainly a good subject changer. That got my attention. "I did not," I said succinctly, taking a long drink.

Whitney was another privileged trust fund baby. She was rich from birth, but for fun she modeled in her spare time. *Barf.* She also happened to be the woman Dante had started seeing immediately after he and Tiffany had called off their engagement.

Her tinkling laugh rang out hollowly. "We should start a Dante's ex club. There are certainly enough of us floating around, right?"

That passive aggressive jab was meant to bring home the fact that we'd both had a relationship with him, and that mine was no more significant than any of his others.

"Oh look, speak of the devil," she said with a smile.

I turned to watch as Dante approached us, looking ill at ease.

Tiffany met him halfway, throwing her arms around his neck as she rose up to say something in his ear.

Images of her wrapped around him assaulted me. Of them, together, naked and writhing. They were graphic, and I'd never get them out of my head.

Seeing him with her gave me that feeling again. My skin humming, bile rising in my throat.

But then—he recoiled from her, moving around her without so much as a hello.

Well, whatever he was doing with her for this twisted little trip, he was not playing the same games as he was with me. If I had thrown myself at him like that, I'd have been over his shoulder and carried to the nearest bed in about three seconds flat.

It was something, some sad sop to my ego. I made a vengeful note to use that against Tiffany the first chance I got.

chapter twenty-five

PAST

Tiffany was only a despised name in my head for years before I actually met the girl.

When her parents started sending her to stay at Dante's house for a few weeks every summer, I was already solidly turned against her.

It is a fact that I never gave her a chance.

Blind hatred will do that.

Dante was kinder than I was, or at least that's what I told myself back then. He tried not to hold their mothers' crazy ideas against her.

When I first got wind of it, we were alone in Gram's parlor right before dinner. We were sitting side by side, waiting for her to finish a phone call.

He had a hold of my hand when he told me the news.

I wrenched it away.

I was already his girlfriend, already possessive of him and sure of my ownership.

And so I threw a fit.

"She's staying at your *house*?" I was trying not to raise my voice. It was the thing I'd been dreading since his mother had told me about her.

He shrugged, looking helpless. "She's just some girl I don't know. My mom invited her. It's not like I can stop them, but who cares? I'm hardly ever home. The only thing I do is *sleep* there.

That sounded ominous enough to me. "If you stay in that house with her, I'm breaking up with you," I told him.

He did not like that. I'd never threatened him with such a thing, never even thought of it before.

"Are you kidding me?" he spoke low, temper flashing in his eyes.

He tried to grab me, but I evaded him, standing up and walking away. "You let me know when you decide what you want to do."

Of course he didn't let me leave like that.

He caught me, picked me up, and carried me back to the couch. He had me pinned on my back, face looming over mine when he said. "Stand down, tiger. Who do you think you're talking to? Whose side do you think I'm on?"

I was *not* standing down, still fuming, face turned away, lips trembling. "I don't even know."

"You do. Pretend all you want, but you know I'm on your side. Don't you?"

"No." I knew I was pouting like a brat, but I felt so helpless. I couldn't stand the thought of him sleeping in the same house as that girl in the picture.

A picture I'd kept, buried somewhere in the bottom of a drawer, my fear of what she represented not buried nearly as deep.

He was the only thing of value in the world that belonged to me, and the thought of losing him made me feel impotent and weak. Made me want to lash out at anyone and anything. Even him.

"What do you want me to do?" he whispered right into my mouth. "I'll do whatever you want. Don't you know I'll do whatever you want?" His voice was cajoling. Seductive. Completely unfair.

And as he spoke, he was shifting on top of me, moving his hips until he was lying flush between my thighs and we were both breathing hard.

He shifted, grinding against me. "Anything you want," he repeated, "but don't threaten me with that again. It's not okay. It's not an option. Don't you know it's not an option?"

I had, but I didn't know how to pull my punches when I was blindly lashing out. "I don't want you sleeping in that house with her," I told him.

He had his lips on me now, was placing deep, drugging kisses on my cheek, my jaw, my throat, as he said, "Okay. Fine. That's easy. I'll stay with Gram until she leaves. Is that all?"

I nodded and he started kissing me. With a groan, I kissed him back, wrapping my arms around his neck and my legs around his hips.

He groaned into my mouth and kissed me deeper, grinding harder against me.

We made out like this just about every chance we got, but we normally weren't this shameless about it. We usually found someplace where we knew we were alone before we did anything like this. The fight had distracted us both.

"Dante, get off her," Gram's exasperated voice broke through the air.

He leapt off me like she'd burned him.

I sat up, straightening my clothes as I looked guiltily at her. More than anything, I wanted her approval, and I hated the idea that she'd look down on me for finding us like that.

But she just rolled her eyes at me. "Boys!" she said, throwing her hands up. "What on earth will we do with this one? Too brazen for his own good!"

I smiled, sending a disgruntled Dante an evil look. I even stuck my tongue out at him. He'd been blamed for the whole thing, and I couldn't make myself be sad about it. It *had* been his fault.

Over dinner Dante casually asked Gram if he could stay over for a few weeks.

She didn't hesitate. "Of course. Any time. You don't have to ask. You're welcome here, always. You too, Scarlett. Come for a sleepover any time you like."

Dante and I shared a look, both of our minds going to the same place, which was he and I sleeping under the same roof, quickly followed by thoughts of us in the same bed.

I blushed and looked away. It was a hopeless fantasy. My grandma would never let me sleep over at Gram's, especially if she had an inkling that Dante was there.

"How about it?" Dante asked me later as he walked me home. "Want to have a sleepover with me at Gram's?" He was grinning ear to ear.

My whole face went red. "Knock it off."

He laughed, backing me into a tree, pinning me there

with his big body. "You don't want to have a sleepover with me?" he laughed some more. It was contagious, and I found myself smiling up into his face.

"I swear sometimes Gram still thinks we're ten years old," he told me.

"She didn't think that when she found us dry humping in her parlor earlier," I said wryly.

His eyes did something fascinating when I said that. "Dry humping, huh? As opposed to what? Wet humping?" He wasn't even smiling anymore, his body crowding me.

"Stop," I told him.

"When are you going to let me wet hump you, Scarlett?" he was laughing again, which was good. For a second there he'd seemed too much for me to handle.

"Shut up," I told him, my usual retort for being teased.

"We're almost to your house," he told me, though we really weren't since we weren't even moving anymore. "Aren't you going to kiss me goodbye?"

"Are you going to stop teasing me?"

He leaned in close. "Never." He kissed me.

I wrapped my arms around his neck and kissed him back. We were good at it by then, we'd done nothing but practice lately. It was a new and dear hobby.

And I was *very* good at giving him a little then backing off, never letting him get too far since my grandma had put the fear of God in me.

I won't deny that the thought of another girl as competition had more than a bit to do with it, but we got a little more carried away than usual. He was grabbing my butt, holding me against the tree while he ground his hardness into me, rooting around for my softness through our clothes.

I brushed my breasts into his chest, rubbing them back and forth against him until he made the noises I liked best.

My nipples were so hard and sensitive and I couldn't seem to stop doing it, brushing them back and forth, making him feel what he was doing to me.

He ripped his mouth away, panting as he pressed our foreheads together. "Jesus," he muttered, a refrain that let me know he was reaching his limit.

Licking his lips, I started pulling my shirt up. Since that first time, when we'd been caught by my grandma, my breasts had been pretty much off the table, but I decided right then to put them back on it.

He pulled back to watch as I exposed my bra, his hips moving in little movements that I doubted he even knew he was making.

I unsnapped my bra and pulled it apart, letting my breasts swing free.

"God," he said, reaching for them.

I let him fondle me while I watched him through heavy lids.

"Does this feel good?" he asked me, kneading at my flesh.

"Mmmhmm," I hummed. So good. "Does it feel good to you?"

His breathing was heavy, his hips circling as he started tugging on my nipples. "You have no idea." He bent his head down to me. "Can I?" he rolled his eyes up to look at me.

I bit my lip and nodded, covering his hands with mine to lift myself up to his mouth.

He started licking my nipples, sucking and tonguing them, back and forth. It felt so good, especially with the way he was moaning while he did it, but he stopped abruptly, setting me down and backing away, a hand dragging through his hair.

"Your grandma's going to be home soon," he told me, eyes still on my bared breasts. "I don't want to get you in trouble." He paused. "And I don't want to freak you out by taking it too far. I'm feeling a little too crazed not to do something you're not ready for."

"Okay," I said, because he was right about all of it, so I couldn't argue.

I straightened and started working at getting my ample boobs back into my bra.

Dante happily helped me, bending down to nuzzle between when we had them back in place. "Can we . . . hang out at your grandma's tomorrow? We'll meet at Gram's. I—" he paused voice thickening, "need some time alone with you. More than a few minutes in the woods."

I kissed him, then kissed him again. "Of course. We can watch a movie or something."

He looked amused. "Whatever you want to call it."

But when I showed up at his gram's the next day *she* was there with him.

I turned around and started walking home.

He caught up to me, stopping me with a hand on my arm. "Stop. Just meet her, okay? She's not that bad. Just come get introduced and we'll make an excuse and leave, huh? But there's no need to be rude. *She's* not rude. Trust me."

I was fuming, but I went back with him.

If only to get a closer look at the girl his family wanted him to marry.

Dante introduced us.

I mumbled out a surly, "Nice to meet you."

She seemed unfazed, beaming at me. "Nice to meet you too, Scarlett."

We did not leave right away, much to my chagrin. Instead we stayed while she chatted with Dante and I glared at them both.

She was very sweet, even to me. And she had an obvious, extreme crush on Dante. She looked up, up, up at him like he was the center of her universe.

I knew the look well. I wore it often myself.

Meeting her didn't help. I hated her more than ever. The sweeter she was, the more it made me sick to my stomach. I'd wanted her to be awful, and ugly.

But she was beautiful and good.

It made no sense.

I was a fighter. A warrior of a girl.

She was a delicate flower. A shrinking violet.

Why did her timidity cow me? How?

Self-disgust resonated through me, and I steeled myself.

Just because she was something I couldn't understand, something he might like, that didn't mean I'd back down.

I studied her while they talked, eyeing her head to toe. She was thin in the way that models are thin, not an ounce of fat on her, but still some shape, even if it was just the way her skin molded around her bones. She'd look good in anything. She had no breasts to speak of, so she was basically a walking clothes hanger.

Everything I wore pulled across my breasts, drawing eyes, making things fit worse than they should have.

And her hips were nonexistent. That I hated even more. Breasts, particularly big perky ones like mine, were well beloved by boys, and more importantly, well beloved by Dante.

But fleshy, shapely hips? It was anyone's guess. Mine were a handful and then some.

I had mentally catalogued every inch of her by the time either of them turned back to me.

They seemed to be getting along, which made me sick. What if he liked her more than me?

Maybe he'd had enough of sharp tongues and rough edges. Maybe he longed for someone soft.

I couldn't even stand the thought.

I turned around and started striding away.

"Did I say something?" I heard Tiffany asking him.

"Nah. We just had plans. Catch you later."

I heard him running up to me, falling in beside me, but I ignored him.

"You don't have to come with me," I bit out. "Go back to your new *girlfriend*. Do whatever you want. I don't even care anymore."

I swear I could hear him grinding his teeth, but he didn't respond at first. We were into the trees before he spoke.

"*What the fuck?*" finally burst out of him. "What is it with you? I was being polite. We talked about nothing for five minutes with you right there. I was just being nice."

"You and I were supposed to have plans. You weren't supposed to bring *her* along."

"I didn't! She came by Gram's house to say hi to me. The timing wasn't good, but it was a perfectly normal thing to do, unlike how you're acting right now!"

I rounded on him. He'd hit a nerve and I wanted to hit him back. "If you don't like the way I'm acting, if you don't think it's *normal* enough for you, then leave me the hell alone. If you don't want to fight, you followed the wrong girl! Go follow *her* instead, if that's what you want!"

He made a noise of deep frustration. "It's not what I fucking want! What is your problem? Why do you turn *everything* into a fight?"

"That's what you think I do? Turn everything into a fight?"

"Sometimes it feels that way," he responded with no hesitation.

"That's all you think I am," I returned dully. My jabs were delivered furiously, but his always hit harder. "One messy fighter of a girl and apparently now you're sick of the challenge. Why do you even bother with me?" I started walking away again, because I didn't know what else to do. I just wanted to go somewhere and lick my wounds.

He didn't let me get far, but when he tried to touch me, I fought him.

He wasn't deterred, hugging me from behind, pinning my arms to my sides. He buried his face in my neck. "Not true," he finally spoke.

He was out of breath from the struggle. At least I hadn't made it easy on him.

"You're letting your insecurity get the best of you," he continued. "You're a fighter, yes, but that is far from all that you are. And I do see all of you, Scarlett. You're more to me than a challenge."

"What, then? What am I to you?"

He moaned and kissed my neck, which was about the fastest way he could weaken me. "My angel."

"Lead us not into temptation. Just tell us where it is; we'll find it."
~Sam Levenson

chapter twenty-six

PRESENT

Dante joined me at the butler's pantry, pouring himself a fresh scotch.

Tiffany hung back a beat, looking unsure, before she approached us and reclaimed the glass of liquor she hadn't been drinking.

Dante gave her a less than friendly look. "Can you give us a minute? I need to talk to Scarlett. Alone."

She did something odd then, something I didn't understand. Her fake nice facade slipped for a second, and she gave him a very hard look that felt to me like a warning. "You sure you want to do that?" she asked him.

I was looking back and forth between them, for once completely lost on the nuances of what was going on.

"Absolutely," he pronounced, turning his back on her.

I smiled as she walked away. "You two don't seem to get along so well anymore," I noted gleefully.

"We sure as hell don't."

"You were engaged to her," I pointed out. I was provoking him purposefully. He knew it and I wanted him to.

"I was engaged to you, too. Didn't do me much good, did it?"

"Who do you think you're talking to? If it did you no good, it's on you."

"Oh yeah, that's right," he noted bitterly. "I forgot I've been painted as *that* guy. Serial fiancé. Because that adds up to you. I'm the guy that makes promises and doesn't give a damn about them, right?"

"Of course you are. Are you *denying* it?" I felt my temper boiling up from the bottomless place inside of me, that place that was so full of rage it could feed itself indefinitely. It was only ever looking for an excuse to erupt.

He didn't deny it, at least, which was perhaps the best way to defuse my ticking time bomb of a temper.

We gave each other a moment of silence. I didn't realize Dante was stewing in his own temper more than giving space to mine until he said, "How long have you been seeing him?" He was looking down at his glass.

I just stared at him. Somehow, even with all of our history, knowing the ins and outs of him, he still managed to surprise me. "Excuse me?"

"Man-bun from your apartment. How long have you been seeing him?"

"I'm not doing this with you." I was infuriated at the very notion that he thought he was entitled to know even *one thing* about my love life.

"Does he mind *sharing* you? Does it bother him to go to your house to see you while you're still filled with another man's cum?"

It was an effort not to show him the reaction he wanted, but I kept my expression neutral, my tone even, "My God, you are out of line."

He was leaning with casual ease against the counter, his posture nonchalant.

The eyes he turned on me were not nonchalant.

They were livid. Wild. "Did you *fuck* him after I left?"

"You're a lunatic," I spoke quietly and vehemently, "an absolute raging *lunatic*," I repeated, "if you think I owe you one *single* answer about any part of my life."

"He was in that TV pilot with you years ago. Have you been seeing him since *then*? *For years?*" There was so much accusation in his voice, as though he had any right at all to feel betrayed.

The sheer gall of it floored me.

"That is rich," I enunciated slowly. "Here you are, staying in a house with a virtual stable of your exes, and you have the nerve to act possessive of *me*?"

His jaw clenched, he stared me down.

"*You* have me sleeping under the same roof as the home-wrecking *whore* that *ruined* us, and you have the balls to think you deserve answers from *me*?"

He looked genuinely taken aback. "What the hell are you talking about?"

"Tiffany is staying here. At Gram's house. With *me* here. Don't act like you didn't know."

"I *didn't* fucking know! Why the fuck is she staying here?"

That knocked some of the fight out of me, and I found myself studying his face for deceit. "You really didn't know?"

"No, I really didn't, and it makes no fucking sense. Why wouldn't she stay with her parents?"

"Renovations, she said."

"Bullshit. That place is a mansion. There's no way they don't still have spare rooms. And if somehow that isn't a lie, why doesn't she stay with my mother? Those two are practically joined at the hip."

These were all my thoughts exactly, but I hadn't expected *him* to be so baffled by it.

In spite of my better judgement, I felt myself warming to him. I took my glass and tapped it to his. "It looks like she's planning something. Don't be surprised if a naked girl that's shaped like a fourteen-year-old boy slips into your bed tonight."

He smirked and toasted me back. "I'm not too worried. I had no intention of sleeping in my *own* bed tonight."

A familiar burn started up just under the surface of my skin. I couldn't mistake what he meant any more than I could stop my body's reaction to him.

And I wasn't sure if I wanted to. Because again, fucking him meant fucking *with* him. Having Tiffany sleeping in the house had only upped the stakes in our little battle of head games.

But I just smiled blandly at him. "Luckily my room has a very good lock."

His grin widened. "Good. No one will bother us, then."

I straightened, setting yet another empty glass down. "On that note, I'm going to mingle."

"Wait," he said, snagging my arm and pulling me back. His finger went to trace over a spot on my collarbone where I'd missed one of the fuzzies from earlier. Carefully he brushed it away.

I shivered.

He glanced down at my nipples as I did that, watched

them harden, protruding clearly through the thin material of my dress. He didn't take his hand away, instead tracing down to circle one of the sensitive buds, rubbing it under his thumb.

His eyes were heavy-lidded on my breasts, his breath coming hard. I was very aware of the effect my body had on him, and he was in a state right then.

He was easily led in matters of the flesh, and I thought I could have gotten him to do anything when he had *that* look in his eyes.

I decided to use it against him.

"I can't believe you let me inside of you *bare* and I only got to have one taste," he uttered, voice low, guttural. "I wasn't at my best. I want a do-over."

I leaned into his touch. "Yes, *bare* inside of me. You didn't even pull out. How was it that you described it? Oh yes, the eloquent—*filled me with your cum.* You obviously weren't too drunk to remember a *few* things."

"Jesus," he breathed, coming unhinged, backing me into the high wooden counter, leaning into me, rubbing his big body against mine, his erection a clear impression against my hip. "I'd have to be dead to forget *that.* And I'm going to fill you up again. And again. Stuff you full of cock and cum until you beg me to let you rest." He started kissing my neck, outright fondling me now.

Dammit, he played a good game. He almost had me sucked in before I caught myself.

I gripped him through his slacks, stroking him hard, not an idle touch but one meant to make him lose it. "I don't think I can wait," I told him, pumping at him in earnest. "You should go up to my room, strip down, and wait for me."

He pulled my hand away, peeled himself off my body, and looked at me, really looked at me.

I smiled at him.

"Christ, you're messing with me, aren't you?"

With an evil laugh I walked away. "And while you're at it, hold your breath," I called over my shoulder.

Mingling was not nearly as fun as tormenting Dante, but I applied myself to the task nonetheless.

That lasted about five minutes. I hated talking to strangers, and that was really the best case scenario. It was the non-strangers, the familiar faces from my childhood, that I *really* couldn't stand.

I ran into one of the police officers, Mandy's father, the sheriff, in fact, almost right off the bat.

I detested him. He'd helped to plant my distrust in cops, which I felt had been to my detriment. Who could you turn to if not the police?

I smiled at him, not letting an iota of my animosity show. I really couldn't afford to have him notice me overmuch.

As I've said, I have a very healthy fear of cops.

"Hello, Harold," I said.

His beady eyes narrowed on me, the fleshy folds of his face nearly swallowing them up. He'd been overweight since I could remember, but he'd really let himself go since the last time I'd seen him.

He studied me for a few moments, trying to place me. He scratched his bushy mustache as he said, "Do I know you?"

Typical. His daughter had tormented me for years, he had covered for her, and he didn't even remember.

"Scarlett Theroux. I went to school with your daughter Mandy."

Ah, that got him.

He fingered his jowly beard, eyes running over me. "Well, you look like you landed on your feet. How 'bout that?"

I didn't know about that, but I was hardly going to argue with him. "How 'bout it," I drawled wryly.

"Have you, erm, caught up with my daughter? I remember you guys were friends."

I almost laughed. "Yes, we caught up in the kitchen. She hasn't changed a bit. It's like she's caught in a time machine."

His uncomfortable smile faltered. He cleared his throat. "So, um, how's your dad doing? He hasn't given us any trouble for a while. That has to be a good sign."

My own smile faltered. "There's absolutely no proof that Jethro Davis is my father."

"Well, the man himself claims he is. No one *else* is claiming it, so I'd say that's some proof."

"Do you usually take the claims of known criminals as proof? Is that how police work is done around here?"

Dammit, I'd riled him. In all fairness, he'd riled me first.

He pulled at his ill-fitted suit collar, eyes darting away from me, face flushed and angry. "Excuse me," he said gruffly, "I see someone I know," and ambled off.

Mingling: 1

Scarlett: 0

And it only went downhill from there.

My next victim was someone I thought was a stranger at first.

He was a short, portly guy, around my age. He shuffled up to me looking nervous as hell, and my first impression was that he seemed kind of sweet.

"Um, hi," he said, looking down at his feet. "I saw you in that lotion commercial. It was—you were—you did a really good job."

I smiled at him. "Thank you. That's a nice thing to say."

He finally looked up at me, flushed, and looked back down at his feet. "Do you, um, remember me?"

I studied him. Nothing about him was familiar to me, but I'd lived here from birth to adulthood, so there were plenty of vague faces I'd forgotten. "I don't, I'm sorry. Do we know each other?"

He gave a little half shrug and just kept staring down at his feet. He looked so utterly pathetic that I found myself feeling sorry for him. "What was your name again? Maybe that will jar my memory."

With much effort he choked out, "Tommy Mann."

I stiffened, the smile freezing on my face. I knew that name. I studied him again, trying to find traces of the boy he'd been.

I vaguely saw it. He didn't look good. He didn't take care of himself. He was pale in a way that gave the impression he didn't leave his house much. But it was in there somewhere, that boy who'd been just one in a long line of the vicious kids that had singled me out for abuse as a child.

My lip curled in disdain. "Did you ever outgrow your habit of punching girls half your size?" I asked him. "In the *face*," I added for good measure.

He actually answered the question, talking to his toes. "Y-y-yes," he stuttered.

And *dammit* that almost made me feel sorry for him. I had a soft spot for stutters.

"I always wanted to say I'm sorry for that, but they switched you to the other class after that, and Dante told me if I ever got within five feet of you for any reason that he'd pound me into next year."

That I believed.

"But I'll say it now. I have no excuse for myself. I'm very, very sorry. I know how it was for you. I know it wasn't easy. I didn't have any friends myself, and I was a weakling and a coward. I don't even know why, but I was trying to fit in and picking on you seemed to be the thing to do."

That I also believed.

"Like I said, I have no excuse. To this day I'm ashamed of myself for it."

I didn't know what to think of his apology. I wasn't used to them. I just felt strange. Conflicted. Did he expect to be forgiven with a few short sentences of remorse many years after the fact, sincere or not? Would I be crazy for holding on to a grudge for all these years, or a complete doormat for accepting his decades late apology?

I decided (begrudgingly) that a late apology was better than none at all. He was far from the worst of the goons I'd had to deal with back then. At least he'd left me alone after one offense.

And I *had* kicked him in the balls really, really hard.

"Apology accepted," I told him quietly, if begrudgingly. I wasn't used to forgiving people. It was a muscle I'd never had to use before.

I couldn't say it felt particularly pleasant to work it out for the first time.

Still, I was rather proud of myself. I'd made it through one confrontation that had gone kind of well, all things considered.

But then Dante.

He appeared just as I was about to move on with a feeling of accomplishment.

He stepped up beside me, wrapped a proprietary arm around my waist, and leaned down, down, down to short, terrified Tommy.

"What did I tell you, Tommy?" his voice was quiet and menacing. "That looks closer than five fucking feet to me."

Tommy stammered out an apology and took off.

I was sitting somewhere between exasperated and annoyed as I shrugged out of Dante's hold and turned to look at him. "I had that under control," I told him. "He'd just apologized and then you scared the crap out of him."

He was completely unrepentant as he shrugged his broad shoulders. "You are talking to the wrong guy if you think you're ever going to get me to feel sorry for any of the punk kids that terrorized you."

Well, now. How could I get mad at him for that?

"You can't buy love, but you can pay heavily for it."
~Henny Youngman

chapter
twenty-seven

PRESENT

As much as it was torture to see Dante, it was always sort of inevitable. A fact of life. At some point we'd find each other, clash again, and run away, trailing blood in our wake.

But Nate was different. I hadn't seen him in years, and in my mind I'd never thought I'd have to face him again.

Also, he'd never wronged me. There was nothing I could pin on him aside from my own guilt at how I'd treated him.

I didn't know what to expect. But if I'd had to guess, him walking up and enfolding me in a big tight hug would have been far from the first thing I'd have come up with. And that's exactly what he did.

I was returning to the theatre room after a trip to the restroom when I ran into him.

I didn't know what to say to him. I didn't know what to do.

"It's been too long," he murmured into my ear.

Still recovering from the shock of him, I was only just then returning his embrace.

"How are you?" I asked him softly.

"Not too bad," he said in that almost delicate voice of his that hadn't changed a bit. It was a voice made for reciting poetry, soothing and lyrical.

We pulled back and looked at each other. I smiled tremulously at him. It really was nice to see him, particularly nice since he didn't seem to hate my guts like he probably should have.

He looked close to the same. His angular face was handsome, his features symmetrical. He'd always been a skinny kid and he'd grown into a slender but graceful man. He was tall but not towering at just under six feet.

His blond hair was longer. He wore it in a kind of artfully messy way where it fell into his face, but it looked like that was the design of it.

I brushed one silky strand behind his ear.

"I don't even know how you do it, but somehow you're more beautiful than ever," he proclaimed with his sweet smile, touching my cheek. He had a way of saying things with such vulnerable sincerity that you couldn't help but be moved.

How had I ever thought that this sweet soul should be relegated to the role of casualty? Why had I thought that was okay?

Because Dante.

Because war.

Still, I'd take it all back if I could, if I'd had any clue the extent of the damage I was doing.

Nate held both of my hands in his and just looked at me for a while. "I can't tell you how good it is to see you," he told me.

"Really?" I asked him.

"Really. Truly."

I caught Dante watching us from across the room.

I tilted my head to the side. The man still managed to fascinate me. Right then he was losing it. His hands were in fists and he was trembling.

Nate followed my gaze. He jerked a bit when he saw who I was looking at. "He still won't talk to me," he informed me wanly. "Won't come near me, and he says that if I try to go near him, I'll be sorry. I believe him."

"I'm sorry," I stated simply.

"It's not your fault. I made my choices. I'm accountable. I love him like a brother, but looking at it with a bit of perspective, I don't think it could be any other way. There can be no peace between two men when they're in love with the same woman."

I flushed and looked away. "I'm sorry," I repeated lamely, a wave of guilt washing over me.

"Don't be. The past is the past, and I'm doing much better now, I promise."

"Yeah?" I looked back at his face.

"Yes. I mean it. I'm doing well enough that I wouldn't mind a phone call from you every now and then."

I nodded slowly, still studying him. "All right. I can do that. I'd like that."

His smile brightened, and he took out his phone. "Tell me your number. I'll call and you can save mine."

I spouted mine off, and a beat later, heard my phone vibrating in my little clutch that I had draped crossways over my torso.

"Sounds like I got it," I told him. "I'll be sure to save it."

He held one of my hands in both of his. "We'll leave it at that. I don't want to agitate Dante any more than necessary. I hope to hear from you soon."

"You will," I promised.

We air-kissed cheeks, and he slowly moved away.

Dante avoided me like the plague after that.

I was fine with that. It was rare when I got to observe him from afar, so I took advantage.

He seemed particularly standoffish, and not just towards me. Or at least, the majority of it wasn't. His family got the honors on this particular occasion.

The way he looked at his mother when she came near him was almost worth being here for. I got an absolutely diabolical kick out of it.

She was a level of bitch that I liked to refer to as *fuck that*.

As in, upon seeing her, your best option was to say '*fuck that*' and flee in the opposite direction.

Even at a funeral. Especially at a funeral.

I wasn't sure what she'd done lately, the sky was the limit with her, but she seemed to have permanently alienated her only child.

I wasn't surprised. She seemed to me to be capable of anything.

I honestly didn't think I'd have a hard time avoiding her. She hated to acknowledge that I even existed.

I didn't factor in the one annoying little detail.

I had something that she wanted now, and of course she'd figured it out right away.

She strode right up to me so suddenly that I didn't even have escape as an option.

Adelaide Durant was hell on wheels disguised as a delicate flower of a woman. She was pale and petite with masses of pitch black hair and eyes the same ocean blue as her son. She had an ageless beauty that seemed to take less blows from time than was fair. If the smooth lines of her face hand been made of karma, she'd look like a withered old hag by now.

Her hobbies were golfing at the country club, playing chess, and ruining lives.

She was a master manipulator. Like mother, like son.

"Give me back my ring." She got right to the point, her tone sharp with impatience.

She thought she could still intimidate me.

Didn't she know she had nothing left to damage me with? She couldn't hurt me anymore with Dante. He wasn't my soft spot to wound anymore.

I smiled. Over my dead body would she get that ring in her clutches. "It was *never* yours. It was Gram's, and she gave it to Dante, who gave it to me."

"Give it back to Dante. It's not right for you to keep it. Even someone as low-born as yourself should know that."

I shrugged and gave her a rueful smile. "Nope. I guess I'm too low-born even for that."

"You're a fool if you think I will let that stand. Don't you know anything? I *never* lose, especially not to a piece of trash gold digger like you."

I looked at Dante, who'd just walked up behind her. "It looks like your son wants a word with you. I'll leave you to it." I gave him a bright smile. "Excuse me. I apparently have some gold digging—things—to do."

Without an ounce of remorse I escaped to the theatre room.

The screen in the theatre room had started to show a documentary about Gram, one of the few docs about herself that she actually liked.

Currently some TV producer was being interviewed. He'd just been asked about when Gram met Grandpa.

I had that story memorized. It'd been one of her favorites.

She'd been a bratty starlet who was too jaded to believe in love. He'd been the heir and grandson of the man who had founded one of the most successful department store chains in the states.

He'd set eyes on her at an industry party and become instantly smitten.

Here's where the producer being interviewed went into detail about how Gram lit up a room, how she drew people to her like bees to honey, especially men.

But Grandpa hadn't been just any man. He was beautiful. He was larger than life. And, after hearing her tell one of her famous stories to a crowd at the party, he was determined to make her his.

According to Gram and the pictures I'd seen, he was the near spitting image of Dante, so it was easy for me at least to see why she hadn't been able to resist him.

And his courtship of her had been famously tumultuous.

Gram herself was interviewed on the doc at that point, with a soundbite about Grandpa. "He was the most determined, stubborn, ruthless son of a bitch I ever met. I didn't stand a chance from the moment he decided he was in love with me," she told the interviewer, followed by her delightful laugh.

My eyes filled at the sound.

"And when did he decide he was in love with you?" the unseen interviewer asked.

She laughed again. She was at least sixty in the video but still vibrant, still beautiful, still absolutely gorgeous with vitality. "Well, the first time he set eyes on me of course. Have you seen me?"

Even the interviewer was laughing at that and I was smiling through my tears.

"How did he court you?" they asked her.

"You name it. I couldn't even walk into my house because of the flowers for a good three months. Little gifts sent to me everywhere I traveled, little thoughtful things that let me know he had bothered to learn my tastes. And of course some not so little things," *she wiggled her brows,* "well they were little, but they came in light blue boxes from Tiffany's if you know what I mean. But the gifts were just a small part of it. They were thoughtful and cute, but it was the man himself that was impossible to resist. He gave me his time, and insisted I give him some of mine, which wasn't easy to arrange at that time, but we did it. And then—the way he looked at me when I told a joke, the way he smiled, and laughed, and always had a comeback that surprised a giggle out of me."

"How did he win you?"

"By making me fall for him. How else? There are not many men that love the way he did. I just don't think many humans are capable of that kind of devotion, but once you get a taste of it, especially if you're a vain thing like me, it's completely addictive. I didn't stand a chance. He made me less jaded, less insecure. He softened me in a way that I needed *at that point in my life. The industry has been wonderful to me, don't get me wrong, but just then the harsher aspects of it were turning me brittle. He brought me back."*

I quietly got up and left the room.

"Love is the whole and more than all."
~E.E. Cummings

chapter twenty-eight

PAST

We were in my grandma's trailer, on the sofa getting hot and heavy again, and every farther bit we went only led to more. It was a one-way street, the progression of it. Once the top was off, it came off every time, once the bra was off, it came off whenever we were alone.

I was straddling Dante and rocking against him as he felt me up, kneading at my flesh, and soon that was not enough either.

I pulled my mouth away.

He let me, but I could tell that he really, really didn't want to.

I smiled at him and took my shirt off.

His breaths grew into jagged pants, and I loved the way his hungry, adoring eyes drank in the sight of me.

To reward him I took off my bra.

"Jesus," he muttered before bending down and taking one sensitive tip into his mouth.

This I could hardly take. I needed something, more, anything, but couldn't articulate any of it because I wasn't quite sure what it was.

So I just kept rocking on top of him while he licked and sucked at my sensitive breasts, his hands cupping them, kneading them, feeling at every inch of flesh I'd bared until he had it measured and memorized, all the while making noises like he was losing his mind.

Eventually he laid me on my back and brought his lips back to mine.

"Take your shirt off," I told him. I needed to feel his skin against mine, his chest against my breasts while they were still wet from his mouth.

He straightened and did it, then paused for a moment, his hands going to the button of his pants.

I'd known he was growing by the day, getting less lean and more bulky, but it wasn't until then that I saw just how muscular he was now. Looking at him then I saw not a trace of the boy I loved. Instead I saw the man he was becoming. A man I knew even then that I'd spend my life being infatuated with.

I watched unblinking, legs sprawled apart, wearing nothing but my shorts.

He squared his jaw and took his hand away then crawled back between my thighs still wearing his jeans.

I wasn't sure if I was relieved or disappointed.

This was even better than before with him on top rubbing hard between my legs, our chests smashed together, his mouth hot and hungry on mine.

His hands explored me again, reaching every place they could with our mouths melded together.

He shifted off me and slid his fingers slowly, tentatively up my inner thigh.

I squirmed, hands in his hair, kissing him for all I was worth.

When I didn't stop him, he reached higher, grazing his fingertips up into the legs of my shorts.

I stiffened a bit but still didn't stop him.

My shorts were tight, and his big hand going into the leg hole made them tighter, but somehow he managed to get it in there and then he was grazing my sex lightly with his knuckles.

I was intimidated, but it felt good, so I rubbed myself tentatively against the top of his hand.

He moaned into my mouth and turned his wrist until he held me in his palm.

I rubbed and rubbed against him until his hand was slick from the contact.

"Jesus," he muttered at me. "You're wet."

The way he said it, like it was so significant, was foreign to me, but his tone just about did me in.

He started pushing one of his thick, blunt fingers into me and I stiffened like a board, my nails digging into his scalp.

"Mmm, God, *oh God*," he breathed at me, pushing the finger in deeper and deeper, until it started to hurt.

I whimpered when he just kept pushing. He stopped at my noise but didn't pull it out.

He didn't budge either, just stayed where he was, panting on top of me.

"Does it hurt?" he finally got out.

"A little. What are you *doing*?"

He moaned and started moving his finger, pulling it out slightly then moving it back in again, though not as deep this time. "Just tell me if you're not ready, okay? I just want to feel you with my finger. I just want to push in a little deeper, okay?"

I was *not* ready, but I found myself saying, "Okay."

He pushed it deeper until he'd reached that spot, and he was hitting against a small barrier and the pain thrummed inside of me again. He moved his finger lightly from side to side, feeling at it, exploring me without delving any deeper.

I was sure we'd gone farther than I was ready for, but I couldn't bring myself to stop him.

The desperate noises he was making as he felt me for the first time were intoxicating.

I'd have given myself to him right then just to keep him in that state.

For love. For passion. For calculation. Take your pick. Each one applied.

He started thrusting in and out, in and out, stopping just shy of the barrier, but it wasn't the best angle with how his hand was placed and after a few frustrating minutes, he pulled it out with a curse.

He panted on top of me, fists on each side of my face keeping him aloft.

Watching his pained face, I reached down and felt him through his jeans.

I'd never seen it before, but the shape of him even through his clothes fascinated me. He was so hard and there was so much of him straining to get out. I rubbed at him earnestly, learning his shape, squeezing and pulling at him through the stiff material.

Abruptly, cursing, he sprang off me and was gone, down the hall and in the bathroom with the door closed.

I stood up and followed him, not bothering to put my shirt or bra back on.

I listened at the door for one beat, two, and realizing

he wasn't going to the bathroom, I slowly opened the door.

He was at the sink, one hand braced on the wall.

He had his jeans unzipped and pulled down far enough to bare his thick, naked sex, and he had it in his hand and was frantically stroking it, yanking it hard enough that it looked like he was hurting himself.

His eyes snapped open, and he stared at me like a deer caught in headlights. Then his eyes shifted down to my breasts, and he started jerking faster.

I bit my lip, stepped inside, and shut the door behind me.

He pinned me against it and started kissing me, grabbing my hand and pushing his cock into my palm.

There was lotion by the sink, and he pulled back briefly to squirt some into my hand before he brought it back to his straining sex and started jerking himself off with both of our hands.

I tried to keep up, but I was clumsy with inexperience.

Still, it didn't take much before he was finishing, just a few hard, long, *fast* motions before warm wetness was shooting out of his tip and against my naked navel.

I loved it, loved the look of madness in his eyes. Reluctantly I let go of his twitching member to put my arms around his neck and rub against him.

With a groan, he rubbed back, his hardness still spurting liquid onto my belly as he palmed my breasts and took my mouth.

Eventually he pulled back to look at me. "Did I freak you out too much?" he asked, studying my face intently.

I pulled back slightly and looked pointedly down. My hand went to touch him. He wasn't as hard now, but he wasn't soft either and I started playing with him.

He moaned and cursed, then started praising, growing harder by the second in my curious hand.

"No," I finally answered. "Actually I think I'm becoming obsessed." I squeezed his tip experimentally. "With *this*."

"Let's go to your room," he murmured thickly, hands still at my breasts, kneading. I swear he'd have played with them every hour of the day if it were possible. He was at least as obsessed with those as I was with his newly discovered sex.

I was intimidated but I didn't protest. I needed something more. More touching. More of his naked skin on my naked skin. Something. Anything. I couldn't have walked away then if I tried.

When we got into my room, he moved to the foot of my bed. His jeans were still undone, but he'd tucked himself away, and as I watched, he zipped and buttoned them closed. After seeing him bare, I wondered how he even fit into his pants.

"Take off your shorts," he told me softly, eyes on my large, trembling breasts. "And come here."

I tried to do both at the same time, fumbling at the button of my cutoffs and moving to stand between his sprawling legs.

With a moan he started sucking at one of my nipples, his hands going to help me.

"I'm not ready to go all the way," I told him breathlessly. I didn't want him to think I was a tease.

Well, at least not a tease that wasn't being honest with him.

"I know, angel," he said with his lips still on me. "I just want to touch you, okay? I want to take care of you like you took care of me."

I moaned and wiggled out of my shorts, but I left my panties on because I couldn't imagine getting naked in front of him just like that.

He left them on, his fingers playing with my sex first over the material, and then he was pulling it aside and pushing into me.

I gasped. It was such a shocking sensation that I couldn't imagine ever getting used to it.

He didn't seem to notice my reluctance, his whole being concentrated on feeling me with his fingers.

"Jesus, you're so wet," he groaned into my chest.

My knees were going weak as what he was doing to me started an ache inside of me that I didn't know how to relieve.

"I want to lie down," I told him.

He moaned and I crawled onto the bed. When I was on my back, he started pulling down my panties.

I stopped him, I don't even know why, instinctually, I suppose, but he just paused, bent, and started sucking on my nipple, then began to pull them down again.

When he had me completely naked, he sat up at my hip and started playing with me again, his eyes intent on what he was doing.

I squirmed. I needed something, I wasn't sure what, but he wasn't doing it. He was jerking his finger in and out of me, his breath ragged, his eyes looking like he was about to lose it again.

"It's too much," I told him. "The pressure's too much."

His hand froze. "What should I do?" he asked, looking as lost as I was.

"It just . . . hurts. Your finger's too big."

He looked horrified. "My *finger's* too big?"

I thought about this. "*That's* never going to fit inside of me."

Something happened to his face, it fell and lifted as a shudder wracked through him. "Jesus." He pulled his finger out of me with a curse. "Fuck. I need to go to the bathroom again."

I sat up and stayed him with my hand. "Don't. Stay here. I want to see."

"I don't want to freak you out."

"Do you do that every time after we . . . make out and stuff?"

His mouth twisted into a sheepish smile, and he couldn't look me in the eye. "*Every* time. At *least* once. Hell, at least *twice*."

My eyes widened. "How long's *that* been going on?"

"You don't even want to know."

I kind of did, but I dropped it as his hands went to the button of his pants.

"What should I do?" I asked him as he rose and shed his jeans.

He tilted his head down to give me an amused look. "Honestly? You could do anything and it'd work for me. Just sit there and watch me if you want."

I shook my head. He wasn't getting it. "I want to do it. I want to get you off myself."

His eyes closed and his head fell back. "Jesus. You're going to kill me today, aren't you?"

I grinned. It was like nothing else, the power I felt at how desperately he wanted me.

I lay back down on my back and feeling daring I spread my legs apart. "Come lay on top of me," I told him breathlessly. "We can feel each other while I . . ."

"Jack me off," he said gruffly, climbing between my legs. "Say it."

"Jack you off." He went a little wild kissing me for that.

He had to get up briefly to grab lotion, and we got carried away.

It started with my hand, but as our bodies rubbed together his tip was brushing against my sex, then pushing at it. I moved him with my hand so he could rub along me without going in.

I would have let him go all the way, in fact a part of me desperately wanted it. Just wanted to say screw it and have each other completely.

But I didn't. My grandmother had ingrained in me too deeply the fact that as soon as you gave yourself to a man he wouldn't want you anymore.

And more than any other thing I needed in my life to survive, I needed Dante to want me. To crave me. To love and adore me.

I was obsessed with keeping him obsessed.

As we rubbed against each other, I found just the spot where the ache came from, and I took the softest part of his blunt tip and started rubbing it there in clumsy movements, then in little circles as I got the lay of it.

Dante didn't last five seconds like that, his tip mashed up against my mound.

He came again with a rough curse and I loved it. Loved making him lose his control and his mind.

He was panting over me, his eyes on where we were touching. He braced himself with one fist on the mattress, the other going down to my hand on him. He was still coming as he fisted his cock and shifted it to my entrance. With a groan, he butted up against it.

I held my breath. *If he's going to do it*, I decided, *I'm not going to stop him.*

He groaned and pushed in just the barest amount, the very tip of him invading me.

But he stopped himself, and with a curse, rolled off me.

I stayed where I was, flat on my back. The ache inside of me had become so powerful that I couldn't stop shifting my hips.

"Try your fingers on me again," I told him.

He sat up and started petting me with his hand, different now, focusing on the area around my entrance instead of just invading.

I showed him the spot I'd discovered. "There," I told him, pressing his finger to it.

He bit his lip and applied himself to the task with utmost concentration. "Softer," I panted at him. He changed his touch, lightened it.

"Mmm, that," I sighed, closing my eyes.

Before long, I had both heels on the bed as I moved against his hand.

He pushed the finger of his other hand inside of me, and this time it was better. This time I wanted it to move.

"Can I go deeper?" he asked hoarsely.

"No," I gasped. "Just keep doing that. Move it. Just like that."

I felt I was getting close to something when he seemed to lose it again.

I glanced down at his lap. I hadn't even realized he could, but he was coming again, jerking into the air.

I hadn't even had to touch him. He was coming just from touching *me*. I reached a hand out, stroking him, feeling it with him, as though with touch I could own his orgasm for myself.

And as he came, and came, he got careless with his hands, jerking his finger harder and deeper inside of me. With a stifled cry, he shoved it in to his knuckle.

I jerked, my eyes shutting tight in pain. "Dante!" My voice was an embarrassing yelp.

"Jesus, I'm sorry," he panted, and he sounded it. "I didn't even know I could do that. My fingers *are* too big. *Jesus.* I'm sorry."

I glanced down as he pulled his finger out of me. It was bloody.

I closed my legs and turned away. "I'm not supposed to start my period," I told him, mortified. "I don't know what happened."

He started kissing my back and stroking me like a cat. "That wasn't your period. Jesus. I'm sorry. I broke your barrier. Your hymen. I didn't mean to, I swear. I thought it would only break when we had sex. Did I hurt you?"

"A little bit. Nothing major. It just surprised me."

His breath was getting heavier near my ear. "Can I look? Are you too sore for me to keep trying? I want to look at you. I want to get you off."

I let him cajole me onto my back again, let him push my legs apart and look at me, because it seemed to be driving him wild again, and I was absolutely addicted to driving him wild.

And just as strong of a motivation; I wanted him to get me off. I wanted to know what it felt like; the thing that put that madness in his eyes.

It took a long time, it was unfamiliar ground for both of us, but he was patient and curious, and he worked me with his hands until he wrung my very first orgasm out of me.

He kept his fingers in me as I clenched on them, a look of wonder on his face.

"Does the hymen thing mean I'm not a virgin anymore?" I asked him later.

"It means that you're mine," he said intensely, kissing me.

I had the most ridiculous, impossible thought then: *I've just planted the seeds of my lifetime obsession.*

I'd never need more than him. He fed all of my needs. He was just difficult enough to challenge me, but tender enough to make me feel safe.

Dante and I fit together perfectly. I'd been made for him and him alone. The idea of even looking at someone else in that way was intolerable to me.

"I can resist anything except temptation."
~Oscar Wilde

chapter twenty-nine

PRESENT

I lay very still in my old room, but I wasn't sleeping.

I was battling with myself, beating back all the memories this house, this town, and particularly this room brought back.

I was especially vulnerable to distraction just then, because I *needed* it. Anything was better than the old memories, even if it meant making new ones to torture myself with.

And so when a quiet Dante came creeping into my room, I did the foolish thing.

I should have turned him away.

I did not do that. I did the other thing. The foolish one. I let him have me again.

And again.

In my defense, I was unutterably weak at that moment, too desperately in need of not just distraction but comfort.

And Dante came in the form of both.

So what if it came with a price?

A heavy price. Of torment. Regret. Bitter nostalgia.

I just chalked it up to my self-destructive streak taking its obligatory pound of flesh. My flesh was so weak; it always paid the price with little to no hesitation.

Just the opposite. My weak flesh paid it eagerly.

This wretched night was no different.

He was a large man, but he'd always had an uncanny ability to move with quiet grace, and so the sound of the door shutting and locking behind him was louder than the quiet shuffle of his feet.

My first reaction was fury. Of course it was. He was such a presumptuous bastard. The sheer, brazen nerve of him coming to me, *here*, like *this*?

But he knew me so well. This entire day had been an ordeal for me. Perhaps he sensed my weakness, the lengths I would go to just then for a powerful diversion. For a few guaranteed moments of blessed oblivion.

And also, though this reason was harder to admit, it was just as significant. If he was with me tonight, in *this* room, that meant he wasn't in another room . . . with *her*.

He didn't say a word as he quietly shed his clothes, but I could feel his eyes burning into me, could tell he knew I was awake though I kept my eyes closed and my mouth shut.

Neither of us needed words to sense the other's avid attention.

When he was done, he put one knee on the bed, and then the other, crawling over me.

Still silent, brazen as hell, with no hesitation at all, he began to strip *me*.

Hating myself, hating him, needing him, despising that need, but still helpless against it, I didn't stop him.

I was panting now in my fury, in my runaway, out of control lust.

He tugged my shirt impatiently over my head, tossing it aside, his hands going to my skin. I could feel his thick, bare member poking into my leg.

With a stifled groan, he ran his hungry fingers down my body, from my jaw, over each bone of my collar to the tops of my breasts, across each pebbled nipple, slowly, reverently along every bone of my ribs, down to my navel, until he reached my hipbones, where he unerringly found the top of my panties and slipped them off with one smooth pull.

We weren't quiet by then, we were both making noises we couldn't hide, gasping, panting loud enough to fill the quiet, but still we didn't speak.

Without even one kiss, he turned me on my side, straddled one thigh and raised the other high over his shoulder, and pushed his pulsing, engorged length against my entrance.

Foreplay or no, it didn't matter. I was wet and pliant, slick, steady beats of arousal pulsing between my thighs. I was already beyond ready for him, and he hadn't even had to check. He'd just known, damn him.

He shoved his tip in, then more, and more, inching forward steadily, not stopping until he was buried to the hilt.

The pressure then was almost too much. He bore into me so deeply and intensely that I felt split open, exposed and raw while he held himself there, at the deepest part of me, his heavy tip smashed up against my cervix unrelentingly.

Tears stung the back of my eyelids, and I couldn't beat them back.

I couldn't handle it.

His possession was so extravagant and so absolute. In that moment I couldn't hide, even from him, how it devastated me.

And in the dark room, with only the barest sliver of moonlight illuminating it through the shades, he still saw my tears.

His blunt thumb traced over each one softly.

"Shh," his voice soothed me. "Shh. I'll make it better."

He dug a fist into the mattress, his other hand cupping my face almost gently as he leaned forward heavily.

And he began to move.

And my body began to quake. A body quake that took me over completely, turned me upside down and inside out.

It was almost too quick for me like that, at that deepest angle with his unstoppable thrusts that put me into exquisite distress with every dip and plunge.

He crashed into me relentlessly.

Possessing my flesh every time he bore into me, and ruthlessly taking everything in his path as he withdrew.

My hand reached up to grab the wrist of the hand that held my face, my nails digging in as I got closer to my end.

My grip was as savage as his was gentle, scoring deep scratches into his flesh.

More marks I'd be leaving on him, more proof of my ownership that wouldn't fade with morning.

I tripped over into my release with a helpless sob.

It was so good. Nothing could compare.

Sex with Dante was so acutely satisfying that it felt both essential and damaging.

I wanted to thank him and curse him out both.

I did neither. It was something. At least I didn't *say* anything I'd regret later. Instead, I only *did*—many, many things I could regret later.

He wasn't far behind me, rooting deeply just five, six, seven more heady times, keeping me worked up and in distress with him, clenching around him, coming even while it felt I might peak again.

He held himself deep as he emptied inside of me, staying there while I milked out every last drop, holding my legs split open like that, stretching me so wide and for so long that I knew I'd be sore in several places come morning.

I could have slept after that. Could have passed out cold and slept deeper than I had in months.

In fact, I tried to, but he wasn't finished. Not even close.

He'd only just begun to slake his great thirst on me, to assuage his terrible hunger.

He pulled out of me slowly, with great hesitation, dislodging himself with regret, lingering at it, moving not just out but around, shifting inside of me, making his presence and its exit known and felt.

When he was finally free of me, he flipped me onto my back like a rag doll, pushed my thighs wide apart and climbed between.

He started kissing my neck, making his way down until he was licking my nipples.

My back arched off the bed.

"So responsive," he murmured into my skin a beat before he sucked one needy nub into his mouth. "So sensitive. Never get enough," he muttered, his big hands pushing my breasts together so he could *feast*.

He kneaded with his big hands and suckled with his perfect mouth until I was crying out his name.

"Yes," he said against my nipple. "Say that to me, Scarlett. Say yes. Yes, Dante." He went back to sucking.

"Yes, Dante, yes," I complied.

"Now say please for me," he urged. "Please, Dante."

I was scratching at the top of his back, but I couldn't hold back what he asked for, "Please, Dante."

He groaned, moving up my body. "I want to feel your naked breasts against my chest when I take you this time.

Without an ounce of resistance, my body in full rut, I let him have me again, our chests rubbing together, his weight heavy on me, in me, my face in his hands, his mouth possessing mine.

I cried when I came. He kissed my tears away.

It was just too bittersweet, the pleasure and the pain of it, and at my very weakest, when all my defenses were stripped away, there were things even I could not deny.

The brutal, unrelenting truth was all too apparent to me in these moments.

I belonged to him. I was his.

I'd never stopped being his.

It was a cruel, unbearable, and undeniable fact.

He dragged my pliant, naked body into the adjoining bathroom, drawing a bath and tugging me in to straddle him.

I tried to lay my cheek on his chest, but he gripped my face with both hands and started kissing me. Not an idle, satisfied kiss, either. His mouth devoured mine like he hadn't just had me. Twice.

His hunger reignited my own, and in spite of myself

I was grabbing his neck and kissing him back with equal fervor.

I'd never been able to get enough of him like this, when he was so wildly passionate for me. Hungry to the point of desperate.

As ever, I answered that hunger in kind.

I don't need food. I don't need air or shelter. I just need this, my body told me with each fevered throb.

His proximity. His touch. His own all-consuming need. Nothing felt more vital to me.

He held me captive like that for a very long time, with his gentle hands and his desperate kiss, devouring me from the outside in, insinuating his all-encompassing craving into every part of me until I was a mindless slave to it.

Eventually the kissing led to more. I had my thighs on either side of his hips, and gradually he worked me closer, his hardness pushing insistently between my legs, ramming teasingly, and then harder against my sex, finally entering me, working in slow inch by slow inch, sucking in each needy breath I gasped out as he invaded me, my cunt sucking in each needy thick inch of his cock.

I tried to move on him, to create the friction that would relieve us both, but his hands let go of my face, snaking down to grip my hips and hold me flush and unmoving, keeping still and buried to the hilt.

All the while, his mouth was unstoppable on mine, kissing, licking, sucking, gasping out the words he knew would get to me the most and the fastest.

I was whimpering by the time he let up, his hands on my hips working me against his thick length in small, jarring movements.

"More," I managed to get out, but barely. Passion

made him vocal, but for me it was the opposite. I was a blithering mess of in-articulation when I was this far gone.

He rewarded me with a few more hard thrusts then began to pull me off.

I protested, but he shushed me, gave me one last long kiss, then lifted me clean out of the bath and perched me on the lip of it.

Gram had given me one of the best suites in the entire mansion, and the bathroom had a garden tub set in a corner with a scenic window. He set my back against the glass, leaned down between my thighs, and went to work.

I gripped my fingers into his hair, head falling back, eyes drifting closed.

His mouth, *God*, his mouth. It'd been so long.

Pulling me open, his tongue and fingers clamoring inside, he finished me in seconds.

I was still reeling when he rose. He propped a foot up near my hip, gripped both hands into my hair, and pulled my slack mouth within licking distance of his thick tip.

I started to get it then. He wanted to do *everything*, wanted to have me every way before the night was through.

I knew him well enough to know he'd have his way.

Neither of us was going to get a wink of sleep until he'd gone through his hit list, which was mind boggling and extensive.

He carried me back to bed and laid me down. When he straightened and started to move away, I wondered if I'd been mistaken and he was actually done.

But he was just turning on the lights.

Of course he would. The intrusive bastard wouldn't let me hide anything from him.

As he moved about, I admired the view. Even the fresh scratches I'd left all over his back. Every inch of him was the benchmark of my personal preference.

I'm so fucked, I thought, my eyes drifting closed.

But the bastard didn't let me sleep.

He kept me up until the sun was rising and every *inch* of my body *ached*.

"I might let you sleep after this round," he told me, kissing my shoulder.

He was on my back, groin flush against my ass, my legs spread wide, his clenched fists on the mattress on either side of my head.

I was in exquisite, tantalizing distress, my face in the pillow, mouth opened wide in a silent scream as he rutted *hard* and *deep* into my sensitive flesh.

His pace increased as he got close, his thrusts getting almost too rough to bear.

He lifted my face from the pillow with a firm hand in my hair, bending down to kiss as close to my mouth as he could reach, and, buried to the hilt, he emptied himself deep.

He stayed inside of me, hips flexing as he rubbed out every last twitch of his orgasm.

"Jesus," I groaned, as he pulled out of me with excruciating slowness. It was just too much.

And still he wasn't done. He kissed his way down my back, pushed my knees up on the bed, and fitted his head underneath me.

I braced myself on my elbows, moving my hips as he ate me out yet again.

My body was still vibrating with pleasure as he flipped me onto my back and straddled me.

"You're a beast," I panted, and it wasn't an insult.

He pinned my wrists above my head, staring solemnly down at me.

A million things were pouring out of his ocean eyes at me.

I didn't even have to say it aloud. We stared at each other and thought the words, a silent conversation with nothing but our starving, devouring eyes.

It doesn't matter what's happened tonight. It doesn't matter that we mourned together, and made ourselves and each other feel better for one bittersweet night.

I can't forgive you. I can't and won't trust you again. You betrayed me and it can never be made right again.

Also, I can't forgive myself. The things I did to hurt you, to survive after you left, and of course, the things I did to take revenge for the things you did, have damaged me beyond all repair.

But we didn't say one word out loud. Finally he bent down and kissed me, and it was so soft and so tender as to be devoid of passion.

It held something else, something even more dangerous. A thing I was afraid to even *think*.

He pulled back with a gasp and started panting like he'd been underwater.

After that, he let me sleep.

"If two wrongs don't make a right, try three."
~Laurence J. Peter

chapter thirty

I woke up to a steady knocking on my bedroom door.

I cast one bleary-eyed look at Dante, who appeared so deeply asleep as to be unconscious.

"What?" I called out, and even then he didn't twitch. He'd always been a sound sleeper.

He slept like a guiltless baby, the bastard.

No answer. Just more knocking, and still more, going and going in a precise, continuous rap. Not hard, not soft, not fast, not slow, just steady and determined.

Whoever it was seemed to have no intention of leaving until I answered that door.

But the thing was, I really didn't want to. There was a limited number of people it could be, and not one of them I wanted to see this early. Or ever.

I wasn't even dwelling on what they'd discover when I opened that door. It was bad enough that *I* knew what I'd succumbed to in the dark, lonely hours of the night. I certainly wasn't thrilled with the notion of anyone else discovering it, but there was no way we could hide it.

First of all, we were both naked. Dante didn't even have a sheet to cover him. He was sprawled out on his back, exposed to the air, sleeping the sleep of someone utterly capable of trust, which was ironic since he'd been the one to rob me of mine. The Bastard.

Second, the room reeked of sex. *I* reeked of sex. I'd lost count of the things we'd done over and through the long hours of the night, and the evidence was everywhere, most particularly inside of and all over my well-used body.

Third, the room looked like it'd been ransacked. The bedspread was over by the window for some reason I couldn't remember, every knickknack on my dresser had been knocked over or off, and Dante's pants were literally directly in front of the door, like he'd left them there to send a message.

I wondered idly if he'd had the possessive foresight to leave a sock on the doorknob.

I glanced around, trying to decide what there was to be done about it, and also, where the clothes I'd gone to bed in had ended up. All I could see were *his* clothes, and they seemed to be everywhere, making it impossible to miss that there was a naked man in my bed even if I'd gotten rid of the naked man himself.

"Open the door, Scarlett," a soft female voice that I'd recognize anywhere called.

My entire sated body stiffened.

Well, hell. I wasn't going to hide this from *her*, of all people. In fact, if I ever *had to* set eyes on her again, this was the demoralizing setup I'd have chosen.

I stood, negligently wrapping a sheet around the

essentials, but not bothering to cover too much. Let her see what he'd picked over her last night. Let her see what she could never compete with. Just as her rail thin body always brought out my worst insecurities, I knew my over the top curves made her feel just as inadequate.

How could a man desire two women of polar opposite looks? I'd often wondered. And worse, *which type does he prefer?*

Though some part of me, my gut I guess, always knew that it was me.

He was a slave to this body, helpless against every curve and hollow of it. If there was one thing I was certain of about him, it was that.

I swung the door open wide as I answered, hiding nothing. Well, nothing in the room. On my face was pure stoicism.

On my face I hid everything.

My hate. My contempt.

My jealousy. My fear.

"Good morning, Tiffany," I said, deadpan.

And since Dante was sleeping and not dead, finally something jarred him out of his enviably peaceful slumber.

With a jerk he sat up. I watched his body flex with the movement, gaze darting from that drool worthy sight up to the dawning horror on his face.

I couldn't decide which thing I liked looking at more.

"What the *fuck*, Tiffany?" he snarled, the horror turning to something darker, something I liked even more if for different reasons.

As he began to scramble to find something to cover himself with, I turned back to the bane of my existence.

I saw her face when she noticed his back.

I saw her go pale as she took in every scratch I'd left on him.

She shot one hostile glance my way.

I feigned a cringe. "Ouch. Those looks like they hurt," I said with a mock sympathetic pout.

"They do," Dante grumbled, still looking for clothes.

The chain around his neck and what hung from it were conspicuous when he was naked and moving like that. I didn't imagine she could miss seeing them any more than I, and that didn't make me sad.

"What do you want?" I asked her, trying to make my tone neutral but landing on borderline rude.

I hated that she was still shamelessly watching him.

I was starting to understand the phrase *claw her eyes out.*

"I just had to see this with my own eyes, though I still can't quite believe it," she said, directing the words at Dante's naked back, using a tone with something in it, some bit of ownership for him that I simply could not tolerate.

My hands were in fists, and I knew it wasn't a good sign. My temper was quickly running away from me. "Are you kidding me?" Disdain dripped off the words. "Did you think we needed your *permission?*"

For that, she looked at me.

I took a step closer to her. "He was mine before you ever had him, and even when you did, know this, a part of him was *still* mine. You *never* got what I had. You had what was left when I was done with him. Even last night, and it was a *long* night, what I got from him had no piece of *you* in it."

For that, I got the reaction I craved. In her dilating pupils, her shortened breath, her quivering lip, I saw how I'd annihilated her with a few brutal sentences.

Good. I had no mercy for her. She'd helped to ruin everything I cared about, helped to make me less whole.

But still, she didn't speak to me, didn't address my words.

"Did you think I wouldn't know?" she asked *him*, a world of accusation in her voice that I for one thought she had no right to. "We're sleeping under *the same roof*. Did you think you could keep this from me?"

It took him so long to answer that I thought I might scream, but then, "I think it's none of your fucking business," he told her in a tone so black and deadly and overflowing with scorn that it made me shiver.

"You think that?" she glanced at me, her scathing eyes at my throat.

Even then, I didn't catch the significance.

"What else don't you think is my business?" she asked, something pointed in her tone that I didn't catch right away.

It was the sort of thing that would float around for a while before it parked itself in my consciousness.

"I think none of it's your fucking business and it *never* was," Dante thundered back, his gorgeous temper coming out to play. "How's that? Clear enough for you?"

"You're going to regret this," she said, and I couldn't tell if she was speaking to him or me.

Either way, I took exception. I opened my mouth to lay into her again when she added.

"You go to bed with trash, Dante, and you can expect things to get *dirty*."

My mind went a little hazy for a time.

Only seconds, I believe, but certainly enough time to do some damage.

When I was cognizant again, a naked Dante was

behind me, arms wrapped around my chest, holding me back.

Tiffany was in the hallway clutching her bleeding nose with both hands, a boxer clad Bastian apparently appearing from nowhere and holding her back, as though *she* might attack *me*.

I thought it was cute that anyone thought I needed protection against her. The prissy, entitled bitch couldn't fight her way out of a paper bag.

"Get out of here," Bastian told her sternly. "Quit fucking *instigating*, and go." He aimed her down the hallway and nudged her until she started to haltingly move.

"You're going to regret this," she sobbed as she stumbled away.

"Come back here," I snarled at her, trying to heave myself out of Dante's impossible hold. "Let me do a few more things I can regret, you fucking home-wrecking whore!"

There was an awkward, pregnant moment when she was gone, punctuated only by the sound of my rage-filled, panting breaths, when it was the three of us left in the hallway, none of us dressed.

I noticed that Bastian looked pretty freaking edible when he was half naked right about the time that we all realized my sheet had slipped down to my waist in the struggle, leaving me topless.

Dante started cursing as he yanked it back up. "Avert your fucking eyes," Dante barked at Bastian.

Bastian, who'd clearly only shown up to help, raised his hands in the air and started walking away with a muttered, "You're welcome for the help, brother."

"Wow," I said when we were shut back into my room. "You know that's the first time I've put my hands on that little princess bitch."

"Yeah?"

"Yeah. She never does her own dirty work, always keeps her hands clean. She's an instigator, not a fighter."

"Don't I know it," he said succinctly, not looking at me.

"You really hate her, maybe even more than you hate me."

"I never hated you. I was just *extremely* upset with you for a very, very long time.

Whatever he wanted to call it, it had felt a lot like hate, but I didn't get into that with him. Instead, "What'd she do that you hate her *that much*? Did she sleep with Nate too?" It was supposed to be a joke, one in very poor taste, but a joke.

He flinched.

My brows raised and I tried to fake a smile. "*Oh ho.* She did? Is that what happened?"

He cut his hand through the air in a way that had me taking a step back, though I was already several feet away from him. "I don't give a fuck who she sleeps with."

"You sound defensive," I accused, trying not to let my tone sound as wounded as I felt at the idea of *him* getting jealous over *her*.

His angry eyes studied me. "Not at all. I said the exact fucking thing I meant. I don't give a damn what or who *she* does."

I didn't miss the implication in every word he said. "So did she or didn't she fuck Nate? Now I'm confused."

His hands were in fists now, his shoulders heaving. "Now you sound like the jealous one. You're the one that brought up fucking Nate! Would it bother *you* if she slept with him?"

I couldn't help it. Meeting his rage filled eyes steadily, before I could stop myself, I gave him the truth he didn't deserve. "I don't give a damn what or who *he* does."

Oh no. Now I'd done it.

He was up, approaching me for that, something spilling out of his eyes that I couldn't stand. "That thing with him, was it only to hurt me?"

"Stop it."

He was on me, hands in my hair, our faces pulled close, though I refused to look at his. "Tell me. Please. For so long, I didn't think I could forgive you for that. I was sure I couldn't, but, fucked up as it is, if you tell me you did it to hurt me, tell me you did it to break me, tell me anything as long as you tell me you didn't *feel* something for him, before or after, then I can forgive it."

I was trembling, head to toe. In rage. In fear. "Stop it. *Fuck you.* I don't owe you *anything*. We were done when it happened. You betrayed me before I *ever* betrayed you."

"Promise? Do you swear it?"

"I don't owe you anything," I repeated.

"Please. Tell me you did it to hurt me. Tell me it only happened after *I* hurt *you*. Please." The arms holding my head angled to his were trembling as badly as I was.

Our combined shaking felt powerful enough to move the ground beneath us, to bring down the house that held us.

"I don't owe you anything." I had to force out every gutted syllable.

"I'm begging you. Have you ever seen me beg? *Begging* you. Tell me, lie to me if you have to, but tell me you did it hurt me. Tell me he didn't mean anything to you."

My hands were gripping his now for support. I thought I might collapse otherwise. This was why he always won. He used every weapon at his disposal, created new ones for his cause, until I felt too defenseless to fight him.

"I did it to *hurt you*," I admitted, the words wrenched from my soul.

He tried to kiss me, but I fought him, heaving away.

"What about you and her? Was *that* only to hurt me?"

He looked so crushed at the question that I lost my breath.

He couldn't even meet my eyes.

"Answer me. I answered you, so you answer me, you son of a bitch. Was that only to hurt me?"

"I'm sorry." His voice was unsteady. "It's complicated."

I should've known better than to ask. The wound had been festering but at least it hadn't been *fresh*. Now it felt opened anew, and it hurt much more.

Of course, that wasn't what I'd wanted to hear. I wanted an answer as uncomplicated as mine had been.

The Bastard.

But I'd known the answer before I asked it. The timeline didn't add up. He'd betrayed me with her before he ever had a reason to want to hurt me like that.

"I hate you," I told him, quietly and vehemently.

"I hate that I still love you." Just as quiet, just as vehement. Far more destructive.

God, with just a few words he'd almost defeated me. I was a sore loser, though, so I did my best to recover and limp away.

I was nearly clear of the room, one foot already in the bathroom, when he finished me.

"I hate that I'll never stop," his voice was soft but no less impactful.

I went into the bathroom and locked him out.

I was in the shower before I realized what he'd done. I'd gone to bed with one chain around my neck and woken up with two.

I held up the newest one. It was a key.

The bastard had put it on me while I slept.

He'd keep me chained to him in spite of everything. This I knew. I hadn't needed proof.

chapter thirty-one

PAST

We were at our old swimming hole. We hadn't meant to come here, we'd just been walking and talking and stumbled upon it, and once we saw it we remembered.

The spot was nothing new to us, and it shouldn't have been so strange, except that it'd been a long time since we'd been here, years at least now that I thought about it, and I didn't have a swimsuit.

Still, when we were kids I'd gone swimming in my T-shirt all the time. Dante never said anything about it, in fact, even though I was sure he had more swim trunks than he could count back home, he'd usually just join me in his shorts, and even though I knew he only did that to make me feel better, which should have made me feel worse, I appreciated the gesture.

My shirt now was too short for me. It barely reached the top of my high-waisted, too tight jean shorts, but

I didn't care. I figured my underwear covered at least as much as most bikini bottoms, and I had a nice flat tummy that seemed to draw Dante's eye whenever the least bit of skin was exposed.

We couldn't be near each other these days without him fixating on me. And if I showed a bit of skin, well, that was even more gratifying.

I absolutely ate it up. I couldn't get enough of his attention.

"We doing this?" he asked me with a smile.

In answer, I unsnapped my bra through my shirt, wiggled out of it, then shimmied my shorts off. Wearing nothing but a thin white, almost half shirt and lavender panties, I made a dash for the water, leaving Dante behind.

I didn't look back at him until I was fully submerged to find him still staring at me.

I smiled. He was slack-jawed and hadn't so much as shrugged off his shirt. "You coming in or what, slow-poke?"

That seemed to shake him out of it, and I had my own moment of slack-jawed staring to do as he peeled off his shirt and then took off his jeans.

He joined me in nothing but his boxers. He was about three steps into the water when I rose out of it, watching his eyes on my body, the way he swallowed, how his breathing changed to ragged.

And my eyes moved down his body to stare in fascination at what his boxers couldn't hide.

What I saw made me realize two things at once—how badly he wanted me, and how quickly this was going to get out of hand, both of which galvanized me into action.

With a cocky grin, I strode by him to the shore, past

it to the wall of rock and started climbing. It was a short climb and easier than it looked. The wall of rock was dotted with almost perfectly placed handholds and inside each one a nice thick patch of spongy moss had grown big and strong enough to grab and hold. I scaled the wall and made it up onto the rock in less than a minute, just like old times, as though it hadn't been years since we'd done this.

I waved to him from above. He hadn't moved, and I'd caught him again very obviously staring at me.

I glanced down at myself. With my thin, white shirt wet, I may as well have been topless. Actually, somehow it felt even more indecent than that. Almost without thinking, I tried to cover myself with both hands but as I did, I realized that grabbing handfuls of myself was even worse.

I looked at him again. He was still frozen in place, staring intently. He looked like he wanted to devour me whole.

With a trembling breath, I let go of my breasts, letting them bounce free, straining against the thin, wet material of my shirt. With a smile I took a running jump off the rock.

He was on me the second I surfaced, hands on my hips. He yanked me to him and started kissing me, his hands slipping around to my ass, pushing my sex flush to his.

I clung to him, kissing him back. I felt drugged, past all good judgement, in a state, and the look in his eyes had put me there.

He dragged me to the shore, out of the water, and onto the ground. He got on top of me, shoving his hips between my thighs.

He was a wild man, shoving my shirt up, grabbing handfuls of me, rough noises escaping from his throat.

My hand went for him, delving into his boxers to cup him.

One of his hands snaked down and started dragging off my panties.

We knew each other's bodies well by now, but it never seemed to be enough.

He wrenched his mouth away from me and moved down my body. When he came back up, I was naked from my shoulders down and his boxers were gone.

"Let me put it in inside you," he groaned into my mouth when he was on top of me again. "Just for a second. I won't come. I just want to feel you."

I couldn't say no. In spite of my better sense, if I even had such a thing, I couldn't say no to the desperate plea in his voice.

"Okay," I said tremulously.

"Are you sure? You can say no. You *should* say no if you're not ready."

"Just for a second, right?"

"Yes. I don't . . . have condoms or anything. I won't come inside you, I swear."

I nodded, craning my neck to look down and watch what he was doing.

He used his hand to guide himself to my entrance, angling his tip to snag in just right.

I was wet, and he'd already taken care of my hymen, but it was still uncomfortable. He was too big and I was too tight.

It took him a long time to stuff his thick length in. If it was uncomfortable for me, it seemed to be excruciating for him going by the noises he was making.

He shoved in until his hips were flush against me, buried to the root. He held still there for a time, panting on top of me.

My body started to adjust. It was still uncomfortable, but that discomfort was starting to be overshadowed by the ache inside of me. The ache was growing fiercely, and my body had come to expect relief from it. I started shifting under him, getting a feel for the overwhelming fullness of it, trying to find the angles that made my stubborn tightness loosen enough to bring me pleasure.

As soon as I moved, he lost his mind.

He cursed, jerked out halfway, shoved all the way back in hard enough to jar a cry out of me, pulled back, pumped in again, once, twice, before he yanked completely free.

He was apologizing over and over as he rolled off me and onto his back.

I followed him, hand going to his hard, twitching length, stroking him, rubbing out every last drop of his release.

We'd had a lot of practice by now. This had pretty much become the thing that consumed all of our free time in the last few months, and I knew just how to touch him, just what he liked.

He pulled my hand away slowly, eyes closed, still panting, but within thirty seconds he had me on my back, his hand between my thighs.

He set his mouth on my skin and started kissing his way down my body.

I couldn't stop panting as he got lower, and lower. Fitting his shoulders between my thighs, he put his mouth on me for the first time.

He was unskilled, but he'd always been a patient learner. With some instruction, a shift here, a tongue there, he kept at it until he made me come against his lips in the most powerful orgasm of my life thus far.

"That's my favorite thing so far," I told him when I had the breath to speak again.

Grinning the most self-satisfied smile I'd ever seen him wear, he climbed up my body and started kissing me.

My hand went to his member. He was hard again, and I started stroking him.

This time, though, he didn't let me jack him off.

He rolled onto his back.

I sat up, leaning over him, hand still on him, still squeezing and stroking.

His palm came up and cupped the back of my head, nudging me with a light touch down his body.

Knowing what he wanted, I'd wanted to do it for a while, I was just always afraid to give him too much, I moved down.

When I was hovering over his arousal, I licked my lips and shot a look at his face.

He was watching me with heavy-lidded fascination.

I licked my lips again, and the hand on my head gripped my hair and pushed me down.

I wasn't good at it. What I lacked in skill I tried to make up for with enthusiasm, but as I bobbed my lips up and down on his length, I kept gagging myself.

Still, it was his first feel of my mouth so it didn't take much. I'd barely gotten the hang of it, my hand helping my mouth, catching the rhythm of stroking and sucking, before he was shouting a warning, and then shooting down my throat. I didn't know what else to do, so I swallowed.

He was still coming in slow pumps when he pinned me on my back and started kissing me.

"I love you," he told me, over and over.

I'd never get enough of hearing those words come out of his mouth. It still seemed so impossible, so unlikely, that a perfect boy like him could love a trashcan girl like me, but I believed him.

"I love you too," I told him. There was nothing in the world I was more certain of. Not one thing. Not the sky or the moon, not the earth or the sun.

He was my constant. He held the vast majority of my faith in the palm of his hand.

With stuttering slowness I told him so.

His answer was to kiss me top to bottom and then go down on me again.

After he'd finished me that time, he climbed on top of me, laying naked and heavy there.

With a groan, I pushed him onto his back and he let me.

"I think I'm ready," I told him, pressing my breasts to his chest, rubbing my nipples into his skin how he loved. "I want you inside me. I want you to *finish* inside of me."

He groaned like I was torturing him. "Jesus. Now you tell me this, when we're in the middle of nowhere?"

"I didn't mean right this second. I just meant, in general, I think I'm ready." I tried to sound more sure than I felt.

The way he looked at me then made my chest go tight with emotion. He cupped my cheek as he said tenderly, "Don't rush for me. I can wait as long as you need."

Sometimes it was like he could read my mind. Lots of times, in fact.

No one would ever know me like he did. Understand and indulge the darkness and the lightness in me. The good and the bad. The strong and the weak. Take all of the parts of me that were toxic and soothe them with the perfect antidote.

We had all of the ingredients of forever love.

And on the immediate heels of that was a debilitating and destructive insecurity. Did he feel the same? Was it even possible for him? Was I enough to make *anyone* feel the way he made me feel?

"Do you love me?" I asked him.

"What do you think?"

"I think that's not an answer."

"Because you know the answer. I've told you many times just today. Of course I do. I'm not sure how I'd get through even one day in this world without you in it. Why I'd even want to."

I studied his face while he uttered every word and found that I believed him.

All I had to do now was make sure he never stopped feeling this way.

But we were never meant to last. If only my heart had known that.

"Love never dies a natural death."
~Anaïs Nin

chapter thirty-two

PRESENT

I was in the kitchen, rummaging around for coffee like an irritated bear looking for honey when a now dressed Bastian joined me.

He still looked pretty freaking edible. Leo was a crappy as hell father, but he sure made good-looking sons. The Durant men were all of a size, uncommonly tall with straight, broad shoulders. Bastian was dark where Dante was golden, but they still shared a certain look, something sinister around the eyes, with pretty mouths and straight, sharp teeth. Starkly handsome but *villainous*.

It was my own personal kryptonite.

"Hey," I greeted him, tone bordering on friendly, because he was maybe the only person in this entire house that I didn't despise.

"Hey there," he returned, tone and smile beyond friendly into outright warm.

My body was facing the coffeemaker, hips leaning against the counter as I waited for the coffee pot to fill.

I was serious about my coffee, especially the first cup of the day. I'd basically been watching the pot filling drop by drop, mug ready to pounce the second it finished.

Bastian was clearly a coffee enthusiast himself, joining me right there, actually *exactly* right there. He didn't even find his own space, instead he invaded mine, pressing himself against my back as he reached above me for a coffee cup.

"Don't take this the wrong way," he murmured into my ear, "but it felt ruder not to mention it—you've got a world class rack. It's going to be hard for me to forget about it."

"Well, Bastian, while we're not being rude I guess I'll mention that you looked pretty outstanding without your clothes on."

"You didn't even get to see the best part."

"Regrettable," I remarked, because flirting with hot guys was in my DNA, even if they were blood related to the hate of my life.

"Well, it doesn't have to be."

I bit my lip to keep from smiling. "You trying to get Dante to kill you?"

"He can try. Besides, you guys aren't actually back together, are you?"

"Hell no, but you're thinking of it reasonably. Try to think of it from the mind of a Dante."

"I see your point. Something's always confused me though. With the way he so obviously feels about you, the way you feel about each other, why did you break up in the first place?"

What happens when two people of terrible pride fall for each other?

Terrible things.

Destruction. Chaos. Pain. Sorrow.

War.

"You'd have to ask him," I finally responded. "It was his idea."

"Well, he's a fool then. Want to know who isn't a fool?"

I was outright grinning at him over my shoulder. "Do you want me to guess or are you going to tell me?"

With a boyish smile, he pointed at himself. "This guy."

The coffee was finished, and I poured us both a cup. "Good to know," I said, turning and handing him his.

His smile died suddenly and he glanced around as though making sure we were alone. "Seriously though, I wanted to ask you about something that's been bothering me for a while."

I shrugged. "Go for it." Worst case scenario, if I didn't like the question I wouldn't answer it.

"Have you ever wondered why Leo and Adelaide never got divorced?"

I shrugged. "I've no idea."

"They *despise* each other."

"Yeah. They seem like a perfect match. They're both pretty easy to despise."

"True. But I'm starting to get the distinct impression that things are even more messed up than they appear. I think Adelaide has something bad on Leo. I think she's blackmailing him and has been for a very long time."

Was I surprised? No. Was I disgusted? Yes.

"Nothing that woman could do would surprise me," was my response, "but I don't know one way or the other.

Why did you think I would? Adelaide hates me more than anyone. I'd hardly be the one she'd tell her dirty secrets to."

He shrugged. "I figured it was a long shot, but you're one of the few people associated with this crazy family that might actually tell me the truth. I thought maybe if Dante knew something that he might have confided in you at some point. Because you know he'd never tell *me* anything."

"He never gave you a fair shot," I said absently, my mind on Adelaide and blackmail. That woman was capable of *anything*.

It was terrifying.

"He didn't, but there's still time. Maybe I'll grow on him. And I get it. All he ever wanted was our father's approval, and being the firstborn and legitimate it must have felt particularly demoralizing to be treated the way he was. What he's never understood is that our father only sees our mothers when he looks at his sons. We get treated, loved or loathed, based on whatever connection he had with the women he impregnated."

I thought about that, and it added up perfectly. It was so horribly simple for something that had brought so much sadness to a young Dante. "And he *loathes* his wife," I murmured.

He nodded.

"You're a good guy, Bastian. I hope someday you and Dante can find some middle ground."

He smiled but it was weaker than his other efforts. "I keep hoping."

"It's strange that your father never had any daughters," I added, watching his face.

"There's always that rumor that Durants only have boys."

I knew firsthand that rumor was absolute rubbish, but I nodded. "There is that," I said evenly.

"But that's only a rumor. I think my dad probably has at least a few daughters. He just never bothered claiming the girls." He saw my face and his mouth twisted. "I know. Believe me, I know. My dad is a piece of shit. What can I say? You don't get to pick your father."

"What's with this cozy fucking scene?" a familiar voice boomed from the doorway of the kitchen.

Bastian and I had been huddled close together. It was completely innocent. Well mostly. We just hadn't wanted to be overheard. But at the sound of Dante's voice we sort of jumped apart guiltily, which didn't look innocent at all.

Because I liked Bastian, in fact, I liked him more the longer I spoke to him, I set down my coffee and moved forward as Dante did, intercepting him before he got close to his brother.

I pushed into his chest, getting his immediate angry attention for myself.

"Are you fucking kidding me with this?" he raged, pointing a finger at his brother. "You've still got a whole night's worth of my fucking cum inside of you and you're already, what the *fuck* was that, *rubbing up against my brother?*"

My brows shot up. Wow. He'd gone full out crazy without much provocation. Bastian and I hadn't even been touching when he walked in. *Had it looked like we had?* I tried to picture the angle he might have seen as I said, "Calm down. We were talking and you're acting like a nutjob."

For that he pointed his furious eyes at Bastian. "I'll show you a fucking nutjob. She is *off limits*. Do you fucking hear me, brother?"

Bastian looked completely unfazed, which somehow just made me like him more. "I'm well aware of how you feel about her, *brother*," he shot back, holding his coffee mug in both hands like he sensed no threat at all.

I pushed at Dante's chest. He didn't budge but that hadn't been the point. Getting his attention back to me had been, and it worked. He turned his gaze on me, and I could tell he was about to lose it. "You need to take a walk, Dante. Walk away. Remember your anger management steps."

He didn't like that, but he responded to it, backing away and glaring at me.

When he was gone, I retrieved my coffee. It wasn't hot enough anymore, so in silence I poured it out and fixed another.

"It never made sense to me, the way it went down with you two," Bastian said quietly.

I could feel his eyes on me, but I didn't look at him as I shrugged. "Didn't make much sense to me, either. Well, anyway, nice chat. I'll see you around, yeah?"

"Yeah. Take care, Scarlett, okay?"

"I always do, not that it helps me a damn bit. You take care of yourself."

"I will."

I started to leave, taking my mug with me.

I was at the doorway when he spoke again. "Will you do me a favor?" he called out.

I stopped and looked at him. "Sure," I said lightly before I even knew what it was. I must have trusted him. That wasn't like me.

"Ask Dante sometime, if you can, what he thinks about his mother and *blackmail*," he said, his voice so intense that I found myself staring at him. Was he referring to

Adelaide and his father, or something else? I couldn't tell, but the words he was saying felt directed at me very pointedly.

I kept steady eye contact with him when I answered, "I'll do that."

"Good. Very good. Keep me posted."

chapter thirty-three

PRESENT

I couldn't seem to help myself. I followed Dante, tracking him down in his room.

I knocked, he didn't answer, but I could tell he was in there, I heard him moving, so I just opened the door.

It's a fucked up fact that I can't resist him when he's angry. I love it when his fury turns him savage.

I love to watch him fight and rage. Wipe blood from his lip, his eyes seeking me out, the rage in them bleeding harder.

Dante more than anyone knows this about me.

He started shaking his head when he saw me.

I shut the door behind me and approached him.

Licking my lips, I reached up and touched his shoulders.

He flung my hands away. "Don't touch me!

Nothing he could say would have drawn me to him

faster. I was in his space, rubbing against him, completely ignoring his words and concentrating on his body.

"Stay away from me," he ground out.

I leaned forward and kissed the soft cotton covering his chest.

He backed away, eyes wide.

"You're freaking out for no reason," I said calmly. "You're imagining things. There is nothing going on between Bastian and I. We were just talking. You are overreacting."

"Why were you huddled so close? Why did he have you backed into the counter like that?"

"We were exchanging sensitive information."

He moved further out of my reach, going to sit on the edge of his bed. "What information?"

"I'll tell you when you've calmed," I said, following him. While he watched, I stripped off my shirt, then my bra. I tugged off my thong but left my skirt on.

I straddled him there, standing against him where he sat.

Groaning, he buried his face between my breasts, one hand going to cup my rear under my skirt, the other working at the button of his pants. With jerky movements he freed himself.

He cupped my breasts, pulling me down until I was on top of him, bending to follow my nipples as they sank down out of his reach.

I rode him like that, on the edge of his bed.

After, we fell into a heap and went to sleep.

I woke up curled into his chest, his hand stroking over my hair.

"How long did I sleep?" I asked him.

"A couple hours."

"I don't know what I was thinking. I need to get ready for my flight."

"You've got time."

"Oh? Is it a late flight?"

"Hmm," he said, and I thought it was an affirmative noise, but I glanced up at him suspiciously. He sighed. "You can't leave yet. The reading of the will is tomorrow."

"I'm not staying for that."

"What if she left you something?"

"If she left me anything, have it donated to that charity she set up for Grandpa."

No, I wasn't insane. I just would not, could not, profit off her death.

Sure, I was broke most of the time. I'd lost track of the times I'd spent my last twenty on a tube of M.A.C. lipstick, or maxed a credit card on a cute pair of shoes, but that was my problem and there was no reason someone else should bail me out of it, even if that someone was Gram.

"My God, you are as stubborn as ever."

"Are you surprised?"

"Not remotely." He paused. "Tell me about Anton."

I'd completely forgotten about that. And of course Dante had known his name all along, the fucking stalker. "You're never going to drop this, are you?"

"Never," he agreed.

I sighed. It was too ridiculous to keep up the pretense. "He's just a friend. A good one. Demi called him my boyfriend because she's a sweetheart and that's what friends do when one of their girls is locked in a room with her ex."

He was stroking my hair, kissing the top of my head. "You were messing with me," he breathed.

"Are you surprised?" I asked him, nearly laughing. Didn't he know how this fucked up little song and dance went?

"I shouldn't be, that's for sure."

We lapsed into silence, him stroking my hair over and over and, likely because I was sated and sleepy, it soothed me. And I let it.

I don't know why precisely it came to mind. Because I was feeling vulnerable, I suppose, and spiteful, as usual. Also, we hadn't talked like we had for the last few days in so long, since before the breakup.

Tiffany was still after him, and I didn't mind giving him another reason to hate her.

"That day," I began, my voice small. "When that cop pulled me out of school." I would not, *could not* describe it in more detail than that.

He'd gone stiff as a board, but he nodded that he knew which day I meant.

Of course he did.

"I saw her on the way out. Tiffany. I said something to her, because she was the only one I saw. She was supposed to tell you that I was leaving with him. Did she?"

I was only telling the truth and asking a simple question. Had I known it would do some damage?

Well, yes of course. That had been the point.

Had I known he would lose his mind?

No, I actually hadn't.

But he did. He lost his ever-loving mind.

First he started to shake. Top to bottom, *shake*.

His trembling hands lifted me off him, he stood, and buck naked, strode from the room.

I didn't follow him, but when I heard things starting

to break, I didn't have to wonder who was breaking them.

With a sigh I got dressed and went to investigate.

Ah, that made sense. He was in the guestroom Tiffany had been occupying but, lucky for her, she wasn't occupying it now because as I stood there she approached.

She was holding an ice pack to her nose.

That made me smile.

Bastian was behind her, Leo behind him.

"What the hell is going on?" Leo's voice boomed through the hallway.

I almost rolled my eyes. "What, did you get interrupted in the middle of screwing one of the maids?" I asked him in a taunting, baby soft voice, "Does that make you grumpy?"

I'd always had a problem with Leo, dating back to childhood when I'd first realized how he treated Dante. Any chance I got, I antagonized him.

Bastian stifled a laugh. I smiled at him.

"*You*," Leo hissed. "You've been nothing but *poison* in this family since my mother dug you out of the trash."

My brows went up. Usually it took more to get a rise out of the old lech. "Yeah, cause otherwise you're all just a bunch of teddy bears."

Bastian was outright laughing now.

"Can you two stop bickering and tell me what is going on in my room?" Tiffany butted in.

"That is not your room," I said, not even looking at her. I was in a hell of a mood, every boom and crash I heard behind the door I guarded was only egging me on. "That is a *guestroom* that you insisted on staying in, even though *no one* wants you here."

"Oh for Christ's sake," Leo muttered, striding to the door. "I want to know what's going on."

I blocked him, moving to stand in front of the knob. "Dante is having a moment, and everyone needs to leave him the fuck alone." I looked at Tiffany. "Especially you. Trust me when I say that you don't want to get near him right now."

"*Me?*" she pointed at herself, doing her usual innocent routine. "What did *I* do?"

I rolled my eyes. "What, you want me to make a list? Please. Save it. No one here believes your act. Take it somewhere else. Somewhere far away from Dante unless you feel like getting strangled today."

As though to punctuate that, something very large broke with a screeching crash in the room behind me.

"Oh forget it," Leo muttered, turning around. "That boy is as melodramatic as his mother, I swear."

"That's right, princess, don't worry your pretty little head about it. You just go back to screwing the housekeeper!" I called to his retreating back.

He flipped me the bird and kept walking.

I enjoyed getting a low class rise out of his privileged ass, and so that made me smile.

"What happened?" Bastian asked me. "What can I do?"

"Nothing, he just needs some time." I pointed at Tiffany. "And it would be best if he doesn't set eyes on her."

I could hear him breathing in there, hear his ragged panting breaths as he struggled with what I'd told him, and I actually started to feel guilty.

Such a little piece of information, but I knew I should have kept it to myself.

"I'm not going *anywhere*," Tiffany huffed.

As though he'd heard her, Dante opened the door, or

as I liked to call him when he got like this, Hulk Dante.

Except even the hulk wore shorts.

His entire naked, agitated body was vibrating with rage as he caught sight of Tiffany. *"You,"* he snarled, tossing a suitcase clean over my head and into the hallway.

It hit the floor and clothes went flying everywhere as it busted open on contact.

"What on earth?" she exclaimed.

"Get out!" he shouted at her.

Even *I* was a little wary to approach him when he was like this, but I did it, setting a firm hand in the middle of his chest.

"Dante, you need to calm down," I said, trying my best to be a soothing presence, though soothing had never been a strength of mine.

I was much, much better at agitating.

The current Hulk Dante was a case in point.

He just kept staring at her, thick black hatred pouring out of his eyes in menacing, palpable waves. "Get the fuck out of here!" he shouted at her. "I don't ever want to see your face again!"

She looked like she'd just been slapped. She swayed on her feet. "What? But, why Dante? What did I do now?"

In answer he disappeared into the room, reappearing a beat later with another suitcase, this one smaller.

It received the same treatment as the first. And then came her purse, shoes, a blazer, a dress.

I looked at Bastian.

"I guess I'll go ahead and load up her car," he said helpfully, and proceeded to gather a huge armful of clothes into the large suitcase, and holding it closed, he lifted it and started down the hallway.

"Thank you," I called to his back.

After Hulk Dante had emptied the guestroom of every one of her possessions he came back to hover in the doorway.

No further, because I was blocking the way, acting as a barrier between him and the object of his rage.

He let me. I was tiny compared to him, minuscule, but he let me hold him in his place with just my will alone.

"What don't you understand about *get the fuck out?*" he screamed at her, the sound of it booming through the house like the roar of a lion.

Her chin trembled. "What did I do?" she asked, and started to cry.

"What did you do? *What did you do?* What *didn't* you do? You think I don't know? You think I buy your innocent act? You and my fucking manipulative bitch of a mother *ruined my life!*"

"I'm going to tell your mother about this. I'm going to tell her e*verything* I've seen here."

"You do that, but you do it *fast*. Because if I have to look at you for one more fucking *second*—" He took a step toward her, but I was in his way, shoving into him, cutting off his tirade and pushing him back into the room.

He was a brick wall of a man, but he let me do it, let me distract him.

As much as I loved to watch him rip into her, as much as I'd love to see her *throttled*, I couldn't sit idly by as Dante got himself into serious trouble.

Also, he was unhinged, unpredictable when he was this out of his mind, capable of forgetting important realities.

Like the fact that he couldn't confront her about what I'd just told him, no matter what.

No matter what.

There were skeletons in our closet that the world could never know about, and if he went down this path with her, it would lead her straight to them.

I kept pushing at him, backing him step by step into the room, and when we'd cleared the door, I shut it behind us.

I walked into his chest, eyes closing as I wrapped my arms around his ribcage.

He was panting, shaking, so upset that instead of accepting my embrace, he raised his arms so they wouldn't touch me.

"Don't touch me. You don't even know. You don't even have a clue," his trembling voice said to the air.

"What are you talking about?" I asked him absently, my hand going down to cup his scrotum.

His head fell back, and I could feel his agitated body trying to calm itself.

I had just the thing. I got down on my knees.

He didn't touch me as I sucked him off.

What do you know? It worked.

I rose, licking my lips, eyes on his face.

His eyes were still adrift, lost to madness, but my tongue darting out caught his attention, and he seemed to snap back into himself.

He grabbed my face with both of his hands and started kissing me.

Eventually I pulled back. "I need to start packing. I'm going to find a flight out tonight. I can non-rev if I have to."

"You're not going anywhere tonight."

"I'm not?" I don't know why, but at this point, I was only amused.

"Try to leave. See what happens to you."

"If you ever looked at me once with what I know is in you, I would be your slave."
~Emily Brontë

chapter thirty-four

I have no excuse for myself. No justifications that don't ring hollow.

I let him keep me there.

I could have escaped, could have fought him harder, could have easily talked Bastian into getting me away. It would have made the brothers come to blows, but it would have worked.

I didn't do any of that.

This was the whole problem, the entire reason I was so stubbornly devoted to hating Dante's guts.

Because when I didn't, I was too weak to fight him. Just a few days in his proximity and I didn't even have the will anymore.

Without the hate, I forfeited all of my power against him. I lost and he won.

Even knowing it was temporary, transient, even knowing it was all a *lie*, that when it finished I'd be in much, much worse shape than when we'd started, I let him keep me there for another day.

It's no secret how we spent that day. We locked ourselves in my room and barely came out even to eat.

The day went too fast and the morning came too soon. The sun rose and drama was not far behind it.

Something had happened between Bastian, Leo, and Adelaide in the middle of the night, the details of it shrouded in mystery, but word had it that Dante's mother was throwing a fit to end all fits, so much so that the reading of the will was postponed.

I was in the kitchen pantry scraping together the ingredients to make crepes when Dante told me the news.

"God, she's crazy. I can't stay another day. I have work. I need to leave tonight."

His answer was to grab me and kiss the breath out of me. "No," he said simply.

I bit back a smile. "You know there's a term for what you're doing here, right?"

"Kidnapping," he supplied without an ounce of shame or remorse.

But a few hours later he changed his mind completely, did an abrupt about face.

I was soaking my sore, overused body in the bath. He'd gone downstairs to grab some water, but I fully expected him to join me when he returned.

He burst in the door, looking agitated. "You need to get packed. You need *to go. Now.*"

I sat up, completely caught off guard. "What? Why?"

"It's my mother. She's gone *crazy,* and she's on her way over. I don't want you here when she gets here."

I waved an unconcerned hand in the air. "Who cares? I can handle her."

Because what could she even do to me at this point?

He set his jaw. "I'll start packing for you, but you need to get ready *fast.*"

My dismay was turning to anger as he shuffled me out of Gram's house like a bomb was about to go off.

"What the hell is going on?" I asked him as he peeled out of the driveway.

We were just pulling onto the main road when Dante's mother passed us, careening around the corner like a maniac.

I watched her go by, staring at the strange tableau.

Tiffany was sitting in the passenger's seat, and she stared right back.

"She won't follow us. My dad's still there, so she'll go after him," Dante reassured me.

"What the *hell?*"

"I don't want her coming near you when she's like this. She's deranged right now. Capable of anything."

We were silent for a long time. "Why are you always trying to protect me?" I finally asked him quietly.

He turned his head and looked at me, something bleeding out of his eyes, something intense and so tormented that I had to look away. "Because it's my job."

I didn't say the thing I was thinking, but my thoughts felt so loud I knew they spoke to him without the aid of my voice.

Who's going to protect me against you?

I thought he was taking me to the local airport, but as he drove for a while, I realized he was headed the opposite way, straight out of town.

"I know this is a silly thing to ask your kidnapper, but where are you taking me?"

His mouth twisted and his hand went to my leg, but

he wouldn't look at me. "Seattle. We'll get a hotel there. I'll let you fly out in the morning, but not yet."

He glanced at me, his brilliant ocean eyes deeply unhappy. "I'm not ready yet," he stated, squeezing my knee.

I wasn't ready either, but I didn't tell him that.

It was just over a two-hour drive, and we took it in silence.

I, for one, kept my piece because I didn't know what to say, didn't know what subject could be broached that wouldn't lead to something volatile or hurtful.

I didn't feel like messing up the fragile, temporary truce we seemed to actually be succeeding at.

His motivations were a mystery to me, but whatever they were, he barely said a word, the only part of him communicating was his constant hand on my knee, and it spoke in a continual, soothing stroke and occasional tight squeezes.

I didn't touch him back. I reclined my seat, brought my arms up to my chest, and stared straight up, wondering what to do with myself.

I wanted to turn my brain off. I wanted to be numb. I wanted to take back every inch I'd ceded to him in the last few days.

I wanted tomorrow to never come.

Dante wasn't messing around. He checked us in to a Four Seasons, and I smirked when I realized he'd booked the Presidential suite.

"Doesn't the waste of this make your frugal, little conservationist heart bleed a little?" I took the dig at him, voice mock sympathetic, as the bellhop situated my bags. The suite was spacious, beautiful, and had to cost a small fortune. It was very un-Dante to flaunt his wealth in such a way.

He just smiled ruefully, eyes aimed out the window at the spectacular harbor view. He waited for the bellhop to finish, handed him a bill, closed and bolted the door behind him, and dragged me to bed.

We didn't leave the suite until morning.

Dante woke up early with me and while I packed and got ready, he just sat on the edge of the bed watching me, his unhappy eyes following everything I did with uncanny focus.

Finally I stopped, staring at him. "What? You're making me nervous. Shouldn't you be getting dressed?"

He was wearing nothing but his boxer briefs. He was leaning forward, the muscles of his torso bunching and flexing with his every breath.

Superficial creature that I am, it distracted me to an extreme degree. Contrary creature that I am, I was trying not to show it. "What?" I asked again.

He just kept staring.

With a huff, I went back to getting ready. The closer I got to actually being ready though, the way he was looking at me, the way his eyes were *screaming* at me, and the screaming was getting louder and louder, until they were trying to melt me from the inside out, became too much.

"Stop it," I told him, zipping up my suitcase. "I need to leave soon, and you need to stop looking at me like that."

But he didn't stop. And it was too much.

I was stepping into my shoes when I said, "I'm ready."

A desperate sound escaped him, and *that* was too much.

Too much. Too much. *Too. Much.*

"I don't want to do this anymore," he spoke, each word gutted. "If I could forgive you, could you forgive me?"

"*What?*" I could barely get my voice to work for that one word.

"For all of it. Everything. Every last horrible thing we've done to each other. I'm so tired of this war. I'm so done lashing out at you, and I'm ready now. Ready to forgive you. Even for the worst of it. *Especially* for that."

I was shaking. "*You're* ready to forgive *me?* Oh, that is rich."

"Yes. I'm ready. I can forgive you. Can you forgive me?"

It was so completely out of left field that I had no response. The idea of him forgiving me was so implausible on its own.

And the idea of *me* forgiving *him* was so completely and wholly foreign that it had never even crossed my mind.

Could I forgive him?

I didn't know. I'd never tried.

I'd just assumed it was an impossible task, and one he'd certainly never asked me for before this moment. "I think we've proven that what you're asking is impossible," I finally said, cutting each word out of myself in big gory chunks.

I'd backed so far away from him that my back was to the wall. My hands were in fists at my sides.

He stood up and my whole body jerked. I put my hands up as though to ward him off, but he didn't take even one step forward, and when he spoke, he spoke passionately and to the ground at my feet. "All we are is proof that love can survive anything. You and I, we're heavy hitters, but even at our worst, we still couldn't break this bond. If you're honest with yourself, we didn't even come close."

I was weakening, my mind trying to find a way to reconcile what he was saying, to accept it and believe it, though I'd never admit it aloud.

But I didn't have to. That was the worst thing about Dante. He knew me too well. Every in and out of me. Every lie and truth. He and I alone held the keys to my destruction.

As I've said, lovers should have secrets.

I asked the one question that would put an end to this madness. "Will you ever tell me *why?*" I didn't have to elaborate. He knew what I wanted to know.

Why did you throw me away?

And . . .

Why did you let me give you every part of myself just so you could toss it all back into the trashcan that it came from?

But particularly . . .

How? *How could you break my heart?*

"I can't give you an excuse," he said in a careful voice that *trembled.* "But I'm asking for forgiveness. Please. I don't make sense without you and you don't make sense without me and you *know* it. We only ever worked together. How long did you think it was going to last? Scarlett without Dante, Dante without Scarlett? You and I going about our lives as though the other doesn't exist? Who are you kidding? Who are we without each other? Apart we're not ourselves. And it's been long enough. I've been *punished* long enough."

Had he?

And—*had I?*

And—couldn't he at least *try* to make up an excuse? Even if it was bullshit, even if it was a complete lie, couldn't he at least *try?*

I didn't know how to respond to him. I didn't know what to say.

I didn't know what to *think*.

He had completely weakened me, utterly destroyed any resolve I thought I'd built against him, and when he started to move to me, I couldn't find the strength to get away.

He crowded but barely touched, his hands going around me, under my hair, feeling at my nape.

Time froze as he unfastened one of the chains around my neck, took the ring off, and put it on my limp finger.

"I know this is sudden to you. I know it's a shock. I'll give you time. There's no deadline on your answer, but it's out there now, what I want, how I feel, though that was never much of a mystery if you were paying attention."

"It doesn't even make sense," I pointed out tremulously. "We don't live near each other, and you know damn well it can never work long distance between us." We'd tried and failed it once. Some part of me blamed that distance for our downfall. It was my ego, I supposed, that was certain that he never would have turned to *her* if I hadn't been so far away.

"I'll move to L.A. If you say yes, that you can forgive me and give us another chance, I'll move tomorrow."

I was looking down at the diamond on my finger, Gram's diamond, that she'd passed down to Dante, that he'd given to me once upon a time when I'd still believed in the conquer all power of love.

I couldn't stop shaking.

"Don't say no," he pleaded. "Don't say anything. Just think about it. I'll wait for you. However much time you need, I'll be here waiting."

And then, he backed away.

We barely touched, barely said another word when he dropped me off at the airport.

I didn't look back as I headed into the terminal, but that insidious thing inside of me was raging again, every step I took that led me away from him, it *raged*.

I was on the plane before I let myself cry. I pulled a blanket over my head, and God, did the tears fall.

I'd folded in on myself, my body failing under the weight of one simple realization: I needed to change. I couldn't go on like this. Hatred alone was not enough to fuel a person through life. I needed to find some version of peace.

What could I forgive for the sake of love? What could I get past for the simple justification that I wanted to be happy again?

My answer stunned me. Rocked me down to my soul.

More than I'd ever thought I could.

"Never make a decision when you are upset, sad, jealous or in love."
~Mario Teguh

chapter thirty-five

I didn't make him wait long before I called, though some part of me thought I should make him suffer longer, I just didn't have it in me.

I shut my eyes tight at the sound of his voice. I was in my bedroom at my apartment, sitting on my bed. I'd only gotten back from Seattle the day before, though I'd made my decision before my plane even touched down.

"Dante," I breathed, my voice close to a sob. I felt so emotional and so desperate to get it out that I didn't even wait for an opening. "Dante. My answer is *yes*. I want you to move to L.A." I didn't say anymore. I didn't need to. If he came here for me, I'd be his. We both knew it, and I'd never been any good at expressing my feelings over the phone.

He was gasping on the other end, breaths so ragged that they punched into my ear like he was shouting.

"Scarlett," he said once, his heart in his voice, hiding nothing from me.

But then, a few beats later, the strangest thing happened.

The tone of the call changed, the connection faltering as it lessened in quality, the background noise getting just a touch more static.

He'd switched it to speakerphone.

It was like déjà vu.

My hand pressed to my chest as the air seized in my lungs.

This has happened before, my mind recalled in horror, not even having to place the memory, because it was burned right there on my frontal lobe in a spot I could never misplace.

And his voice, when he spoke again had been stripped of all emotion. It was detached to the point of cold. "I'm sorry, Scarlett. I've thought about it, and it was all a mistake. What I proposed . . . is impossible."

"What?" I breathed. "I don't believe you."

"Don't you?" he asked, his indifferent tone ringing out hollow.

"And this was what? You messing with me? *Revenge?* Why would you do this?" My voice broke on the last word.

"You and I can never work," he said simply.

My eyes were on my shaking hands. "This is really what you want?" I asked, and as I heard the words come out, heard how pathetic they were, I wanted to snatch them back.

"It was silly to think we could be together again. I'm sorry I put you through that, but it is impossible."

And with that, he hung up.

A few days later, I pulled myself together enough to send him a small care package.

My return gift to Dante was not as fun as a pair of Louboutins, but it was far more valuable, and the note that went with it felt satisfying as hell when I wrote it.

Dante,
I know you love meaningless gestures. how's this one for you?
Enjoy. thanks for everything.
S, aka the hate of your life
p.s. there is not one more fucking thing we need to talk about.
ever.
p.p.s. lose my number.

chapter thirty-six

PAST

A twist came my way senior year, one I couldn't have foreseen but that I'd be feeling the reverberations of for a very long time.

Tiffany's wealthy family purchased a great amount of acreage right next to Gram and Adelaide's estates and they built a huge house and moved in over the summer. Next thing I knew, Tiffany was going to high school with us.

I hated it.

And what was worse, Dante had become *friends* with her. He said hi to her now when we ran into her, *smiled* at her, he even chatted and *joked* with her. When I'd called him out on it, he'd said, "She's not that bad, tiger. We've snubbed her for years for no good reason aside from spiting my mother. Don't you think it's time we grew up? She can't help that my mom's a psycho any more than I can. Give her a chance. She's actually pretty cool."

I didn't take that well. I gave him the silent treatment for two days, would barely look at him, but then it occurred to me that if I withdrew from him, he might turn to *her*.

I approached him at his locker. He was surrounded by people, as he always seemed to be lately, but I ignored them all.

Tiffany was lingering near him, talking to some girls. I knew she'd do that. She'd become a part of his circle of friends, I was certain of it.

The thought had been my last straw and why I had decided to approach him right *then*.

He smiled warmly when he saw me. He thought I was over my snit, and he was happy about it.

I didn't smile back but moved right into him, smashing my soft chest against his hard one.

He put his arms around me, and I lifted my face up to him. He was not into public displays of affection, but he gave me a brief peck on the mouth.

I wasn't having it, so I reached up and pulled his head back down to mine. I rubbed my body against his and started kissing him.

With a quiet groan, he started kissing me back, his hands going to my hips.

After a few beats he pulled back with a curse, "Jesus, what's gotten into you? Not here."

He wouldn't let me move my hips, but I was brushing my breasts lightly into his chest, back and forth, over and over.

"Not fucking here," he gritted out. "Guys!" he barked at the jocks he called his friends these days. "Give us a minute, will you?"

They left and the girls that were with them followed, Tiffany sending one long, steady stare my way before she joined them.

I met the stare, pressing my body harder against Dante. *Mine*, I told her silently. *My man, my territory.*

"What was that?" His voice was quiet and incredulous.

I glared up at him. "What? Are you embarrassed of me? I'm pretty sure everyone at this school knows we're together."

That pissed him off royally, I could tell. His hands tightened on my hips and his eyes shot daggers at me. "You know better. Don't say shit like that. And yeah, of course everyone knows we're together, but look at you right now. The fuck me look on your face, grinding on me in broad daylight in front of a crowd? I don't want other guys seeing you like this. I don't want them to have this picture of you in their head when they're fantasizing about you because I know that every fucking one of them does. The assholes can use their imagination; they don't need a picture like this."

I was sure he was right about at least one of them. The way Nate looked at me, even just before the guys had cleared out, the gaze he'd cast my way, one of sheer longing, I was well aware I was the star of his fantasies.

"I think Nate is in love with me." I had a habit of goading his jealousy, because I couldn't get enough of it.

"I think so too. Try to go easy on him, will ya?"

"Aren't you jealous?" I was pouting. That was hardly the reaction I'd been expecting.

"No. I trust you, and I don't honestly think he can help it. I know I can't."

I pulled his head down to me and started kissing him again.

After a few drugging moments, he pulled back again.

"I need you," I said into his ear.

"*Jesus*, Scarlett, we have class in like five minutes."

"You can't skip one class to give your girlfriend what she *needs*?" I breathed.

For that, he crowded me into the locker. "Oh, I'll give my girlfriend what she needs all right, but I highly doubt we'll only miss one class, and just for the record, I'm a little disappointed in her."

"Why?"

"She hasn't spoken to me for two days because she's jealous when she, of all people, has *no right* to be jealous."

I pulled back to look at him. "I don't?"

"You don't. No right at all. Other girls, other *people*, aren't even on my radar. I don't notice them. I don't *see* them. I don't care about anybody but you and you *know* it."

With a coquettish smile, I took his hand and led him out of the building.

We walked through the parking lot and then into the woods. The elementary, middle school, and high school were just minutes from each other, and all of them backed against the same large stretch of forest. It was a longer walk through the woods to get home than it used to be when we were younger, but still only about twenty leisurely minutes.

"Where should we go?" he asked me. "*Dammit*, I should've driven today." His brain had gone into full-on rut mode.

"The forest," I decided. Usually we went to my grandma's house. I hated that place, but it was always abandoned until the evening so it was too convenient not to use.

He grunted, not sounding pleased with the idea, but when I started pulling him, he didn't resist.

We didn't make it far, maybe five minutes in before we were all over each other.

"We need to walk the rest of the way," he told me between drugging kisses. "I don't have any condoms on me."

"You don't? Why the hell not?"

"Because normally I don't need them at school, and I especially didn't think I'd need them *today* with the way you've been giving me the cold shoulder."

"Whatever. It's fine. You can just pull out."

He groaned and started kissing me again, but quickly pulled away. "We've discussed it, and you know that doesn't work. You need to get on the pill and until then, condoms."

I started rubbing him with my hand through his jeans. "Just once won't hurt. I want to feel you *bare*."

"Fuck," he cursed, yanking away from me.

I smiled and turned around, unsnapping my cutoff shorts and pushing them off.

"What are you doing?" he asked me when I went down on hands and knees.

I straightened, shrugged my shirt off, then my bra and lowered again. "I'll let you guess," I told him.

He cursed and cursed, but it wasn't long before I heard him taking off his clothes, and then I felt him behind me, his chest against my back.

He kissed my neck. "I can't believe I'm doing this. You could talk me into anything."

"It'll be fine," I assured him. "Just pull out, okay?"

"Okay," he panted and pushed his tip into me.

We both groaned.

He palmed my breasts and moved deeper.

"Oh God," he breathed and rammed himself home.

He'd been getting better about lasting longer the more we had sex, but this time it was like our first time. He only made it a few rough thrusts before he was pulling out of me, coming in warm spurts against my ass, kissing my back and telling me he loved me.

Well, at least he'd pulled out.

"Sorry. Fuck. Sorry." His fingers were playing with my clit, his other hand still fondling my breast. "Don't worry. I'll take care of you."

I squirmed. My knees were already sore and I knew they'd be marked up from the hard ground, but I didn't want to move. I just wanted to stay like this until he was ready again.

"More," I told him thickly, moving my hips.

"So greedy," his approving voice rumbled onto my skin. He pinched my clit lightly as the fingers of his other hand pushed into me, two fingers thrusting steadily. I tilted my hips until they were hitting just the right nerve.

"Don't stop," I gasped when I was getting close.

He stopped abruptly.

"What did I say?" I snapped at him, unfinished and surly with it.

His answer came in the form of his recovered cock breaching me. He picked up the steady rhythm again, but this time it was so much better with the thickness of him.

I'd just started to come, my sheath clenching around him, when he pulled out again.

I straightened, turned, and pressed myself against him, grabbing his spasming cock and helping him finish with my hand, pulling his blunt tip to smash against my sensitive clit as we both got off, his warm cum coating my tender flesh in continuous pumps.

It was so good that I kept ahold of him, giving him open-mouthed kisses as I squeezed him, not ready for it to end.

He pressed me onto my back, spreading my legs open wide.

He had my breasts in his hands, pushed together while he licked my nipples when he reluctantly pulled back. "We should go somewhere. To your grandma's probably. She'll still be at work, so . . ."

I pulled his head back to my breasts, aiming one aching nipple at his mouth. I didn't want to go anywhere. I was already worked up again, and it was still a solid fifteen-minute walk. I didn't think I could wait that long and I told him so.

With a loud pop, he let my nipple out of his mouth. "It'll take me more than fifteen minutes to recover," he pointed out.

I bit my lip and pushed his head down just enough for him to get the hint.

He smiled and put his mouth on me again.

"God, if the girls at school only knew, *mmm*, that you could do this to them," I told the sky as he kissed his way across my body. "They already want you something *fierce*, and they have no idea, *mmm*, that you're like this, *mmm*."

He came up for air long enough to say, "For the record, I'm not interested in doing this to anyone but you."

His head was deep between my legs, and I was just on the edge of release when he pulled away.

"What!" I cried out. It was no time to be stopping.

He moved up my body, and grinning, shoved into me again.

My sated body was still vibrating, his heavy weight

on top of me, when I blinked my eyes open and caught a movement at the corner of it.

I froze.

Dante was oblivious at first, still moaning as he finished on my thigh, his mouth busy on my neck.

I tapped his shoulder, then tapped it again.

"Mmm?" He made the noise between kisses.

"Someone saw us," I told him, shivering.

His head snapped up, his entire body lifting off me. "*What?*"

"Someone was watching us," I clarified. I pointed to the spot in the trees. "I don't know for how long, but I saw somebody when I opened my eyes. They were watching us, but when I spotted them, they disappeared.

"Did you get a look at them?"

"It was a big man. I think it was that homeless guy, the one that's always sleeping by the river, closer to the middle school. Remember?"

Dante was not happy about that. He cursed fluently as he got dressed, then impatiently stuffed me back into my clothes since I hadn't been hurrying fast enough to suit him.

He dragged me around as he checked the immediate area, but there was no sign of the guy by then. "I don't like it. I should find the pervert and put the fear of God into him."

"I don't honestly know how long he was watching. He might have just stumbled upon us, and I just happened to catch sight of him before he could leave."

I moved into him, hand rubbing his chest. "Let's forget about it. Let's go to my grandma's." I cupped him. "We weren't done, were we?"

His head fell back. "Jesus, you're going to *kill* me."

We didn't make it back to school that day, and even knowing he'd catch hell from his coach for it, he skipped practice.

The next day we couldn't even look at each other without the past day's sensory memories ruling us. I lasted until just after third period.

"I'm so sore," I breathed into his ear.

His answer was a very satisfying, half-stifled moan.

"I can't sit down for another class, so I'm skipping," I continued.

His hands squeezed my hips, and I may as well have been reading his mind.

"You know what's not sore, though?" I asked him.

His only answer was a few helpless pants into my ear.

"My mouth."

"At this rate," he told me later. We were in my bed, his naked form spooning me from behind, "I'm going to get kicked off the team."

I didn't tell him that that wouldn't have made me sad. He knew how I felt about football.

It was just a few weeks later that it happened.

It is so sad and so terrible how the most random and senseless things can set about your destruction.

Walking home alone that day was a complete fluke. Nothing but a temperamental whim on my part. Something so silly, some petty, jealous fit over Dante being too nice to Tiffany, and I'd gone into a rage and decided to go home early, ditching out while Dante was at practice, and sulk by myself.

When I think back on it there's always some significant

echo, some resounding weight to the steps I took alone into the woods that day.

But I couldn't say if I noticed it then, only that it has attributed itself quite securely to my memories.

It is a powerful echo, one that aches with regret and a million what ifs.

What if I hadn't gone that way? What if I hadn't gone alone?

What if I'd waited for Dante to walk with me?

Any of those things could have prevented so much heartache, so much pain, and the domino effect of destruction that followed.

One thing was for certain, whether it was memory or retrospect, those footsteps would reverberate like gunfire through the rest of my life.

BOOKS BY R.K. LILLEY

THE LOVE IS WAR DUET
BREAKING HIM
BREAKING HER

THE WILD SIDE SERIES
THE WILD SIDE
IRIS
DAIR

THE OTHER MAN
TYRANT - COMING SOON

THE UP IN THE AIR SERIES
IN FLIGHT
MILE HIGH
GROUNDED
MR. BEAUTIFUL

LANA (AN UP IN THE AIR COMPANION NOVELLA)
AUTHORITY - COMING SOON

THE TRISTAN & DANIKA SERIES
BAD THINGS
ROCK BOTTOM
LOVELY TRIGGER

THE HERETIC DAUGHTERS SERIES
BREATHING FIRE
CROSSING FIRE – COMING SOON

THE BISHOP BROTHERS SERIES
BOSS - COMING SOON

HERE'S A TEASER FROM THE FOLLOW UP TO

breaking him.

"If you prick us, do we not bleed? If you tickle us, do we not laugh? If you poison us, do we not die? And if you wrong us, shall we not revenge?"
~William Shakespeare

breaking her

PRESENT

Scarlett

I was drunk. Good and stinking drunk.

We were at the crew hotel in Seattle (not my favorite town) on a layover, and we were trolling the lobby bar.

Okay, *I* was trolling the bar. My girls were just there for moral support.

No wait, that wasn't all. We were supposed to be celebrating. Something great had happened, I had to remind myself.

I'd just landed my first starring role in a feature film.

Yes, that was it. We were *celebrating*.

Also . . .

I was planning to make up for the fact that I'd just spent *way* too much time being a pathetic, lovesick fool, moping in my room, hiding in my bed.

Hating myself. Wanting to disappear.

I'd barely scraped myself together enough to make it to the fateful audition that had landed me the part that might change my life.

Even when I'd gotten the news (that I was finally, at last, going to star in a movie!) I'd barely felt even a stirring of happiness.

The last round with Dante still had its hold on me. I'd let him do his worst and the wounds he'd inflicted were just not healing.

But I'd vowed tonight that I was done with that.

I was on the hunt for a stand-in punching bag. I had decided about three drinks ago that I'd feel much better about myself if I put at least one man between me and my last memory of Dante.

I was looking around, a pout on my face. "No cute boys," I told the girls.

Demi agreed.

"I'm not sad," Leona said, studying me. "I don't think I want you to find a cute boy when you're in this shape."

They were sitting in a booth and I was standing next to it. I was not in a sitting mood. I was in a sway to the music and get some male attention mood. I just wished there were some males around worth being noticed by.

I'd already shot down two that just weren't cute enough. More specifically: Reject Number One wasn't tall enough and Reject Number Two looked too wholesome.

I didn't like wholesome, never had. I craved sinister categorically.

"Don't speak too soon," Farrah said, eyes aimed at the door. "I'll let you have him if you want him, but damn, I sure don't want to."

I turned to see. And smiled.

It was my lucky day.

Either he was actually looking for me or it was a hell of a coincidence, but Dante's half-brother, Bastian, had just walked in the door.

He was standing there scanning the room and it didn't take him long to zero in on me.

He grinned.

I tilted my head and grinned back, then pointed my chin at the bar, heading there with a bouncing little strut.

He beat me to it, and watched me approach, his eyes all over me.

I was glad I'd turned myself out well.

My minuscule nude dress was basically man catnip. It hit all the right buttons—deep cleavage that left very little of my abundant breasts to the imagination, short skirt that showed off my sky-high legs, and the whole thing was fitted to show off my tiny waist and hourglass figure, the color giving the illusion that I was close to naked.

Pink platform stilettos and sexy bedroom hair didn't hurt my situation, and my makeup had been on point before I'd gotten sloppy drunk. Who could say now? Who could care?

Not me. My lipstick was probably smeared, my mascara bleeding down my face, but I felt sexy as hell either way.

"Hello, stranger," I said when I got in earshot of Bastian. "You look good enough to eat."

And he did. Three-piece suit, dark, messy hair, five o'clock shadow, a handsome as hell Durant face, and a devilish smile.

Yeah, he'd do.

"Look who's talking," he retorted, eyes on my catnip dress. "My God, woman, you are trouble, aren't you?"

I went to hug him, because drunk, and breathed into his ear. "You have no idea."

"Unfortunately, I don't." He sounded truly regretful about that as he put his hands on my hips and set me back just the slightest bit. "I'm sure you've guessed, but I came here to talk to you."

"How did you know I'd be here?" I asked him, cocking my head to the side.

His mouth twisted ruefully, and when he did that, he reminded me so much of Dante that I wanted to smash something over his head. And cry. And run away. And kiss him.

"Facebook. You and your friends love to share your locations, and, you know, I live here."

I scrunched my nose up. "Facebook stalking me, are you?"

He was unapologetic. "Yes. It's a helpful tool. Actually, I was going to fly down to see you soon, but this worked out much better. Well, it did if you're up for a serious talk that I'd like you to remember in the morning."

"I'm not up for a serious anything," I told him and, because drunk, I pressed my mouth to his.

He made a little noise in this throat, a hungry one, and I licked his lips, brushing my breasts against him.

He set me away, but he was breathing hard.

"You taste good," I told him.

He smiled but not like he was happy. "Do I taste like revenge?"

"*Exactly* like that. It's delicious."

"Trust me, you beautiful, edible, *dangerous* creature, I would love to take you up on that, but it's a line we can't cross."

"There's no line I won't cross," I said, meaning it. I was feeling self-destructive to a desperate, limitless degree. "God, do you know what he *did to me* after we left Gram's house?"

"I heard a bit about it," Bastian said solemnly.

That surprised me. "What did you hear? And from who?"

He sighed. "From Dante. I'm sure you won't be surprised to hear that he's in rough shape."

That bit of unfair bullshit only made me more determined. I moved closer and he let me. I rubbed up against him, my full, glossy lips in kissing distance of his again, teasing him. "Let's make it *rougher* for him, huh?"

"*Jesus*," he said, and it reminded me so much of Dante that I wrenched away.

I leaned against the bar, flagging down the busy bartender.

He didn't make me wait, in fact stopped what he was doing and came to do my bidding with a smile.

I'd been flirting with him all night, but he wasn't my type. He was tall but his shoulders weren't broad enough. Still, the right smile got me some amazing service.

"Hey, Scarlett," he said, his tone when he said my name making it sound like we were old friends or new lovers. "Another scotch for you?"

"You're the *best*, Benny," I told him, leaning forward, shamelessly teasing him. "Can you make it two?"

He nodded, eyes on my cleavage. "Anything you want, gorgeous."

"Wow," Bastian whistled when Benny moved away to get our drinks. "If I was Dante, I would *lock you up*."

"Well, that's *not* what he did," I said, and it was an effort to keep my voice steady. "He threw me away. Again."

"Oh, Scarlett," Bastian sighed, a world of sad sympathy in his voice that made me turn to study him. "I have a few things to ask you and *so much* to tell you. I'm not sure just how drunk you are, but I'm pretty positive that what I have to say will sober you up."

That was an understatement. What he had to tell me didn't just sober me up.

It changed *everything*.

"She burned too bright for this world."
~Emily Brontë

PAST

Dante

I'd always had a soft spot for her. Since I could remember, her flashing eyes and stubborn face were dear to me.

Even before she'd decided we were friends, before our fateful bonding moment outside of the vice principal's office when she first realized I was in her corner, I'd admired her.

Admired that she never backed down. Admired that, with the way she was treated by nearly everyone around her, she never bent, not one iota, let alone came near to breaking.

Her strength galvanized me, made me see the world in a different way.

I had it so easy. My mother was awful, my father dismal, but my life was pampered and I could escape any time I wanted, which was often, and go visit my Gram, who lived a short walk away and made up for both of my piece of shit parents and then some.

I had an anger problem and a bad attitude. This I

knew. But it was Scarlett who inspired me to give those things *purpose*.

The first time I tried to help, she didn't even notice me.

We were in the cafeteria at school. I was in line to get lunch, stealing glances at her.

She was by herself. She always was. She was less interested in talking to other kids than any kid I'd ever seen besides myself. Once, I'd even taken a seat across from her to eat, and she'd still barely said two words to me.

Her thick, brown hair was endearingly messy. She had the perfect face of a doll, but it was always set into hard lines, an incongruous, arresting look but one that I couldn't stop staring at. And I stared a lot. I enjoyed watching her. She wasn't like anybody else, didn't react to things in the same way. I got a kick out of expecting the unexpected from her.

What made other girls cry made her throw a punch. What made boys whine made her snarl like an angry tiger.

Every inch of her tiny frame read: This girl is tough and she does not plan to deal with your shit. Do not mess with her.

So why was everyone *always* messing with her?

They loved to tease her about the trashcan stuff, and I thought that was about the most messed up thing ever. It set my teeth on edge. What an awful thing to tease someone about.

No part of me understood, but then, I'd never felt like someone who fit in, either.

They were serving cheese zombies and tomato soup for lunch, one of my favorites, and I waited in line just watching her and not particularly paying attention to anything else.

I couldn't help but overhear the boys in front of me, though. There were two of them and they were snickering. It was the type of laugh where you knew there was something bad behind it. Something mean, and so I focused on them, listening as they revealed themselves to be just the kind of little shits I had no patience for.

"I swear to God, Jason," one said to the other, "I have five dollars in my backpack and if you do it, it's all yours."

Jason laughed harder. "I'll get into trouble."

"It's five bucks! Just say you tripped and spilled it. Hell, some tomato soup on her head might make her smell better."

They both went into loud peals of laughter. I thought they sounded like nasty little hyenas.

I felt sick. I didn't even have to hear any more, I knew what they were planning and to who, but I did hear more, I listened and collected my food, then quietly followed them.

I set down my tray on the first table I passed.

Jason's giggling friend sat down at the next one and waved him on.

With an evil grin, Jason approached Scarlett from behind, still holding his tray.

With quick furious steps I caught up to him, grabbed his tray, stepped on his foot, and sent my elbow hard into his chin all at once.

He went down with a gratifying cry.

Very calmly, I took his tomato soup and poured it right into his dismayed face.

"Is it funny now, you little *shit*?" I spat at him right before a teacher started dragging me away.

I glanced at Scarlett as I went.

She'd turned at the commotion, looking bored with only a touch of interest in her big, dark eyes as she looked at me, but no comprehension on her face that I'd just saved her from a headful of soup.

Still, that didn't deter me too much.

Her plight ate at me. I'd lie in bed, hands clenched into fists, and stew about it.

I was a lonely, solemn boy, more sensitive than I'd ever admit, and I couldn't *stand* what was happening to her. The casual cruelties. The constant unfairness. The unending *injustice* of it.

Anytime something was really bothering me, I took it to my Gram.

"It's not right," I told my glamorous, doting grandmother. "It's *wrong*, the way she's being treated. The kids are monsters, and the teachers don't care until it's gotten so bad that Scarlett gets herself into trouble. It's every *day*, Gram. Every *day* she has to put up with these little *shits* picking on her."

She was studying my face in a way that I liked, the way she always did when I was reminding her of grandpa. She didn't even reprimand me for cursing, that's how intently she was listening to me.

"You've gotta help her, Gram. It's bad enough the way they talk, but she's got no one at home taking care of her. She needs *clothes*. Soap. Someone to wash her hair and brush her teeth, or ya know, teach her how to do it."

She touched a hand to my hair, purest love pouring out of her eyes. "Yes, yes, of course she does, Dante, my sweet, sweet boy. We will work on all of that."

"They're *awful* at school. They won't let up on her. Maybe if you talk to her about . . . taking a bath or somethin', it'd make it easier on her."

"I will. I absolutely will, you darling boy. I'm ashamed that you even had to point it out, but you leave it to me, okay?"

I nodded. I had absolute faith that Gram would do anything she promised, so I was done worrying about that part of it.

"Thank you," I told her. "But . . . what should I do? How do you think *I* can help her?"

"How about just being her friend? Friends can make life a lot better."

I flushed and looked down, embarrassed to tell her that the girl I was so worried about would barely say two words to me. "I'll try," I muttered.

"And Dante?"

"Yes?"

"You're strong. And brave. I have faith in you. I know you will find a way to help her. If you see she needs defending, *defend* her. Do what you think is *right* and you won't have any regrets."

A few weeks later, I pounded a guy that I heard making a joke about her, and I got my first smile out of her, a conspiratorial grin that let me know she had a newfound faith in me.

I loved that smile.

From that day forward it was my job to protect her. Her feelings. Her body.

Her freedom.

CPSIA information can be obtained
at www.ICGtesting.com
Printed in the USA
LVOW01s0845021016
507014LV00022B/1352/P